WILLIA

NO TIME

Babash - Ryan

© 2003 William Wood
ISBN 1-904706-00-2
The right of William Wood to be identified as the author of this book has been asserted in accordance with Sections 77 & 78 of the Copyrights and Patents Act 1988

First published in Great Britain in 2003
Babash-Ryan, The Shadowline Building, Gainsborough, Lincs. DN21 2AJ
Cover Design by Babash
Typeset and Printed by Babash Ltd

CHAPTER ONE

Taking his first breath after stepping off the plane in Gondo, Capital of the Nile Republic, Martin Thomas felt he was swallowing quenched fire. The air was at once scorchingly hot and soakingly humid. The landscape was flat and brown, with a green rim of short trees beyond the airport. The terminal apart there was a total absence of buildings.

The twenty or so passengers were herded into a dark, hot shed with a tin roof, to complete immigration formalities and to collect and clear their luggage. Those desperate to relieve themselves after the three-hour flight from Nairobi in the little plane were allowed to run across the tarmac and use the tall grass as a screen. Most were too dehydrated to bother.

Some half an hour later, glistening with sweat, the first passengers - Martin among them - emerged from the immigration shed, blinking into the glare of the car park, an area of baked red earth cleared in the bush. Off-road vehicles with the logos of various aid agencies, UNDP, UNHCR, FAO, and competing Christian bodies were parked waiting to pick up their visitors, "expats" for the most part here on short "missions".

"The definition of an expert," a chirpy American was telling Martin, "is someone who has flown over the territory twice, preferably once in daylight."

"Yes," said his equally cheerful side-kick, "and an education expert is someone who knows the same as you, but who has slides."

"Are you an education expert?" Martin asked him.

"Yes, but I've left my slides behind. There's no electricity in Gondo."

"So you'll have to cope with appropriate technology."

"Say, that was some landing," said the education expert. The plane had circled, made its descent and at the last minute had roared up into the sky again scorching the scrub as it scraped over the broken perimeter fence.

"Cows on the runway," the American had explained. "The pilots usually spot them when they circle the airfield."

Martin still felt shaky from the bumpy flight and the exciting landing attempt when the Americans' Chevy pick-up drove in, hooting.

"See you around," they called, as they climbed into the enormous vehicle, which bore the insignia of some bible translating agency. There was something rather fanatical about their gaiety. Almost forced. "You going to be here long?"

"About three years," Martin shouted back.

"We'll pray for you," the slide less education expert shouted, and Martin realised with a shudder that he was serious. He would rather they had given him a lift. There was no one to meet him. In London they had told him to go to Gondo. Well, he had arrived.

He was in Gondo; where they had sent him. And now he no longer had anywhere to go. Find accommodation, open a bank account, rent an office. It had sounded easy in London. It would have been easy in London.

He watched the expatriate groups and the Arab traders disappear into their vehicles. He heard the burst of engines as the plane that had brought him taxied out to the runway. His bowels turned over. Quite literally, he imagined, understanding the cliché fully for the first time in his life. He steadied himself, noticed all the immigration officials drive off in an old van. No plane was expected for another week. He was suddenly on his own. The airport building, like a tropical Marie Celeste floated abandoned on the shimmering ocean of the Savannah. Martin sat on his large, aluminium suitcase and his head span in panic.

It was his honesty that had put paid to him. Honesty, integrity and perhaps a certain courage were his only qualifications. And such qualities were obsolescent in the new ethos, in the culture, as he had learned to call it, of the organisation.

When they asked him at the promotion interview what achievement during the previous year he was most proud of he thought carefully and replied with a modest smile, "I suppose really it was a poem I wrote."

The panel was incredulous. After a pause one of them asked, "What project was that for?"

"Oh no," Martin hastened to add. "It wasn't part of my office work." And he risked a joke, "It gave me far more satisfaction."

The joke fell flat, unnoticed. Two of the interviewers exchanged a glance but a third pursued the candidate's extraordinary confession. "And just how much, Mr. Thomas, did you get for it?"

"How much?"

"Yes. How much is it worth? Your poem? In real terms?"

"In real terms! What a curious way of putting it. I hadn't actually thought of selling my poem. I suppose some small magazine might give me a few pounds if they saw fit to publish it."

"And in your work, Mr Thomas," the chairman of the panel asked, returning to the first question. "Has anything given you satisfaction this year?"

"Well frankly, no," he replied. "That is why I have applied for promotion. I want something more challenging."

"I don't think any of our senior Management posts require a poet?" ventured one of the interviewers. His attempt at humour, earned the same response as Martin's own small joke. To save the little fellow's face Martin said earnestly, "But I'm sure creative leadership is important."

The interview ran on for ten minutes, more he sensed for the form than from any enthusiasm on the part of the examiners. At last the Chairman thanked him for coming, told him they still had people to see for a limited number of places; he would be hearing from them shortly.

Martin was no fool. He realised he had failed the test, presented the wrong image. What angered him was their lack of interest in his record, his experience, and his service to the organization. They had pried into his character, his attitudes. They had been more excited at the results of a graphological test than in his proven commitment.

"Your handwriting shows you to be of an academic disposition, thoughtful, innovative even," one of them had explained. "Would you agree?"

"Do you need to examine my handwriting to discover that?" he had retorted, genuinely amused.

They ignored this question, pointing out that while these qualities were admirable, they did not match the corporate template for promotion. They were looking for risk takers, rather more aggressive personalities, people with drive and ambition. As he closed the door behind him Martin realised he should have told them to look at the candidates' driving licences in that case, and appoint those with the most endorsements.

He was pondering the validity of this approach when the buzzer on the receptionist's desk sounded. The young woman looked at him.

"Mr. Thomas?"

"That's me"

The receptionist spoke into the intercom. "Mr. Thomas is still here. Yes, I'll ask him to hang on." Then to Martin, "They want another word with you in half an hour".

"Do they?" he said in surprise. In the same instant he realised he had lost interest.

6

"It's a good sign. Won't you sit down?" She had green eyes. Green and friendly.

"I don't know," he said despondently. "Half an hour!"

"It's a good sign," repeated the girl with green eyes. "Besides, you may not get the chance again."

"Do you know something I don't know?"

"Not at all," she said indignantly. "But it's obvious they wouldn't ask you to come back for nothing."

"Perhaps you are right," he smiled, to please the helpful young woman. He felt lonely, depressed by his interview. In the same way that ecologists had come to realise that man was despoiling his physical surroundings, Martin Thomas was beginning to think that organisations, particularly official organisations, both national and international and often with snappy acronyms, were polluting the intellectual and spiritual environment. The misuse of words, the "culture" of the organisation being one example, the stultifying uniformity typified by instantly recognisable logos, the obsession with image, corporate identity, the dictatorship of house style and house speak...

"Would you like a cup of tea?"

She was standing in front of him now, slim, in control, above all friendly.

"Yes. As a matter of fact, I'd love a cup of tea. But only if you let me help make it."

"I wouldn't do that..."

"Why not? We both work for the same organisation, don't we? Why should you make me tea?"

She was amused. "That's the spirit. The kettle is above the alcove behind those files."

He was glad of something to do, but he could not stop the angry train of thought roller-booting around in his head. Britwords, the organisation he worked for, was an extreme example of this fad, this trend. It had been set up by the

Ministry of Trade to exploit the country's richest resources, its words.

"English is a very desirable global commodity," the Chairman had said at its launch. "It is in this country's interest to capitalise on the increasing demand for the English language as a vehicle for commerce, travel, the dissemination of knowledge and in a word, domination."

But to Martin it was a pollutant, this influential English. He could remember the time when less developed countries had collected money by storing the toxic wastes of the industrialised North. Now they were encouraged to become the recipients of redundant jargon, international catch phrases, instant opinion; their own literary and philosophical fields were spread with the muck of materialism, while their own once flourishing vocabularies were trodden underfoot.

Some of his colleagues found the cross fertilisation enriching. Martin had only to think of all the official reports he had ploughed through, the heavy clay of international prose, to be profoundly depressed.

He was fluent in several languages himself but would have been the first to admit that in no other language could he achieve the elegance of a cultivated native speaker. There was no reason, therefore, why the aid mercenaries, the fat-cats of modern day charity, the shuttle-diplomats, the politicians and the journalists should write anything memorable in international English, a hybrid language without tits or balls. In any case the image was replacing the word as the international medium of persuasion.

"Hasn't the kettle boiled yet, Mr. Thomas?"

"Oh yes. Sorry, I was thinking."

"Did they give you a hard time?" she asked.

"What? No, no. I was thinking about... oh it doesn't matter."

"You know your trouble, don't you Mr. Thomas?"

"Don't call me Mr. Thomas. I'm Martin."

"Your trouble is that you give up too easily."

"You know nothing about me. What's your name?"

"Alice."

"Alice! Hmm. That's a nice name." He laughed quite spontaneously. "Some names are like that. They surprise you.

"Why, what did you think I was called?"

They were standing by the little sink, trying not to touch, "Go on," she persisted. "If I'm not an Alice, what am I?"

"I don't know. Fiona perhaps."

"Fiona's posh. I'm not posh, am I?"

"Fiona's not posh. It's Scottish."

"I'm not Scottish, either. Anyway, where are you from?"

"Kent, I suppose."

"You suppose?"

"Well, I have a small flat in London. But I was brought up in Kent. In a village."

"It must have a name."

"Yes, the name has not changed since I knew it."

"But you're not going to tell me what it is."

"It doesn't matter any more. It's a different place. Only the name's the same. It's a travesty to apply it now. Like insulting someone you once loved."

"You are in a funny mood."

"Well, I'm in the middle of an interview. Probably the adrenaline."

"Yes, I'm sorry." She poured some water from the kettle on to his tea bag.

"No, I'm sorry I offended you. It was very kind of you to offer me tea. It's just what I needed in fact."

"In fact," she repeated and they both laughed.

"Cheers," he said, lifting his mug.

"Cheers," she replied, watching him as he drank.

"I hope I'm not keeping you from your work."

"What the heck! I'm allowed a coffee break, too. I'll join you." She unspun the plastic lid of the Nescafe jar, took a spoonful of granules, added some milk surrogate and hot water and mixed up the sticky brew until it resembled coffee. They sat on a window seat in the alcove, side by side like two passengers on the tube.

"You don't take sugar," he observed.

"No. Waistline."

"What do you mean? You're slim as a thread."

"As a thread? That's a funny thing to say."

"It's Norwegian but quite unpremeditated. I'm sorry"

"Don't apologise. I'm flattered really."

"You know what you remind me of?" he said, looking at her green eyes. She shook her head, springy black hair a fraction of a second behind the movement of her skull, like a visual acoustic echo.

"A poem. No that's trite. A good read."

"You think you can read me? Like a book?"

"No, no! It's simply that you tie in with what I was daydreaming about just now. How to explain... In our work we read hundreds upon hundreds of reports, of minutes of meetings, of summaries. Well, as you know many of these come from international sources, they are written in what I call commodity English by people whose first, even second language is something else. At best this stodgy great feast of words communicates its message; even a native speaker rarely writes well about Third World Debt or the Diseases of Cocoa. But every so often I pick up a book of poems, a novel, and by comparison with the fodder on my desk at work, the words glisten, the verse gleams. The work rings true, rings sound. I get so much pleasure from it. From words well used."

"Yes, I suppose..." She was lost now.

"Well," he interrupted. "You stand out in the same way. Not because you are pretty. We're not allowed to tell our colleagues that, it is sexist talk isn't it, but you strike me as authentic, genuine. You haven't been putting on an act. You offered me a cup of tea out of a real human feeling."

"I wouldn't say that," she said, laughing away the glitter in her eyes. "I thought you looked tired and disappointed. I thought a cup of tea would cheer you up."

They were interrupted by a buzz from Alice's intercom. She went over to her workstation smoothing her straight black skirt, and then hurried back.

"They want you to go back in," she announced. "Good luck!"

The atmosphere inside the boardroom had thawed a little. The chairman gave Martin a smile of recognition and motioned him to the chair he had vacated a short time ago. "I'll come straight to the point," he said, "You are not the material we want for management positions in the U.K."

Material, am I now, thought Martin.

"We recognised," continued the Chairman, "that you have grown stale in your present job, that you find it unstimulating, routine. There is a post, a difficult... a challenging post in one of our operational zones. It requires someone on whom we can rely, someone with courage and resilience. We do not of course expect an immediate decision."

Any decision at all was difficult since Martin had no idea what was being offered him. He was not a member of the operational cadre and therefore was surprised at the offer to serve in an operational zone, which meant an overseas post.

"The post," explained the Chairman, "is in fact that of Manipulator, Republic of the Nile."

"In any other concern," replied Martin, "wouldn't this be categorised as dumping?"

"I don't follow you," said the Chairman.

"You have just described me as unsuitable material. Now you are proposing to dump me on some Third World

Republic, like a sample of time-lapsed drugs or cigarettes with too much tar content." He said this calmly, detachedly.

"That is a fair observation. To be frank, it is a post we have been unable to fill. And you are single, therefore cheap."

"Thanks for your honesty," said Martin, impressed for the first time. The two men smiled and the Chairman handed over a folder of papers. "Read these, sleep on it and let us have your decision tomorrow. Any questions?"

"Yes, two, although the answer may be in this folder."

"Fire away."

"Does this mean promotion?"

"No. And the second question?"

"Isn't there a civil war going on in the Republic of the Nile?"

"Oh that's been rumbling on for 17 years," said the Chairman almost jovially. "The civil war's the least of your worries."

Martin looked about him.

"The trouble with you," Alice had said, "is that you give up too easily." But he had thought you could at least change money, buy a drink. At least, he had thought there would be people, other people.

"I'm frightened, I'm terrified," Martin told himself in wonder.

"Well, how did it go?" Alice had asked when he had walked out of the boardroom that second time.

"They've offered me a job."

"Super!" she said. "Terrif! Is anything wrong?"

"Alice," he said, "what are you doing tonight?"

"Nothing special."

"Will you come out with me?"

"Where?"

"I don't know. Anywhere. For a meal or something."

"I'd love to," she said.

It was not practical to go home, change and meet later. They went from the office to a restaurant and despite lingering over a cocktail beforehand had finished their meal and a bottle of wine by eight thirty.

"You know," Alice had told him. "I do so admire what you are doing. It's just what I've always promised myself, but I'm not brave enough."

"You've still got time," he had replied. "You're young. For me it's a last chance."

She had laughed. "Don't think of it like that. That sounds so... so doom-laden. Think of it as a first chance."

"I haven't decided to go yet," he had reminded her. "That's why I needed someone to talk to."

"So I was just someone, any old someone to talk to."

"No," he had said. He had taken her hand and squeezed it. "I want this old someone."

She had changed the subject, acquiescing in a way.

"Did they give you all the bumf on Gondo? The living conditions and so forth?"

"It's all here," he had told her, patting the briefcase beside his chair.

"Let's read through it."

"Yes, but not here."

It had seemed natural, convenient to go to his flat. The description of life in Gondo contrasted with their comfortable, simple London routine. Meat is not often available, though a whole goat may sometimes be purchased or a side of a cow, they had read. You are advised to bring a meat cleaver.

There were pages on generators, gas bottles, medical supplies, precautions and preparations, all written for lecturers in the days when the University had flourished.

"Listen to this, Alice," he had said at one point. "The Nile flows through Gondo at a speed of 4 knots and hippopotamuses are common. However, commercial shipping has ceased and river blindness, bilharzia and malaria are endemic." On paper it had all sounded so exotic, so exciting.

At the deserted airport Martin clasped his shoulders in his hands and rocked himself in a despairing mimicry of self-consolation. If there had been another flight back he would have got straight on it. He felt sick.

In London, forgetful of time he and Alice had weighed the pros and cons.

"Well?" she had urged, "What's your decision?"

"Oh, I'm too excited to make up my mind about it now. I'll have to sleep on it." And, caught up in the excitement, he asked,

"Will you sleep on it with me?"

Before they fell asleep, she murmured,

"I don't want you to think I'm this kind of girl."

"Not any old someone," he incanted, "someone special. It's a pity, really..."

"You have decided to go."

"If I do, will you come and visit me?"

CHAPTER TWO

Perched on his suitcase Martin wondered whether he had made the decision for himself, in spite of himself or to impress Alice. No, despite his panic, he was not blaming her. And even inside that spinning helplessness he knew he could not be far from town. That he could walk in if need be. That he had money. That he would not starve. He simply had to take things one at a time. A drink, a room for the night, the search for an office, establishing lines of communication... But first a drink and shelter.

He looked up and saw a vehicle approaching the airport in a coil of red dust, a battered, short wheel-based Landrover, one of the old models with the headlamps close together in front of the radiator. Like the farmer back home used to have. Like an old friend.

The driver was a tubby, unsmiling white man who drew up at the steps where Martin was still sitting with his suitcase.

"Was Ajung on the plane?"

"Who's Ajung?"

Realising Martin was a newcomer the man said irritably, "Seven foot tall, thin as a piece of string, buck-toothed, black as ink."

"Can't say I noticed anyone of that description," said Martin.

"Then the bastard's still in Nairobi. Unless of course he's coming overland. Road train of diesel due in this week."

"Good," said Martin, to keep the conversation going. The tubby man looked at him.

"Where are you going?"

"The hotel."

"The Gondo Hotel? What on earth for?"

"Got to stay somewhere."

"Stay with me. No one stays in the Gondo Hotel. It's not that kind of hotel."

"You mean it?"

"Hop in," he ordered.

"I don't know you. I don't want to put you out."

"I wouldn't offer if I didn't want to. Get in." He made an effort to smile. It was more like a grimace of pain. "I'm Bob. Teacher."

"Martin."

"Is that all your luggage? Bung it in the back. Door's open."

Martin slid his case through the rear door onto the steel floor and hauled himself up beside Bob. He sank into his seat in gratitude. Immediately he shot forward as if stung. The seat back was burning hot.

"Sorry about that," said Bob, "canvass worn away. Metal gets hot. So does the floor. Can't drive her barefoot anymore."

They drove into Gondo. The ribbon of dirt from the airport led to a stretch of tarmac road. "The republic is the size of France," Bob said, "and this is the only bit of metalled road in the whole country."

"How long is it?"

"I'll give you a trip round it if you've got time."

"To tell you the truth," croaked Martin, "I'm badly in need of a drink."

"I know what you mean. It's only three and a half kilometres, actually. Past the Hotel, up to the new Ministry Block. Little spur off to the University and the Market."

"Is that all?"

"Nowhere else to go. That's Gondo. Half a dozen solid buildings, the rest mud huts. Tukuls."

They were driving past a pot-holed entrance to a crumbling, whitewashed shell of a building. Some people were sitting at cast-iron tables under a large neem tree.

"The hotel," explained Bob. "Only building in Gondo that hasn't got a thatched roof."

"It's got no roof at all."

"Precisely. Very convenient if you like fresh air, mosquitoes and Ugandan whores."

"You can stay there, then?"

"Oh, they'll take your money, yes. There's a restaurant of sorts. Legacy of the old days when the Sunderland Flying boats landed on the Nile. Same menu. Brown Windsor Soup, fish, meat and caramel custard you could bounce off the floor."

"Sounds like literally the same menu."

"Probably is. It's also got the first squash court ever built in Africa. Now a grain store."

They went over a rise and turned off down a tree-lined track. Bob told him that this had once been the merchants' quarter. Walled gardens had enclosed orchards of mango and fig and lime trees. The crumbling remains of the walls and some gnarled old mango trees were still in evidence. The houses were substantial and some, despite Bob's earlier remarks about thatched roofs, still had the original terra cotta tiles; others had been patched up with corrugated iron or indeed, with thatch.

"See those little doors in the walls?" Bob said. "They were the toilets. They held buckets of 'night soil' which were collected every night by members of a particular tribe and emptied."

Now the buckets had gone and sewage dribbled thickly across the road. The ditch was black with it, much to the satisfaction of a muscovy duck, shovelling avidly for the maggots with its broad, bony beak.

A little way down the bumpy road Bob hooted and an iron gate, freshly painted green, opened in a newly restored stone wall. A handsome, muscular boy welcomed Bob and closed the gate behind the vehicle.

"Isaiah, this is Martin. He will be staying. His suitcase is in the back." Bob enunciated each word one by one like separately shaped and cut stones of unstrung discourse, in the way English people do who have lived long in Africa. To Martin it was a new phenomenon, yet he was not too tired to observe that Africans themselves did not speak English in like manner.

"And Isaiah... Martin is very thirsty, eh?" The lad, who was probably about 20 years old, smiled, hurried in with Martin's suitcase and returned quickly with two large bottles of tolerably cool Elephant beer and glasses which he set down on a table on the small veranda.

"You've saved my life," said Martin.

Isaiah looked at him seriously. "Perhaps one day you will save mine," he said, and burst into an open laugh.

Martin let the liquid wash round his mouth. He moistened his parched lips with it and emptied half the glass straight off before putting it down on the table.

He looked round. On this side of the wall there was just space enough for one vehicle. In front of the veranda where he sat, papaya and banana plants towered above the wall creating shade, and in the case of the bananas an impression of coolness by the rattling of their fibrous leaves. Pots full of plants, most of them useful rather than merely decorative, tomatoes, aubergines, peppers, kumquats lined the wall. Inside the house the stone floor seemed to be waxed or polished a reddish colour. The walls were rough, thick and washed white.

"This is very nice," Martin said as Bob re-emerged from the shadowy interior.

"Yes. I don't know what we'd do without the smugglers."

Martin realised he thought he meant the beer. "No, I mean the house."

"Yes. I did it up. Probably fix you up with something like this."

Martin's spirits rose. Pretty good if he could get himself sorted out this quickly.

"Mind you," went on Bob, "took me five years. How much time you got?"

"I'll be here some time," said Martin, his panic returning. "I expect."

"None of us have got much longer. The rebels, so-called, are gaining strength so Isaiah tells me. By the way, I've put you in his room for tonight."

"Where will he sleep?"

"Oh, he can sleep out here. He won't mind."

"Does he work for you?"

"He's a student. Works in the morning, goes to school in the afternoon, or vice versa. We do two shifts."

"He's a bit old to be a schoolboy, isn't he?"

"Twenty four. That's nothing. Civil War disrupted education. Still is. Disrupting everything."

"I see," said Martin, but he didn't.

"You married?"

"Not at the moment."

"Then you'll need help," judged Bob. Martin smiled, wondering how his female colleagues in the office so far away now would have reacted. Bob did not even notice. "I can get you a house boy. The deal is they help you half the day, you see them through school. Books, food, shelter, uniform and so on. It's a good deal for both. A better relationship than servant and employer."

Over the next few days Martin learned that Bob's irritability, indeed irascibility was mainly a mask. As he had already proved, Bob was kind and helpful. Martin also discovered Isaiah was not the only student Bob was assisting. There were lots of young men in and out of the house. Some of them like Isaiah belonged, others came to study, to borrow books or to use the hand operated Gestetner.

Since the school was on holiday, Bob found Martin a temporary room of his own in a vacant staff unit. Brusquely, economically he taught Martin the art of survival and his own house was always open, a kind of bolt-hole.

This was just the back-up Martin required but hoped he would not call upon. To help set him up further Bob took him to an Asian run hardware shop where he bought a splendid earthenware British Berkefeld water filter made in Tonbridge, an electric fan from China and a small Japanese generator to run the fan and a few lights. He even changed a sterling cheque into local currency. "Better than the bank. Take all day to cash a cheque there. Literally," said Bob. "Even when you have an account." Finally they ordered a gas fridge.

"Can you get gas?"

"Bottles sometimes. We'll put your name down."

They drove to the Gondo Import/Export Company to do this and more importantly to find out the whereabouts of Martin's Landrover, shipped to Mombasa. Juma, who managed the store, knew there was a Landrover in Kenya and said he expected Big Pete would probably drive it up himself on his return from leave later in the month. Otherwise it would be put on a lorry in the next convoy or await another suitable driver.

"Who's Big...?" began Martin but Bob muttered, "Tell you later."

Since neither the gas nor the fridge would be ready for some time they went to the market to purchase a sack of charcoal, a flat iron, a big clay water pot and some provisions. Back in Martin's temporary home Bob showed him how to keep his filtered water reasonably cool by sinking bottles in the clay pot itself filled with water. Martin realised why Bob had haggled over and bought two empty whisky bottles in the market.

"Never ever throw anything away," Bob advised, "Everything has a use. Especially containers."

The clay pot sweated a little, the moisture evaporated and this kept the water inside a little cooler than the air temperature. More difficult was filling the iron with burning charcoal and ironing the shirts without smudging them.

"Sounds impossible," said Martin.

"It'd be easier with an electric iron," admitted Bob, "But I can find you a boy or a girl to fetch you water, do your washing and ironing. No problem."

"Let me get sorted out first. When I get a permanent place I might take up your suggestion of a house boy." He was beginning to look forward to rather than dread the prospect of home and office building. "Now tell me, who is this Big Pete?"

"Oh, he's the manager of the Import/Export Co. A useful person to know but... You'll see. He's a law unto himself. If he likes you..."

"Why shouldn't he?"

"Well, he's like a great big dog. You know dogs can sense if people are afraid of them and they get more aggressive. Pete's like that. Show him plenty of affection and he'll be your friend."

"Is that necessary? To have him as a friend?"

"Oh wait and see," snapped Bob abruptly, "I don't want to prejudice you."

"Is he an expatriate?"

Bob laughed in exasperation. "God, what's that man got that I haven't got? You've not met him yet and you seem fascinated by him."

"Sorry."

"He's a white Kenyan, Yorkshire origin. I had a set-to with him about one of my female students. Ah, forget it. You'll

21

have to make up your own mind. Gondo is a small community."

When people got to know that Britwords was going to set up an office in Gondo they flocked to Martin with offers of accommodation, help and with requests for jobs. This continued to encourage him. It all seemed suddenly so easy.

He did make several mistakes initially. In the market women sat on the dirt ground behind pyramids of beans set out on a scrap of cloth or a piece of paper. There were all kinds and colours of beans and pulses, heaps of onions and tomatoes; chalky chunks of dried cassava glistening like gypsum in the sun. After a few meals of rice and aubergine and onion fried together and followed by delicious, fresh pineapple, he thought he would try something different. So one afternoon he bought a paper coneful of greenish pulses. He thought he would boil them until they were soft and mix them with a tin of corned beef. He boiled them for two hours but they remained hard. He waited another hour, using more of his precious charcoal. Still no difference. In the end he fell back on bread and the giant pot of Marmite he had brought with him from England and which, together with packet soups, had kept him nourished during this time of trial and error. It was not until the morning, having simmered the pulses until they were dry that he learned that what in fact he had bought were not pulses at all, but coffee beans. They should have been roasted.

More serious and time-consuming was his ignorance of official procedures. He spent days traipsing from office to office to get a residence permit, a work permit, a driving licence and to complete a dozen other formalities.

Finally in despair he dropped in on Bob who said, "It'll be worse when your Landrover arrives." He told him about the roadworthiness tests, the registration, the painting on by hand of his own number in regulation letters and numbers in white paint on a black background, and even then it was likely to be the same number as someone else's.

"You need a Mr. Fixit to do all this. Someone who knows the ropes."

"Do you know someone?"

They discussed a few possibilities but finally Martin decided he would have to take the plunge at once and recruit his own staff. He did not want to employ a casual fixer. Such duties would be included in the job description for his office manager. He wasn't getting anywhere very quickly but at least, he felt, he was making decisions, finding his feet, getting on top of things.

ALICE'S STORY. PART ONE

I was working for this organisation. You wouldn't know it. A kind of export company. They thought themselves very progressive, employed hundreds of women and blacks and called it equal opportunities. No family man, and let's face it, the main breadwinner was still very often the man, could afford to work for them. Not in the London office. The women, you see, worked for pin money, or mortgage money to bring the expression up to date. The blacks were pleased to find employment. It was the 1950s all over again under a respectable guise. Instead of driving buses they were put to clerical and registry jobs in underfunded organisations like Britwords. I'm sure if Britwords had paid us a living wage they would not have been able to boast of their striking equal opportunities record. And anyway all the senior managers were men.

I'm telling you all this to try and recapture my mood at the time. My friends tell me I am normally rational, sensible... Good friends tell me I am too sensible, too careful.

Well, I don't know what came over me that day. I did a very rash thing. I think looking back on it that quite unconsciously a sense of frustration had been building up inside me for some time.

Don't get me wrong. I enjoyed my work. I was P.A., personal assistant, to the Controller of Human Resource Material. He was all right. He called me Alice and I called him Mr. Jefferson until he went on a training course entitled 'You and Your Secretary.' When he came back he got very embarrassed and asked me to call him Alan. He kept asking me what I thought about this and that, even about the way he did his own job. I told him he was paid to think about those things, not me. That's why he received a higher salary. I told him if he wanted to consult me on policy matters he should really pay me a fee. I don't think his course had adequately prepared him for this response, but he muttered something about my having a made a fair point. Oh, I could manage Mr. Jefferson all right. I didn't need to go on a course, 'You and Your Boss.'

But all the same I felt trapped. I was living in Putney with Linda, my married sister. There was no way, you see, I could afford a place of my own. Not on what I was paid. My sister's all right and I was useful to have around for child-minding and helping ferry her kids to ballet classes. But no couple really wants a third party in the home. Particularly not in a small house with children. Not to mention how this third party felt about it!

Oh, and I went down to Kent every other weekend to keep an eye on Mum and Dad. They depended on it. And my sister thought by putting up with me during the week, she was somehow doing her duty by Mum and Dad as well. She was usually too busy with the kids, you see. I went down for both of us. Sometimes I took the kids. So Lyn didn't get a bad deal. I never took a man. Mum wouldn't have liked it.

And then I had a row with this guy I was going out with at the time. The last of many as it turned out, though that morning I was not to know it was the end.

I had to be at work early to prepare all the papers for a promotion board. Mr. Jefferson did not like leaving anything to chance. His senior colleagues attended the board, of course, though he chaired it. And he liked to have everything at his fingertips. Or if not at his, at mine. So I needed to study the files of the candidates, remember their ages, family circumstances, details about their service and so forth.

I must say, on paper I wasn't much struck with Mr. Thomas. He had been in the company for fifteen years. He was a good, steady worker. Mainly on the research side. There was not one adversely critical comment on his file. He was capable, creative but somehow nothing stood out about him. He was a bit of a loner, anyway not what I would call a joiner. I couldn't tell from the photo, likely taken ten years previously, whether I had even bumped into him. Britwords was a large organization. We didn't know half our own colleagues, not even those of us who worked in Personnel, as I still thought of it.

I was pleasantly surprised when Mr. Thomas did turn up, though. He was quite old, really, well past forty. I knew that from the file, but I still had the photo in my mind. He looked a bit like a mild mannered professor, slightly stooping but well preserved. There was nothing threatening about him, nothing aggressive. That was his problem, from a promotion point of view. They liked the bumptious types, the con-men, the over-confident. We used to joke that if you really wanted to get on in the organization you needed to get involved in a monumental cock-up. Then they would promote you out of it.

Mr. Thomas had been passed over for promotion several times; he was in fact in danger of being made redundant though he did not know it. His qualities and his qualifications had gone out of fashion. And as I say he was a bit old.

He came out of that interview so disappointed. God, I've seen worse cases. I've had them crying on my shoulder. Part of the job, you see. But I felt really sorry for Mr. Thomas. Not, I think because he was so crushed, but that in my own frustration I sympathized with the smouldering anger beneath his disappointment, with his sense of injustice. Britwords in trying to be ahead of the game was always led by fashion, by trends. It was never as innovative as it thought it was. You see, it was a bit of a quango and received a sizeable government subsidy. If the flavour of the month was First Steps Initiative or "efficiency savings" or "repositioning" Britwords tried to keep one step ahead. In fact it was led by the nose down the path of political expediency. Oh, I'm talking like him now!

When they called Mr. Thomas back, I was delighted for him. But he seemed to have given up. He seemed so dejected. I persuaded him to give it a second go. He agreed. I offered him a cup of tea. He helped me fetch it. We got chatting. Then they called him back in to the boardroom.

The offer they made him showed just how cynical, how two-faced Britwords could be. Here was a man who they had already found unsuitable for a company that considered itself so modern. Admittedly he was different from the successful younger managers. He was urbane, he spoke languages (quite useful in an export company you would think), he went to classical music concerts, played tennis quite well. I found out later he had never been to a football match or seen the inside of a disco! There was a note on his file recording his refusal to accept a complimentary ticket to the Britword Marquee at Wimbledon, or was it Ascot.

In short here was a man taken on when content and quality had mattered, but who was no longer seen to be of use to a changing organization. Bulk export, mass markets were the order of the day. He was a square peg in a round hole, still insisting that the words themselves were important. So what do they do? They decide against all their psychometric testing methods, against all their test and objective criteria, to send him to a quite differently shaped hole. At least that was the assumption in Human Resources Material. I don't think any of them had actually been there. Britwords offered this man, who had never travelled further afield than Greece, a trading post in the most rugged and remote corner of their neo-empire. Sorry, I'm quoting his words again.

What so surprised, and I admit touched me was that he was actually considering accepting their offer. Touched because I realised the depth of his desperation. Here was a man with the courage to get out of his comfortable rut. Even if that courage was born of despair. Perhaps, because I felt myself similarly trapped, I encouraged him a little bit, too.

The upshot of it was he took me out to dinner and I went back to his flat. I do not make a habit of spending the night with complete strangers, if I can describe a colleague as such. My sister never worried if I did not come home. I was often at Malcolm's place before we split. The truth is I didn't think of Martin as a stranger or as a colleague, I saw him as a kindred spirit. And what the hell, he was leaving for the Republic of the Nile in a fortnight. It was his decision. Though I've wondered since if I did not encourage him.

He seemed flattered at my unconcealed pleasure when, having slept on it, (eventually we did get to sleep), he said,

"I think I'll go."

I was delighted for him. Sometimes I feel guilty. Sometimes I feel I made the decision for him. For selfish reasons, as if by willing his escape I was vicariously removing my own straightjacket. We kissed as if to seal the bargain and we made love again before breakfast. After that I do not think he would have had the face to change his mind. But hell, it was his decision.

Almost immediately our delight evaporated. We were still in bed, retreating into our own bodies and beings when we both realised at the same time what this decision meant. It meant for one thing we would not have many more nights, many more awakenings together. Even then, you see, we had taken a liking to one another. Obviously, or I wouldn't have been in his bed.

And then he said, "Well, I'll go on one condition."

I told him I doubted whether Britwords would listen to any condition.

"I'm not asking Britwords to listen. I'm talking to you Alice. I'll go if you'll come and visit me."

I laughed. It was out of the question. I'd never travelled. Certainly not to Central Africa. I had no money.

"We'll talk about it on your home leave," I said. I was happy. His condition, unrealistic though it was, opened up a future beyond the immediate, frightening prospect of our parting.

He did go. And it was his decision. And I made no promises. I have nothing to feel guilty about.

If anything it was because of him that within six months I was in the Republic of the Nile myself. Long before his home leave fell due.

CHAPTER THREE

Martin stood naked in the dark space that served as his bathroom. He dipped his calabash into the drum of water and poured it over himself with a ripple of pleasure. The water was not cold, but it was cooler than he was. It washed off the dust and it refreshed before splashing on the floor. He had put a grill over the hole to keep snakes and insects out.

Wondering how much more water he would allow himself, Martin heard a familiar engine outside and a beep on the horn. He put on a towel and greeted Bob, who stayed in the cab of the Landrover.

"Got a dinner jacket?" shouted Bob.

"Well, no," replied Martin anxiously. "Why?"

"Invitation. Delia. University."

"Do we have to dress up?"

Bob gave a rare laugh. "In this heat? Shirt, trousers. Both long. Mosquitoes. Pick you up at six."

The University compound was formed of a group of colonial style bungalows that once had housed the expatriate training college. Some bungalows still had the original clay tile roofs, others were patched with tin. Radiating from a central water tower, the houses were sufficiently spaced to afford the present occupants privacy. The general picture was of picturesque decay. Some houses were quite submerged in a spray of purple and white bougainvillaea, most had some kind of shade tree, flamboyant or jacaranda or merely plantain as protection from the sun. A few people whose energies had not been entirely sapped by the heat of the place, for as Martin was finding, survival itself was quite as demanding as the work one was supposed to do, a few people had planted their gardens with cassava or sweet potatoes and ground nuts.

"Question of whether you want to bathe or eat," observed Bob. "Water's short."

"But isn't that a water tower?" said Martin.

"Pump's broken. No parts. Like us, they employ someone to carry water from the river."

Delia was sitting on the front step of her small veranda waiting for them. Her bare arms were clasped round her equally bare legs. She watched them drive up and get out of the Landrover. She raised one hand to acknowledge them and stood to shake Martin's as he walked up the path in the fading daylight.

"Welcome to Gondo," she smiled toothily. She had a generous mouth with teeth that seemed to have been thrown into it pell-mell. Her voice was rich and throaty. "Hi, Bob."

"Hi, Delia. All well?"

"As can be expected."

They were clearly old friends, thought Bob. This tranquil, unhurried woman radiated repose. She poured the men a beer and sat facing them, patient but alert for news.

As Martin took in this scarecrow of a woman in the increasing darkness he had to suppress a smile. She was one of those white women most at home in Africa. She had short straggly hair and thick-rimmed glasses. Her full, almost African lips covered all those teeth. Her cotton frock was thin and creased. As she bent to light a hurricane lamp and placed it between them on a low table he noticed that her unshaven legs were disfigured by the red blotches of insect bites.

Having adjusted the flame to her satisfaction she lent back in her cane chair, knees slightly apart and said to Martin in her deep-squeaky voice,

"I hear you've been recruiting staff. How's it going?"

"I think I've found what I wanted," said Martin, rather pleased with his day's work. Raising his glass he said, "This beer's good. How do you get it so cold?"

"Aha, gas fridge," she chuckled.

"Delia!" scolded Bob, "where did you get gas from?"

"Some of us have our sources," she grinned. The two friends evidently shared a secret that Martin did not understand.

Bit by bit he told them about his day. How he had decided that to start with he needed a secretary and an office manager cum accountant. He had followed Bob's advice and advertised on Radio Gondo. In the absence of TV and newspapers the radio sold time for small announcements every evening.

Martin had weeded through hundreds of applications and today had invited eight for interview.

"And you've chosen them already?" exclaimed Delia in alarm, scratching at a bite on her ankle.

"Yes, on probation, of course."

"Who are they?" she asked, perhaps a little too eagerly.

"Delia knows everyone," explained Bob. "Should have suggested.... Well, none of my business...."

Martin was surprised at their interest. He was after all only trying to establish a trading post. It was not as if he were trying to fill sensitive posts in government or even in a school, or so he believed.

"So who's your secretary? Is she pretty?" teased Delia.

"If she is that is not why I have chosen her," said Martin, defensively. He was offended. He was still imbued with the attitudes of his headquarters with its equal opportunities and a selection process thought to be entirely objective. Provided that was that the correct percentage of minority groups were enrolled, the correct balance of gender maintained and a satisfactory ethnic intake achieved. As for middle-aged white males, they could only be sent to Gondo.

"Come on then. Out with it," urged Delia.

"Her name is, now what is it? Rishti? Ashley? I forget."

"Not Vashti by any chance? About thirty? Sense of humour?"

"Vashti. Yes, Vashti May is her name."

"Vashti may and Vashti will," joked Delia. "You'll have fun and games with that young lady."

"Oh, Vashti! Ex-VC's secretary!" exclaimed Bob.

"That's right. She told me that," said Martin. "Well, you both seem to know her. Have I made a good choice?"

"If you want a bit of excitement in your life. No, she's very good. If she wants to be."

"Habit of disappearing. Days on end," said Bob.

"It could well be she had other duties to perform," hinted Delia. "It was a difficult time for the university. For the VC in particular."

"Or it could have been lack of supervision," said Bob. "The Vice Chancellor was not often on seat himself."

Martin noticed that Delia seemed uncomfortable with Bob's harsh criticism and he intervened diplomatically,

"I think I will be able to handle her. Though I admit she's got cheek. When I asked at the end of the interview whether she had any questions she said, 'Yes, are you married?'"

They all laughed and Delia filled their glasses with more Elephant beer. "And are you, Martin?" she queried, pausing with the empty bottle still tilted over his glass.

"What?"

"Married."

"No. Well, I'm sort of engaged."

"Aren't we all," she sighed.

Martin then went on to describe his second recruit, a deliberate contrast to Vashti. He was a solid, dependable sounding married man with a large family.

"How does he support them now?" snapped Bob.

Martin told him that Ndua worked at the Commercial School but that the school had been closed for two years and there was no prospect of its re-opening.

"That's true," nodded Bob.

"Now don't tell me he is drawing two salaries," said Martin. "We went into that. As long as he puts Britwords first, that's not my concern."

"You're learning," said Delia, picking up the lamp. "Come on. Let's go in and eat."

Before they had finished the meal, a well-seasoned spaghetti Bolognese, the trio was alarmed by the sound of a vehicle drawing up, much tooting and shouting, a door banging and footsteps approaching.

Without so much as knocking a bronzed, unshaven white man walked in. He looked about forty, balding, moustached and his muscles bulged out of a thin cotton waistcoat and tight shorts. While Delia and Bob relaxed at once, Martin was more alarmed than ever when, ignoring the others, the intruder demanded...

"Are you Martin Thomas?"

"Yes."

"I've got your Landrover outside. Bastard got three punctures on the way from Mombasa. That's forty quid you owe me plus delivery."

"Martin, allow me to introduce you. Big Pete, Manager of the Trading Post. Martin Thomas, Manipulator, Britwords."

"As if he hadn't guessed," said Bob. "Hi Pete. Good holiday?"

This was the cue for an astonishing monologue, or pretty well a monologue. Installed back on the veranda with coffee and more drinks, Pete proceeded to recount not the hazardous adventure of driving overland from Mombasa to Gondo, which to those present had become routine, but described his holiday in Britain. It had been his first for five years.

34

"The country's going to the dogs, man, you know that?" he said in a deep voice, half Yorkshire, half that cross between clipped South African and drawling Australian English that is spoken by white East Africans.

"No service. They're all peasants, man, bloody savages," he said of his fellow countrymen. "You can't even get a drink without fighting for it. I mean, here in Gondo, there are no real bars or restaurants and that, but you just sit down, say in Unity Gardens and clap your hands at them. If they don't come running pdq you sort them out, right? Well, in England they don't give a damn about you. They don't want to serve you. They're indifferent. You don't exist. Bloody hell, it's not surprising the country is in the state it is. One pub I went to it took me two minutes to push to the bar. And when I say push, well...." His eyes glinted. "They didn't like it, mind, but it's not right to keep a man waiting for his beer. And the prices! They really try it on. I went to a place for a meal, see. It was good grub, I don't mind admitting it. But when they brought the bill, it came to sixty quid. Sixty pounds for two. Did I make a noise? I tore it up. I did. Then I walked out."

"You were lucky not to be caught," said Martin.

"It's not luck, man. If I don't want to be caught, no one catches me."

"You can't get away with it all the time," said Martin. Delia looked a bit nervous, as if it were dangerous to contradict Big Pete, but he seemed pleased that Martin was taking him seriously.

"Not over there, you can't, you're right," he admitted. "As a matter of fact I got arrested twice. Pigs, all of them. First time was Heathrow. Two customs blokes. Buggers wanted me to pay some duty or other, yeah? I told them I'd smash their heads together if they didn't let me pass."

"What did they do?"

"They didn't argue, Martin. Only two big cops suddenly turned up, out of the blue like. Asked the customs officials if they could be of any help. The buggers nodded at me and the pigs asked me to go along with them. I told them I wasn't going to. I was, I said, going to the duty free shop. So I did and they followed me round. Stuck to me all the time."

Martin thought he sensed an inconsistency here. Passengers pass through duty free on the way out not in. Bob anticipated Martin's objection and chipped in,

"So you got through?"

"Absolutely. Make enough noise, you can bullshit your way through anything. Even in the UK," Pete said to Martin. "The British hate trouble. And I was ready to fight. No kidding. But I tell you, it's getting to be a police state over there. I did get arrested in Leeds."

Whereas the others were all barefoot, Martin and Bob having removed their sandals at the step, Big Pete was wearing size twelve mosquito boots which he proceeded to take off.

"When Pete removes his boots," said Delia in her languid voice, "there's nothing for it but to lie back and listen."

"You lie back, love and I'll take off more than my boots," said Pete with a dirty laugh, before proceeding with his story about Leeds. He had just taken delivery of his new motorbike, a BMW Super Tracker, in London. He drove it up the motorway to get the feel of it. He also had a business contact to meet in Leeds. "Important lunch and all that crap," he explained, flinging off the second boot and downing half a glass of beer.

"I drove round and round for fucking hours looking for somewhere to park. It's a big machine, a Super Tracker. But there's nowt but yellow lines in Leeds so in the end I stood the bike on the pavement outside the restaurant we were to meet in, see. I'd just taken off my crash helmet and jacket, it's fucking cold on a motorbike in England, man, you ought to try it, when this little Asian in a parking warden's fancy dress turns up and tells me I can't leave my motorbike there. I'm very friendly. I tell him I wasn't born yesterday and suggest to him that he hasn't seen the motorbike on the pavement. I told him he should turn round and get his face out of my sight before I smashed it in for him. I warn him, that's all, smiling like. Nothing abusive."

"What did he do?" prompted Martin not really willing to encourage racist attitudes; hoping he was not toadying.

"He went away. The only trouble was he came back with two coppers. Would they listen to reason? Would they 'eck! Where the hell do they expect you to park in Leeds, man? Tell me that. I never did make that lunch."

"You're from Yorkshire, aren't you?" said Bob. He too was relaxed, well fed and enjoying the cool evening. Let the man entertain them. He needed to talk after days on the road. Besides, there was no TV in Gondo.

"Yes, went to see Mum and Dad. First time in years. And the last, I reckon."

"Oh?" said Delia, re-filling all their glasses.

"We had a bit of a misunderstanding. Me Dad told me not to come back until I'd grown up."

"That will be quite a while, then," snorted Delia.

"Delia, you're the only woman that gets away with a remark like that."

"I'm flattered."

"I should hope so."

"So what provoked your Dad's remark?" she asked, preventing matters from turning personal between them.

"Well, they live in this poxy little semi. No room to swing a monkey, know what I mean? So they invite me and my brother(who I never liked - chalk and cheese) and his wife and their dogs and brats. It was cruel, man, cruel. Like caged animals, we were. I'm sitting there, right, well into my second jar when their car draws up outside and these dogs burst in. Monsters. One is a Doberman, the other a ridgeback. A Doberman and a ridgeback from bloody Halifax, that's where they live. The Tunbridge Wells of the North and not a lion in sight. Not Nairobi where you need guard dogs. Halifax!" He made the name sound like an obscenity. "And they were vicious, these dogs, vicious. They were bored with having no one to bite, like, living in Halifax. You could tell they were bored to the back teeth. And they showed me all their teeth when I growled at them.

Well, one of them snarled at me. Now dogs normally like me, they respect me, see. Pack leader. Dogs certainly don't scare me, but this one was vicious. I asked my brother, do you mind taking that thing out of here, calmly, like.

'He's all right,' said me brother.

'Is 'e 'eck!'

'Don't take no notice of his snarling. It's his way. He won't bite.'

Well, for the sake of family harmony I gritted my teeth and the chat began and they said how did I like Gondo. Better than Bloody Yorkshire, I told them.

'He's not changed, has he!' says my smart Alec brother. As a matter of fact his name's Alec. Anyway I moved my arm to pour out a bottle when it started again. The dog growled. Well that did it. I picked up my chair and I held it over my head and I said, 'Do you mind getting that dog away from me? 'Cos if you don't, I'll kill it.' That set the other dog off. There was a hell of a shindig. Anyway Alec took the beasts out and bundled them into the car. Then the bloody kids came in. They're worse than the dogs, I swear it. Alec and his wife are very modern parents. They let their kids do what they like. Well, I put up with it for quite a while. About five minutes. But when the little girl put a sticky lolly in my hair, what's left of it, I told my brother he'd better put the kids in the car and all. I was mad. Because if you don't, I said, I will, and I hope the bloody hounds make a meal of them.

"Of course, that did it. They all left. Mum was crying, Dad was shaking, so I said,

'I think I'd best be going now. Thanks for tea. See you in ten years if you're not dead and buried. Ta-ra.' And I left. Holiday!? It was purgatory. Do you know something; I never thought I'd say this. I'll not say it again, that's for sure, but I'm actually glad to be back. I'm glad. England's too small for me."

CHAPTER FOUR

For months Martin had been too busy, too absorbed setting up his office, hiring his staff, simply surviving to think much about what he was there to do. The lack of any mail allowed time to pass by before he had accounted for it, though in moments of loneliness he missed his private mail and in particular news of Alice. But mail would come, Bob assured him. It accumulated in a freight office in Nairobi and was flown in when a plane was available, bags of it for all the agencies operating in Gondo. Erratic but reliable, unless you were in a hurry.

Martin was already losing any sense of urgency. Everything was so different here.

"You must believe in your product," he had learned on a marketing course. But no one had taught him how to acquire that belief. There was an underlying assumption that British Words, any of them were good for the world. In the Republic of the Nile they nearly all appeared to Martin to be absurdly inappropriate.

He could see, of course, the political advantages of selling British rather than Arabic words from his own government's point of view. The Republic of the Nile was a kind of buffer state between the Islamic, Arab North and the black, Christian South. In fact in the Republic, the people were mainly animists still, with Christianity a comparatively recent veneer. The Republic was still very poor though Western countries were prospecting for oil. The leaders, too, were poor but were beginning to succumb to the appeal of corruption. The countries to the North, some of them already oil-rich, bribed the Gondo Government to build mosques and to open centres for Islamic culture. Sometimes such projects were a condition for trade or aid.

The people, however, harboured a folk memory of great resentment if not of downright hatred for the Arabs, a word used indiscriminately for some of their own lighter-skinned elite as well as for the "true" Arabs in countries to the North. Few of the inhabitants of Gondo would have known that their town was originally founded by the Turks as a trading post, a source of supply for ivory, gold and slaves, above all slave girls. The cruelty of these raids lingered in the collective consciousness. It totally erased the brief intervening period of British Rule.

Many people in Gondo for reasons of expediency or ambition called themselves Gabriel or Mohamed or Fatimah, but they kept their African and their Christian names as well. The resentment against things Arab occasionally broke out in times of shortage in the form of attacks on the stores of the Northern Traders, these clannish men for ever scratching their crotches beneath the folds of their long and grubby galabiahs.

The growing assertiveness of the Arabist government was the reason for an increasingly organized resistance movement based on Gondo, of which Martin was only dimly aware.

Whether selling a few well-chosen words would prevent such abuse, Martin was unable to judge. In his more lucid moments he wondered whether they were any better substitute. The few cartons of words that had come in with the fuel and some office furniture were not particularly well chosen. He could not see that Humpty-Dumpty, known by most British children to be particularly fragile, would staunch the flow of Islamic Fundamentalism, though he considered that there was a kind of Alice in Wonderland logic about his situation.

Other agencies, too, were importing British Words and for a while he wondered if they were not in direct competition. However he soon realised that many of the Christian organizations, attacking the same enemy in a different way, had a predilection for the more archaic items; the European

Community brought in job lots of such gobbledegook that it took a skilled linguist to decipher whether the assortment actually was English or whether it was a concoction from one or two of the other languages misused by the Brussels tower of Babel. The World Bank and its agencies had a monopoly on words to do with finance and economics and structural adjustment; and the U.N. Agencies brought in truckloads of lexicon labelled sustainable development. To ensure the commodities had survived the journey they ran them through the spell-checks in their computers, but since the computers were American or Japanese, the results as far as Martin was concerned were not reliable. In any case, he could honestly say the words were not British.

In these efforts, and in the individual efforts of health and agricultural and rural development agencies, Martin saw opportunities for himself. However hopeless his own task, he did believe that his organization was able to offer better or more appropriate words than such bodies could obtain, even in their own areas of expertise.

Suddenly he saw a real opening. Not only could he interest these wealthy international agencies in his Britwords' sets and packages, but more strategically, he felt there was a role for someone to co-ordinate this massive inflow of information and misinformation, of prejudice and theory, of belief and of fashionable conviction. If managed more efficiently there would be more words to go round.

The project was daunting. And in the final analysis, he would not be judged by the effect on the people of the Nile Republic of these intangible riches. He was held responsible by his masters for the quantity of words he i.e. Britwords could sell. "Value for money" was the government catchphrase and like most government statements meant the opposite. It had nothing to do with giving value for money but everything to do with selling the national heritage, the good and the bad bits of it, for as high a price as possible. The aim was short term. If shoddy goods would sell, sell them. By the time anyone found out they did not work there would be a new government.

Martin had been asked to open an office in one of the poorest countries of the world. Nevertheless it was expected to pay its way, and quality, real value for money, was a luxury Britwords could not allow him. An uncompromising message had been drummed into him on his briefing course. "English is a very desirable global commodity. Get out there and exploit the demand."

Martin pushed aside the remnants of his breakfast, a slice of pawpaw and some rather nasty robusta coffee and milk made with powder and Nile Water. He was still pondering his plan when there was a knock on the door.

A girl about eighteen or nineteen years old stood there. Her worn flip-flops were made of car tyres and her cotton frock was so threadbare it might have torn as easily as a spider's web. It had once been blue but the fabric had faded so much that the small white flowers in the print were almost indistinguishable from their background. But the frock was immaculately cleaned and pressed. The girl who filled it was pretty but unsmiling, her hair carefully, plainly plaited. She could have been a poor Sunday School teacher.

"Mr. Thomas?" she inquired.

"Yes?"

"I'm Margaret Obote." She held out a well-scrubbed hand. He shook it but said,

"This is my private house. The office opens in half an hour."

"I know. I wanted to see you privately."

"What can I do for you?"

"It's what I can do for you. May I come in?"

"Perhaps," he said suspiciously. "You had better tell me your business first."

"May I tell you about myself?" He did not yield and she did not wait for an answer. "I'm a Ugandan. I come from the camp by the river. My people were driven out. We are hungry."

"Doesn't the UNHCR look after you?"

"They have given us tents. We have no food, no money. We are expected to grow food but crops do not come up overnight."

"Margaret," he said, hardened already by all the hard luck stories he had heard, "I am sure you are telling the truth. I am sure you are suffering hardship. But before you continue, let me tell you, I cannot give you money. I cannot employ you. I am only allowed to employ nationals of this country."

"I will work for food."

"I have filled the few posts I had."

"I will do housework. Anything."

He looked thoughtfully at the girl. She was so well spoken, assured and so very thin. Why should she have to do his housework? "How is it you speak such good English?"

"I was a student at Makerere. But I had to flee. The soldiers, you know..."

He did know. The rape and mutilation of female students by the military was known even in Gondo. "Can't you be useful at the camp?"

"Useful of course. But I want to eat. I want money."

"Couldn't you teach?"

"Of course, if I was not Ugandan, if I could get a residence permit and a work permit; and if the Department of Education would pay me. I cannot wait so long."

"People come to me every day," explained Martin. "Men and women, young and old. I cannot help them all."

"So you do not help any?"

"You do not know who I help," he replied angrily, defensively.

The girl changed her tone now, pleading, "I will do anything for you. I can type, I can do clerical work, I can wash your shirts."

"I'm very sorry," he said, echoing her despair, "but so can I."

She took his hands in hers, a gesture that would have been more appropriate the other way round, like her next question.

"Isn't there anything I can do for you?"

"No," he said, freeing himself. "No."

"Is there nothing else you need?" she suggested. "You are a single man, I know. I asked. You may be lonely. I will do anything," she stated baldly.

Martin looked at her. Her thin frock barely hid the contours of her body. There was no spare flesh on her. Her breasts and buttocks were firm and trim, accentuated by the worn fabric. Necessity had given her the kind of figure girls in his country dieted for or went to aerobics classes to achieve. With a little food inside her and a smile on her face she would have been beautiful. She turned slightly, letting Martin's gaze play over her. She saw his hesitation, his weakening.

"May I come in now?"

"I'm sorry," he said. "I would not like to take advantage of you in that way."

"I would be the one taking advantage," she said. "You are not a violent man. You would not abuse me." She was almost crying now.

"No," he said, and tried to shut the door. She held it.

"Please. Please."

"There is nothing I can do. Nothing. Please go away."

She pulled herself together and asked, "May I have a glass of water before I go. At least that."

Somehow Martin had the notion that if he let her in she would stay for ever. The prospect was almost as tempting as it was terrifying. And it was not right. He could not think why, exactly, but somewhere in the back of his mind it was not right. It was abuse, whatever she said. Throughout history the strong had abused the weak. And he did not want her or anyone come to that on those terms.

He returned quickly with a glass of water and half a loaf of bread.

"Just this once, mind," he said, avoiding the reproach in her eyes. She took the loaf and the glass. She drank the water down quickly and handed back the glass.

"Please," she began, but he started to close the door. The girl, Margaret Obote, turned and walked away. Martin felt sick at heart, but he could not have taken her in. Not on such terms. He felt he had acted strongly, done the right thing.

It was only seven thirty in the morning but already hot. The coffee and the conversation had made him sweat already. He went into the makeshift shower he had constructed to freshen up for the office. Under the tumbling water he thought of Margaret Obote again. Her barely concealed figure, the nipples standing proud against the frayed cotton, her vibrant voice.

"I will do anything. Anything."

"Scrub my back, darling," he said between his teeth, allowing the tepid, untreated water to play over his lips. Her hands massaged his back, slipped round his groin, felt lower, eased his pain and his desire.

Martin relaxed his tense thigh and stomach muscles, rinsed himself free of the clinging remnants of his lust and limply turned off the water. He had never felt so disgusted and so lonely.

He dressed, walked across the compound to the building he called his office and despite the airlessness of the building closed the door to his room. There was a heap of mail on his desk. It had arrived the previous day, his first mail bag. He had eagerly cut it open but the contents had been a disappointment. Nothing personal at all. He had hoped by now to have heard from Alice. It had been perhaps too much to expect some lines of encouragement from his Headquarters. All the bag contained were reports, questionnaires about whether smoking zones should be permitted in Britword offices, returns about computer hardware in use, sales surveys, market reports and internal news. The only items of the remotest interest to Martin were some bills of lading for consignments that were due to him and some financial documentation. He began despondently to sort through these when there was a knock and Ndua, his office manager opened the door.

"I said I didn't want to be disturbed, Ndua."

"Sorry, Boss," said the office manager, but continued to stand there. Undecided whether to go or come, he simply waited, his presence hanging in the heat like that of some slow, solid buffalo.

"Well?"

"There's a young man outside."

"There are always young men outside."

"This one's different. He's got his sister with him. She's different, too."

"Can't you deal with it? What do they want?"

Ndua's solemn features came briefly to life. "That's the problem. They don't speak any of our languages; they don't speak much English, either, or Swahili. I think they speak French, Boss."

Martin sighed and pushed aside the heap of mail.

"This is Britwords, Ndua, not an employment agency. I've told you to be firm."

"These people are different."

"Show them in."

Ndua rarely smiled, but the wrinkles in the corners of his eyes revealed his satisfaction. Martin watched him move slowly to the door that was propped open to encourage any draught that might relieve the heat, pushed his chair back from his desk on its castors and crossed his legs. If they came from Zaire, he thought, they would have shared a tribal language with some of his staff. They must be from further afield.

Ndua's bulk filled the doorway again like a dark shadow. "Come," he said over his shoulder. A young man in clean, but threadbare grey trousers and a neatly pressed, frayed white shirt entered, followed by a girl in a blue, European style dress. The man walked over to Martin's desk with a mixture of confidence and deference.

"You speak French, Monsieur?" he asked.

"Yes."

"Tres bien." He shook hands and introduced himself as Jacques and the girl as Therese, his sister. In reaction to these civilities Martin rose to his feet to shake her hand. Such manners reminded him that other worlds existed. He offered the girl a chair. Other than his desk stool, it was the only one in the room. She sat in it as of right, modestly folding her hands on her lap. Martin noticed how worn her frock was and faded - just like the frock the Ugandan refugee girl had been wearing. But judging from Therese's features and coffee-coloured complexion, she was from further afield.

"I'll go and fetch another chair," he said.

"I'll get it," said the young man, eagerly, but Ndua surprised them all by re-appearing with one himself. He set it down with dignity in front of Martin and Jacques, and lumbered out of the room without a word.

"Well?" asked Martin, ensconced once again behind his desk.

"Thanks for seeing us," began Jacques. Martin gave an impatient wave of the hand. The young man got straight to the point. "We need your help."

"I thought you did. I don't know that I am going to be of much use to you."

"At least you can understand us."

Martin looked at him curiously. He could not make out from the lad's features where he might have come from. Like his sister, he was lightly built and lighter skinned than the tribes in the Republic of the Nile or the neighbouring French speaking countries. He could see what Ndua had meant about the girl being different. She was quite beautiful with a cat-like grace. Indeed, her face had that triangular appearance some Burmese or Siamese cats have and her modesty was different from the sideways glancing, self-aware bashfulness of the local girls. Martin rarely came across sophistication among the local population in Gondo and never among the small group of white technicians and aid administrators. He could not place these strange, elegant young paupers.

Their story was simple, and impressive for what they did not tell him. They said that they had been born into a tribe that straddled Southern Uganda and Rwanda and had been brought up as royalty. Their people were educated and had become the administrative class in the land. Due to their skills and influence they had been favoured by General Amin, but after his overthrow were treated as enemies by the Ugandans whom the tyrant had persecuted. They were chased out of the country. Their kinsfolk in Rwanda did not want them and they fled into Zaire. The family was split and Jacques then fourteen years old and his twelve-year-old sister had become separated from their parents. During the last chaotic years in Uganda they had not had much formal education and were too young to have learned English. Now they were faced with new languages and the greater problem of survival on their own in the jungle. Eventually they had found their way to a refugee camp where they had been well looked after for two years. Jacques had learnt a trade.

"I am a good carpenter now," he said a little ruefully and his sister looked up at Martin and nodded earnestly before fixing her gaze on her bare feet. "It was good for Therese, too. She went to the lycee. She was top of her class."

"Yes, I learnt a lot. It was a good school. It was a happy time."

"Why did you move?"

"Refugee camps are not meant to be permanent. Ours was closed, many people were able to go home. We were transferred." He told Martin of a long trek in a lorry north through Zaire. Days and days of thirst, jostling, red roads and green jungle, sleeping under the lorries at night, mosquitoes, dirt.

"It was not good for my sister," said Jacques. "Some of those people are like animals."

Eventually they were settled in another camp but coming from a strange tribe were not accepted by the majority. Therese managed to continue her schooling for another year, would have done well, but they were resented by other refugees.

Their account was interrupted by a knock on the door. Ndua plodded in without ceremony and said in his slow, deep voice, "Someone to see you, Boss." It was part of a pre-arranged code to relieve Martin of unwanted visitors. But on this occasion Martin surprised his office manager by replying,

"Thank you Ndua. Would you ask them to wait twenty minutes."

"You want them to wait?" he said in disbelief. Then he looked at the girl and leered at Martin. "All right. I'll tell them to come back." He trundled out shaking his head.

"I am sorry we are wasting your time," said Jacques, wondering whether to go, but his sister sat on, serenely patient.

"Well, let's not beat about the bush," replied Martin. "I appreciate your position, but what can I do? I have no vacancies."

"No, it's not that. I want help for my sister."

"What kind of help?" asked Martin suspiciously. The thought crossed his mind that they were not, perhaps, brother and sister after all.

"The Refugee Office here has been good to us. They understand our difficulties in the camps. They have given us a room at the Travellers' Hotel."

Martin knew the Travellers', a kind of doss house for overlanders and the few Arab merchants who came South to wring some business out of this impoverished town. A noisy, dirty place near the Customs House where the drivers from Kenya and Uganda waited away their lives squatting in the shade of their huge and mud-spattered lorries. The Travellers' Hotel, not much better than the camp, he thought. As if in echo, Therese said passionately, "It's horrible. I can't go out. I have to lock myself in my room all day. There is no window. It is dark and hot like an oven."

"Voila," said Jacques, "When I am there in the evenings it is supportable. But in the day I am out at the Commission processing papers. They have been good, but there is a lot of waiting, a lot of paper. Sometimes Therese can come with me, but then I must work, too, she cannot come with me. I am a carpenter. They have found me a temporary job at the army compound."

Martin saw the problem that a young African girl would face alone in a hotel full of Arab merchants. "Have you told the Refugee Office?" he asked.

"Of course," said Therese, fiercely, forgetting her politeness for a minute. "They tell us that if we do not like the hotel we can return to the camp. They know we cannot do that. These people hate us. They are fighting our people back home. It is blackmail."

Martin scratched his head. He knew too that the hard-pressed little refugee office with so many people to feed and shelter, had no time to go into individual problems as well. "So what you are saying is, you want somewhere for your sister to pass the day."

"Exactly."

The couple smiled at each other. It seemed that as if stating their modest but important problem they had solved it.

"Could you come back tomorrow?" he asked, and their smiles disappeared.

"No. I know what you are thinking. You'll come back and I'll refuse to see you. It's not that. I think I might be able to help. But no promises."

Martin left his office at two thirty. Before walking across the compound he drove down to the Custom's House. Pete had told him some of his lorries were expected, lorries carrying fuel and possibly a consignment of words. It was the hottest time of day and the decaying, collapsed city centre was deserted. The steel shutters of the merchants' shops were closed and a few of the shop-keepers were sleeping in their angorebs, wooden beds strung with strips of goatskin. A lame donkey stood bad-temperedly in what had been the service pit of a petrol station in better times. Now the garage was just a dirty shell, a cave filled with litter and animal droppings, but shady nonetheless. Avoiding the hole in the dirt road left by a broken drain cover Martin turned the corner, and the peeling, pink facade of the Travellers' Hotel behind its moat of running sewage reminded him of the couple he had spoken to that morning. Theirs was the second hard luck story he had heard that day. He was not convinced that Jacques' story was genuine.

The pair of them seemed somehow untouched by deprivation. So many of the poor, old and young alike who made the hopeless circuit of Gondo's few offices looking for work or often just for food, had been reduced to a cringing, sullen beggary. Jacques' pride had not soured into resentment and he had not pleaded. His sister too had swallowed back her despair. Martin wanted to help them. He still felt mean about chucking out the Ugandan girl. But he remained suspicious. The only way to check it out was to call and see whether they really were registered at the UNHCR.

Next day three lorries arrived with most of their cargoes intact. Big Pete was there, busy seeing to the drivers, exhausted after six weeks on the road, completing the paper-work for customers and officials alike. Everyone mucked in on these occasions. Big Pete ran the Trading Post but it was in everyone's interest to help unload the lorries. They all needed fuel for their generators. Electricity meant cool air and cold beer. Even Ndua leant a hand, not physically, but he volunteered to go down to the market and hire a gang of labourers to manhandle the heavy drums from the lorries. Most of the day Martin, too, was out of the office. In the general excitement he forgot about the refugee couple. In fact it was three days later that Ndua came into his now pleasantly cool office and announced,

"The young lady, Boss."

"Young lady? I don't know any young ladies, Ndua."

"No Boss. You are knowing this one, I think. Come!" he bellowed into the corridor. It was Therese. She was dressed in the same faded frock, but it was immaculately clean and pressed and she had piled her hair up in a scarf. She apologized for not having come sooner, but Jacques had had malaria and she had been tending him. She had come as soon as possible, although Jacques, who offered his excuses, was still too weak to make it.

Martin outlined his proposal. It was nothing very much. He was not allowed by law to offer her money, but if she wanted to get out of the hotel during the day she was welcome to go to his house. Unless he had guests, she could if she liked use the spare room. Martin laid down two conditions. One, she was to invite no one in without his knowledge. Two, she was to return to the hotel at night.

"Is there a shower?" she asked at once.

"Yes. Of sorts. You have to pour in the water at the top first."

"May I use it?"

"Of course."

"And I will study."

"What?"

"You have books?"

"Yes." No shortage of words, either, he thought.

"I am learning English," Therese said in English, with a shy smile. "I want to learn proper English. Not what these people speak." Again that regal disdain. Martin could well understand that Therese and her brother were not liked in the camps. He made sure that she understood the arrangement he was proposing was temporary, just to tide her over her present difficulties.

"Anyway, I will have to ask my brother," she said, trying to conceal her enthusiasm.

"Well, why don't you bring him round when he is a bit stronger. Let him see the set-up. The house is just behind the office actually, in the corner of the compound."

Martin had been lucky about accommodation. True to his promise, Bob had negotiated a lease on a house not far from his own in what once had been a well-kept, tree-lined street in the former merchant quarter. It was the same street, in fact, that Bob had driven him down the day of his arrival. The houses were built of good, locally produced brick, a material no longer made in the Republic. Rubbish accumulated in piles outside the houses, spilling into the black, treacly streams of sewage that issued from many of the buildings. Scabby, curly-tailed dogs rummaged listlessly among the empty cans. Many of the fine trees had been mutilated, in some cases completely felled for firewood for cooking. But one or two houses had been restored and their large gardens brought back into production. Martin planned to make his building habitable as an office and a house. He would turn the walled garden with its shady old mango tree into a literal haven for relaxation and escape from the heat and the dust. Such were his plans at any rate. For the moment his living quarters were a pre-fabricated bungalow behind the original house. The prefab had been temporary accommodation put up by a road building team with money from the World Bank. The old house had served as their office as it now served as a Britwords regional office.

"I love making things grow, don't you?" Martin asked the young pair as they sat drinking tea on the patch of coarse grass he called the lawn. Jacques laughed.

"In our country it is the women who cultivate."

"Oh, I do not depend on my garden. It is more a hobby. I do not think I could live on what I grow. The insects eat half of it. I've not really got it going yet."

"Perhaps I could help you," said Therese. "I am quite strong. If you would like it."

"If you want to. But please do not feel you have to work. In fact as a foreign national you are not permitted to! You are my guest. If, of course, your brother approves."

Jacques did approve, but he set strict limits. On those days when he couldn't pick Therese up, he would expect her back at the hotel by the time he returned from work. They had, he said politely, no wish to impose themselves. They were grateful, deeply grateful for the help, but friendship could only be built on the basis of equality, not charity. One day, when he was established himself, he would return

Martin's hospitality and perhaps then they would all become friends. He spoke without vindictiveness or pride. He spoke with dignity. Martin was pleased, too, that Jacques did not intend to pick his sister up every day, stopping off, perhaps inviting companions along, taking over his house, as Bob had predicted might happen. Martin admired the young man for his spirit and his independence.

Therese, too, was herself very determined. She would not eat with Martin, perhaps at her brother's insistence, but she would accept a glass of milk in the morning and tea when she left. One thing she did use lavishly was the shower. Martin discovered a bore well in the overgrown garden. The water was too saline to drink but there was now a plentiful supply of water to wash in. Therese would spend hours in the bathroom and emerge soap-scented and smiling.

At first, though, she spoke little. Gradually she became more talkative and through occasional anecdotes Martin learned not only of the physical pain and of the deprivation of being a refugee, but of the bureaucracy, of the questions repeatedly asked, answered and never fully believed; a refugee has no past, he has to recreate himself every day. And perhaps the biggest struggle of all is not to hope for too much for fear of another disappointment, yet not to give in entirely to despondency.

Jacques and Therese were hoping to emigrate to North America where they believed ultimately they might find other members of their family. Distant relations in both senses.

"But we have to get on the lists. We have no money," explained Therese.

"Why should you need money?" asked Martin in his naiveté.

"The staff at the office for refugees, they are Africans."

It took Martin a few moment to realise what Therese was inferring.

"Oh, they do it secretly. Their European bosses do not know. But their European bosses are well paid. They do not understand the temptations. The local staff here in Gondo, they do not live much better than us. Who knows, next year if it does not rain, if there is civil war like people say, they will flee south themselves.

"And their bosses?" asked Martin, but he knew the answer.

"They will move on, taking their salaries with them." Therese was very worldly-wise for her tender age thought Martin sadly.

But she became less tolerant as the weeks rolled by. She had been telling Martin that she and Jacques would soon be moving from the hotel. They had been allotted a piece of land on which to build their own hut. Jacques would soon be paid for the benches he had been making. He had already been given a permit and a small grant to set himself up locally as a carpenter. It had barely covered the cost of materials and the rent in the market place of a tin roof on four spindly legs that passed as a workshop. But it was a start. Having completed the job at the army compound, he struck lucky. He got an order to make up six benches and two cupboards for the police station. On completion of this commission he would be able to repay the seed money. He would be truly independent. It was this that had prompted Therese to speak of leaving the wretched hotel and of building their own hut. As they both explained to Martin, they felt they had outstayed their welcome.

But things did not happen quickly in Gondo. The weeks dragged by, Martin when he was at home got used to Therese's quiet comings and goings, but Jacques did not get paid for the furniture he had made. And because he was now working, the Office for Refugees would no longer pay his hotel bill.

In his desperation, Jacques who was normally too proud to ask favours, begged Martin to intervene.

"I'll make some enquiries," Martin promised. He knew the Director, Arne Svenson, slightly: a balding Norwegian who worked himself to exhaustion just trying to feed and shelter the growing number of refugees. He could not be expected, thought Martin, to know the particulars of an individual case.

That evening Martin had the opportunity to discuss the problem with Bob. He explained Jacques' predicament as he understood it, concluding,

"The trouble is, I don't really know the facts."

Bob threw him a shrewd look. "You don't trust them, no?"

"Listen, Bob. For weeks now, I've been giving them something. Okay, I can afford to, but that's not the point."

"They're ripping you off, you mean?"

"Not really. I don't think so. I give them money to get on the list, money for ration books, school fees for Therese, money for books, money for uniforms..."

Bob chuckled. "Par for the course," he said. "How long did Therese stay in school?"

The Office for Refugees, in recognition of Therese's youth and ability, had placed her in a government secondary school as one of a small quota of refugees permitted. At first she had been delighted, especially as she had become more confident with her English, but after a few days she had refused to go to school. She knew more than the teachers, let alone the class of "these dirty people" among whom she had been placed.

Martin had tried to get her moved up to a higher class, but had been told that Therese would have to prove herself first. So school, the fees, the uniform and the books were abandoned. Therese had not mentioned repaying the money and Martin had not asked for it back. Despite this episode he was growing to like and admire this serenely confident girl.

"You want to help them," said Bob.

"Of course."

"No point asking too many questions, then."

The next day, who should come into Jacques' office but Arne Svenson. When they had finished their business, Martin asked Arne if he knew of a young man his Office had set up as a carpenter.

"Yes, I believe he is good. One of our success stories," smiled the Norwegian, rubbing his tired eyes.

"He says he has not been paid yet for the work he did for the police."

"You know him then?"

"A little."

"He probably does not understand the system. The customer would have paid us direct. We deduct a small instalment to recover the seed money and we pay the balance to the refugee. In theory he reinvests this in his business. It works in fifty percent of cases."

"So you got the money from the police."

"Yes, I should think so. And I am sure Iris would have paid the young man by now. If he says she hasn't, either he is fooling you or he does not understand it."

"Who is Iris?" asked Martin.

"Iris, she is one of my local assistants. She's been with us for years, knows the local scene inside out. She's invaluable. I rely on her completely. In fact, I think it was Iris who found the work for your young man in the first place."

Martin returned to his bungalow for lunch and told Therese that according to the Office for Refugees the police had paid over the money. Jacques should have collected it by now. Therese was quiet for a long time, but she was not given to sulking and eventually said to Martin,

"Why does no one believe a refugee?" Her voice was so laden with despair that it surprised and worried Martin, who asked,

"Why? What do you mean?"

"Iris! You know who she is? She is the mistress of the Chief of Police."

Despite this and many other setbacks, Therese continued to look forward to her emigration to North America. Sometimes she would speak excitedly of the new life she would make. Martin listened with a kind of sad admiration at the young girl's ability to keep her hopes alive. Her enforced exile put his moments of homesickness and doubt into perspective.

"Do you ever miss your country?" he asked.

"Of course, but my country does not exist any more. I have to find a new one. It is true that in Canada they speak French?"

She did have memories of her old country, though. On one of the days her brother was unable to collect her, Martin walked back with her along the riverbank. The sun was going down and a relatively cool breeze from across the water made it a pleasant place for a stroll. They passed under some old mango trees, too big now to have been hacked down for firewood like most of the trees around Gondo. The mango trees and the spreading banyans further upstream had been planted for shade by the foraging Turks in the days of the first slave traders. Therese had not walked this way before since it was perhaps not the best route to take alone. She did not react, as Martin did, to the brilliant flash of the kingfishers, the dazzling white of the home-flying egrets, or to the pinkening water against the dark, luxuriant green of the vegetation along the far bank. She seemed lost in her own world.

They walked on as far as the bridge where the townswomen came to bathe, wading deep into the swift flowing, brown water to wash off the day's dust. Those who could afford it soaped themselves and removed and washed their clothes at the same time before returning home, carrying on their heads the plastic containers filled with the river water for domestic use.

The men had their own bathing place on the other side of the bridge, sharing it with the drivers washing their lorries in the precious water. The sight of all these people going about their routine ablutions awoke Therese from her reverie.

"These people are like animals," she exclaimed, and Martin was surprised at the disdain in her voice, at her lack of compassion.

"Surely you have seen worse things in the camps?" he suggested.

"I never saw anyone taking drinking water from the place where they wash; I never saw any woman behave immodestly," she said, indicating the old crone, too weak to venture far enough into the current to cover herself, standing naked and drinking water from the river in cupped hands.

Martin's attention was distracted from this simple sight which so repulsed Therese by a loud hooting and a sight to him more repellent. It was Big Pete, more full of himself than usual after a successful hunting expedition. He had just crossed the bridge in his Landrover, back from the bush. Over the bonnet was strung a young bush buck, in the back, quarters of something even bigger like an eland. No doubt he had bribed the soldiers at the checkpoint and on the bridge with joints of butchered flesh.

He had no room to offer Martin a lift. Indeed, this was not his intention. He merely wanted to show off his kill. He was disappointed to the point of insult at Martin's reaction of outrage.

"I thought these animals were protected," said Martin.

"Don't say you're one of those anti-blood-sport nutters," spat Pete, deflated and angry. "It's culling, not killing, man. I leave that to the military with their bloody automatics. They need a target as big as an elephant. They're drugged out of their minds with fear and boredom, you know that. All bloody Arabs. And scared to death by the black men in these parts." He looked at Therese. "Hi, Sweetheart. What would you do for a nice fresh steak, then?"

Therese, who had been eyeing the carcass with relish tossed her head and walked away.

"Not with you, then?" Pete said pointedly to Martin, who was still shaken by the big man's outburst.

"What do you mean?"

"Your girlfriend! Have I said summat to offend her?"

"She's not exactly my girlfriend, Pete. She's just a kid."

"Since when has that stopped them? Eh? Eh?" Martin refused to let Pete wind him up. The Big Man leered, tooted his horn and drove off with, "I'll see you later, anyroad."

Martin caught up with Therese. "I'm sorry about that."

"You should buy some of that meat," she advised. "It will not keep."

They walked on along the narrow path between the shoulder high grass, heading for the cool, uncrowded stretch of river below the prison gardens.

"We used to eat meat at home," she recalled. "There we had a brick house with a garden. There were always fruit and vegetables. Water came from taps in the wall. We slept on beds between white sheets and we were driven to school by a chauffeur. Will it be like that in Canada?"

ALICE'S STORY. PART TWO

In spite of everything I went through, when I think of the Republic of the Nile, I still retain the pictures painted in Martin's first letters. I suppose then I was romanticising the whole thing. I saw Martin as a pioneer. I read into his letters a sense of adventure. It was with a shared sense of adventure I plunged in myself. One of Martin's friends told me he thought Martin's own state of mind had most usually been blind panic! If so, he hid it pretty well in his letters. I'm sure he was describing the real Gondo. In fact I know he was for I soon experienced it for myself. But the fact remains that some of my most indelible impressions are second-hand, Gondo seen through Martin's rose-tinted spectacles. Impressions of the place physically, I suppose. What happened to us there, to me, is another matter.

Martin could be quite self-deprecating. He laughed at a mistake he made about boiling coffee beans for a stew. Food seemed to pre-occupy him. I remember some of his recipes. Suppers of sweet potatoes and pineapples, or plantains, corned beef and onions, followed by mangoes or pawpaws according to availability. He wrote of a Nile perch the size of a goose. He wasn't exaggerating. Later I was to see with my own eyes a young man wheeling his bicycle from door to door with one of those huge fish folded over the crossbar, mouth nearly in the dust on one side, tail trailing on the other. On paper it all sounded so exotic, succulent. Later, when I was forced to subsist on far less interesting rations, I remembered Martin's early experiments and his recipes fed my imagination.

I pieced together my own picture of the town and surroundings in the same way. He described a trip to the original Turkish settlement where a few brick remains could be discerned near a clump of original shade trees. He wondered about getting out an archaeologist through the company to excavate any early British words.

Panic or no panic, he conveyed his exhilaration during an excursion to a tributary of the Nile, dry except in the rainy season, but where pools of water in its bed attracted hundreds of birds and at dusk animals too shy to approach the Nile proper - antelope, water buck and giraffe. In the Nile hippos and crocodiles were common. But what prevented him from swimming in its fast flowing current was his dread of bilharzia.

He enticed me with accounts of his solitary evening walks on the plains by the airport where marabou storks plodded about like ungainly old men, bent over, with their hands clasped beneath their coat tails, and which flight transformed into graceful, soaring birds. When I spotted my first marabou I recognized it instantly from Martin's caricature. I learned about barbets and honeyeaters so small and erratic in flight they could be mistaken for flitting butterflies, about mannequins the size of bumblebees. He told me how after a shower of rain thousands of caterpillars gave his compound the look of an ocean on a windy day as they advanced across the grass, across the bare earth, across the floors and mats of his home, wave upon tidal wave of flowing, heaving insects on the march.

He tried to help me understand what it felt like living in Gondo. Sometimes he took off those tinted spectacles and gave me a hint of things to come. One letter is burned in my memory, though I never appreciated it fully until experiencing the terrible, oppressive heat of that land-locked country for myself. In his letter he listed examples of what the heat meant. Martin wrote, "You have to sleep naked. There is no electricity, no fan therefore, and what little breeze there is does not enter the mosquito net. You sprawl naked, longing to slip away into sleep. You turn the pillow in the hope the other side will be cooler."

In London this sounded faintly erotic. I was to discover there was nothing erotic about the hot season. Two in a bed made the heat worse. To touch was to sweat. Lovers kept apart for comfort. Cuddling, curling up together after sex is a luxury of a temperate climate. A luxury I did not have time to sample, I hasten to add. I did not know then that what Martin described was in fact luxury compared to what lay in store for me. A pillow indeed!

Other indicators of heat: while you are advised to wear the minimum of clothing you always need shoes because the ground is too hot to tread barefoot. The stones are too hot even to pick up in your bare hands at midday.

A hosepipe lying in the sun ejects scalding water for a minute after being turned on.

Candles wilt in the heat, bending to touch the table with their wicks like Arabs praying on their mats.

Fridges cannot make ice. If the generators are running, the compressors race full time just to keep the metal intestines of the fridge cool.

I devoured Martin's letters, but my realization that he was not getting mine was as slow as it was appalling.

While I was learning the landmarks of Gondo through his letters, the disused TV satellite dish on the outskirts, the huge catholic cathedral and the mosque that vied for dominance of a town of straw huts, called tukuls, the University clock tower from which the scaffolding had never been removed for fear of collapse, the jebel or small mountain that looked down even on the mosque and the cathedral, while I was trying to picture all this, I began to notice other references were missing from his letters. Answers to my questions, for example, reaction to things I had told him. Only gradually did it dawn upon me that he was not getting my letters at all. He must have been wondering therefore whether I was receiving his. That he kept on sending them was an act of faith.

You might say he needed to write it all down in the way that some people keep a diary. That he was writing for himself. Nevertheless I am certain now that during those six months it did not occur to him that I might have lost interest, forgotten him, that I did not want to write. At the time I was frantic to reassure him, to get a message through. I tried to send them through Britwords but there were no electronic communications in Gondo and Britwords mail was not getting through either.

It was not until I made my own journey to Gondo via Nairobi that I came across the mailbags in the agent's office there. I took some of it myself, thus bearing letters to Martin I had written many months earlier. It had not occurred to Britwords, or to me, to be quite honest, to get our own East African Office to intervene. Until I saw the heap of mailbags to different organizations in the Nile Republic spilling their contents across the floor of the Kenyan agent's office, I think none of us realised what a hit and miss business this was. Anyone could and did collect and promise to deliver mail if he or she were travelling to the Republic by any means.

Outgoing letters Martin was able to give to more reliable travellers and they usually got through, albeit in batches.

I heard about some of Martin's friends, about his staff. I learned about the smell of money. In a climate where shirt and trousers are the most men wear, bank notes are inevitably carried close to the skin. Tropical money smells of sweat and is dark and limp to the touch, tearing easily and transferring its dirt to your fingers. When I handled my first fistful of this rag-like currency I experienced a vivid sense of deja vu, until I remembered I had read Martin's own description of it.

He did not send me photographs but he sent me word pictures that I was to recognize later. Of huts so close together, for example, that they form their own maze of shady passages where chickens strut, babies crawl and squat and a goat eats a rare delicacy, an old newspaper, watched by ever nervous cats, beasts that in Gondo risked becoming ingredients in the stew pot.

I got an idea, too, of the magnitude of the disorder even before the renewal of the Civil War. Never again will I complain of unrepaired frost damage in my street when I remember Martin's description of why his fuel supplies had not arrived. I quote from memory:

"On the way up from Uganda eighty lorries, some of them overturned, are floundering in thigh-deep mud. The potholes are so deep a Landrover can disappear into them, the thick brown waters meeting over the roof. The stranded drivers are hungry and sick with dysentery. Despite the three-day cloudburst that turned the road into a sea of mud, they have little clean water to drink. All the surface water is polluted with the diesel and petrol that has leaked from the overturned vehicles; it has not helped that over a hundred drivers and their mates dare not venture too far from their trucks to perform their own natural functions."

When I first read this I was impressed not so much by the message but by the fact that Martin had despatched it. In my mind's eye he was like an intrepid news reporter. My images were of him reporting from the front, not of sick drivers surviving in squalid conditions. But I was to experience enough of those for myself and to learn the hard way the difference between reading about something and being there. I am not ready yet to attempt to write about it myself.

Anyway, when I arrived in Gondo after six months of this preparation, instead of being bowled over by it, I was disappointed. It all seemed so familiar. This impression was soon overwhelmed by events. In one of the mailbags I was carrying, and unbeknown to me, were all the letters I had sent Martin. He did not know I was coming. I was due for an even bigger disappointment.

CHAPTER FIVE

Martin heard the uproar from his kitchen. He had woken late, unrefreshed by a heavy sleep. He had eaten a ripe mango for breakfast and was standing washing the juice from his mouth, hands and wrists when he heard raised voices from the office across the compound. He recognized Vashti's voice shrill with anger. A man's equally impassioned threats answered her. Hardly the tranquil Ndua, thought Martin lethargically.

It had been an effort getting up. He hoped the staff would sort out their differences. He did not feel strong enough to intervene.

He slowly gathered some papers he needed. He heard a thud, a cry of indignation from Vashti and then a yelping screech, a scream, such as he had only heard from a dog hit by a passing car. A man's scream of pain. Furniture was upturned, a door slammed. A man fled out of the compound.

Violence is contagious. Martin's lethargy was displaced by his own fear and anger. He hurried across to the office.

A trail of crimson blood lay still wet on the steps, turning purple where it had spurted on to the beaten earth of the compound. Inside the office the floor and Vashti's desk were also bloodstained.

Vashti was sitting behind the reception desk holding something dark and bleeding in her hands. Her mouth was smeared with blood and her white blouse splattered. She wiped her lips with the back of her hand and looked up at Martin, laughing.

"Vashti! What has happened? Are you hurt?"

"I'm O.K., Boss," she said. Martin looked at the object she was nursing. She held it out to him. "It's his ear!" she said. "I bit it off!"

Martin took the ear automatically. The surprise in his face was replaced by slow recognition which in turn got the push from quick horror. He dropped the ear. Vashti found this dumb show hilarious. While Martin remained silent, gagged with disgust, Vashti broke into a torrent of laughter followed by tears.

Martin was making an effort to pull himself together when Ndua's office door opened and the ponderous man lumbered into the reception area completely ignoring Vashti's distress.

"We actually have a problem," he said to Martin.

"You don't have to tell me that," said Martin. "Look at this mess."

"They have cut off our water," Ndua continued, blind to the bloody disarray of Vashti's desk and person. His sentences came out heavily, at the pace of a buffalo, slow but unstoppable.

"Why?" Martin asked. The water rarely flowed whether it was cut off or not. Most people paid a girl to fetch it in buckets from the river.

"We have not paid our bill."

"Then pay it," shouted Martin above Vashti's hysteria.

"We have yet to receive it," explained Ndua, revealing a trace of irritation that his boss did not appear to be giving him his full attention.

Martin took a grip on himself and on events, He told Ndua he would be with him in ten minutes, but first they must get the office and steps cleaned up.

"For that," pointed out Ndua, "we need water."

Martin sent Vashti into his house where he still had half a drum of water in his bathroom.

"Sorry to trouble you, Boss," said Vashti, calming down and suddenly repentant. "I hope you are all right now."

"I'm fine. Get cleaned up. Later you can tell me all about it."

"Oh it's nothing. That was my husband."

"I see," said Martin, who didn't see.

"He is too, too jealous," she said and flung the ear into a bin.

On the way to the water office with Ndua, Martin tried once more to concentrate on the problem in hand. He remembered Bob's story about having had his telephone cut off in some other African country where they had telephones. Bob had not paid his bill for the simple reason he had never received one. When he had demanded to know why the bill had not been sent before he was cut off, the company admitted it had been unable to locate his address.

"Why didn't you telephone and ask?" Bob had fumed.

"Your phone was cut off," came the inevitable but illogical reply.

Martin's water problem appeared to be similar. Low paid clerks content to sit and pick their toenails had neither the energy nor the inclination to exercise one cell of imagination. They had not been trained to use initiative. The very suggestion would have been an insult to their status. Their job was to sit on wooden chairs, fill ledgers and ignore the queues of anxious customers.

Martin's musings were interrupted by Ndua.

"He will not be back," chuckled the bovine man darkly.

"Who?"

"Miss Vashti's husband."

"What was it all about, Ndua?"

Ndua told Martin that Vashti had been married, divorced and had re-married. She also had a boy-friend. The man who had so recently given his right ear for her was her first husband. He had come in and picked a quarrel.

"Vashti said he was jealous," said Martin.

"Yes."

"But surely, she is re-married..."

Ndua shook with slow laughter. "No he is not jealous of the husband. The first husband has just found out about the lover..."

70

Martin was confused. "And does the second husband know about the lover?"

"If he doesn't he soon will. There will be more blood spilled." Ndua was dabbing tears of mirth from his big eyes.

"Well, I hope it is not Vashti's blood," said Martin. He was feeling nauseous again. Dizzy.

They had reached the public utilities office, an old, brick building. Inside it was bare except for shelves piled high with ledgers whose brittle yellow pages flapped back and forth in the breeze like pale, dry leaves. Behind four separate desks bookkeepers and clerks were silently transcribing figures from or into ledgers. They ignored the two intruders until Ndua passed some dank currency notes to one of the men. Martin pretended not to see this transaction and explained why they had come. He was offered a wooden chair. Although it only had three legs he was thankful to sink down on to it, bracing one of his legs to keep his balance. To his surprise the clerk found the missing bill. The man pretended to examine it closely and said to Martin,

"You have not paid it."

"Of course we have not," said Ndua. "We have not received it."

The official looked at Ndua and shrugged. "I don't know. Maybe you have received it. Maybe you haven't. What I know is that you have not paid the bill."

Martin could see this argument going round in circles for ever. He offered to pay the bill and suggested they re-connect the water at once. This took the official by surprise.

"You want to pay the bill?"

"Yes."

"Now?"

"Yes."

"This bill," said one of the other clerks, "is an electricity bill, not a water bill."

It was Ndua's turn to be surprised. He took the piece of paper. "We cannot pay an electricity bill," he said ponderously.

"You will pay it," ordered the first clerk, who clearly disliked Ndua.

"But my dear," Ndua told him condescendingly, "we have no electricity."

"That is why we did not cut it off," explained the official as if talking to a child.

"But look," insisted Ndua. "This figure, 281 Niles. Where did you get that sum from?"

"From your meter, of course."

Ndua looked impassively around the room like a cow when it lifts it head from drinking. He announced to all the clerks, "That cannot be so. We have no electricity. We have no meter."

"We have no water, either," added Martin.

The whole conversation started up again in Arabic. Martin was lost. After three minutes Ndua explained to him, "They have cut off our water because we have not paid the electricity bill. They could not cut off the electricity, you see, because we do not have any." Ndua himself seemed quite satisfied now that he understood the problem.

"Why is there a bill in the first place?" asked Martin.

"They say they read it from the meter," repeated Ndua.

"We have no meter."

"That is what they say. Here is the bill."

Martin was learning. Things were different in Africa. And it was too hot and airless to argue. "All right," he said, "we'll pay."

Immediately everyone broke out into smiles. White teeth flashed in the dark, oppressive room.

"Of course," added the clerk, "there is a five Niles reconnection fee also."

"You can't win," Martin said to Ndua while he drew out the chequebook from a damp breast pocket, unfolded it and began to write. As he did so he felt a small doubt, a tiny spark of revolt. Why should he cave in to the system? Why should he let them get away with this? Smiling, he wrote out the cheque but post-dated it by two years.

Pleased that his ruse went undetected, Martin rose to go. For a lurching moment his body refused to obey him. It felt heavy like a sack of potatoes. He dragged it out into the sun with him. It was still early, not yet nine o'clock but he felt desperately weak, tired. He told Ndua he was just popping home to freshen up. He would return to the office shortly.

Martin was learning how to cope with the practical problems, the frustrations; he had to some extent begun to control the submerged panic that every evening welled up and screamed let's get out of here, let's go home. He was getting better at improvising solutions, dealing with the unexpected. He had taken Vashti's domestic quarrel in his stride.

But this! This physical lack of strength was a different kind of unexpected which surprised and frightened him. He sat on his bed and a total lethargy invaded him. No, lethargy implies a comfortable kind of laziness. This weakness was an anti-force. He held a glass of water in his hand but to raise it to his mouth required the determination of an elbow wrestler. Getting up from the bed to undress, for he knew now he was ill, that he needed more rest, getting up needed the conscious prompting of mind to body called upon by a swimmer preparing to dive into a cold pool. And Martin did not have that determination. He sank back on the bed, clothed. The numbness in his limbs spread to his mind. Something inside his head seemed to be spinning, whirring like a small fan at the very centre of his skull. He had an overwhelming desire to close his eyes, to sleep. He was conscious enough to realise he was aching all over, his back, the muscles in his buttocks and thighs, his neck and shoulders. Not only his muscles ached, but his bones and the joints between the bones groaned. A quick shiver of panic shook him before he sank, sank down through the bed and blackness closed in over him.

He did not hear the timid knock on the door. Did not answer, and Therese went to her own room.

Later he woke, still unrefreshed, stood up shakily and blacked out again. He knocked a lamp from his bedside table as he fell back, spilling the oil. The noise brought Therese to him and she made him comfortable in the bed before getting a cloth to mop up the spillings.

In her deliberate, unruffled way, Therese nursed Martin through the day. She had seen many sick people and was not worried for Martin's health.

When her brother came to accompany her home that evening the couple could not wake Martin. They left a drink and some fruit by the bed.

He slept most of the next day but found Therese's presence comforting. He could not raise his head from the pillow and this frightened him. Therese said it wouldn't last, laughed kindly at his worries. Back home in England he had had the whole of the National Health Service to reassure him, ambulances minutes away in cases of emergencies, buildings full of medical words to cast out anxieties simply by naming the complaint. The label as cure. Here he had a young girl's word that he would be all right. He wondered what he was doing in Gondo, importing not only medical words, but lexicons, pantechnicons of vocabulary.

When Jacques came to fetch Therese in the evening Martin was asleep again. Jacques suggested his sister sit with Martin through the night. She would be as safe in this house as she was with her brother in their stuffy hotel room and a good deal more comfortable; she would be able to help Martin if he awoke in the night and needed anything. It did not occur to either of them to seek help from Martin's office. To the refugee pair the local people were ignorant, inferior beings. Besides, Therese and Jacques were used to keeping their own counsel, to looking after themselves. That they had sought help from Martin was exceptional and his illness gave them the opportunity to repay his kindness, to redress the balance.

By morning, after sleeping for nearly two days Martin found his lethargy had lifted. He was desperate for a cup of tea. On his way to the kitchen he surprised Therese still in her body wrap asleep on his settee. He remembered having seen her in his waking moments and began to understand she had nursed him through the night.

"Are you feeling better?" she smiled, getting to her feet, big feet he thought, for such a slight and pretty girl. Like a lioness.

"Yes, I must make some tea, though. Will you join me?"

Therese insisted on making the tea and the breakfast. Martin went to the shower where he discovered he had a bright red rash from his collarbones to his groin. But he felt fine. A good night's sleep and he was right as rain.

He gulped down his tea, watched in fascination by Therese, and he ate several slices of bread covered in honey that Therese had bought in the market. The honey was thin and clear but contained in its sticky tresses dead bees and bits of burnt bark. Wild honey, stolen while the bees were smoked out of the long hives hung in trees.

"This is the best honey I've ever tasted!"

"Because you are hungry. You 'ave not heaten for two days!"

"Two days!" What do you mean?"

It took a while for Therese to explain.

"Didn't you call a doctor?"

"Where is there a doctor? You are better, isn't it?" She replied, adding as an afterthought. "Someone called last night, very late."

"Who?"

"A lady. I told her to come back when the office opens."

"You really have been looking after me, haven't you?" he said, not wondering why a lady should want to call on him very late at night. He lifted Therese's hand and kissed the inside of her wrist. She withdrew it at once, but cradled his kiss in her lap with a shy smile.

CHAPTER SIX

Fortified by his breakfast Martin tried to stride purposefully across to the office. He had two or three day's work to catch up on, but he was interrupted by Isaiah, one of Bob's houseboys.

"Please sir. Mr. Bob says you are please to come to the school, urgently."

"What is it, Isaiah?"

"Emergency."

As they drove into the school compound Bob came out of the classroom block and led Martin into the room he called the library. It was a Portakabin provided some years back by the World Bank. Temperatures inside reached over 50 degrees centigrade during the day and the books it was supposed to house were still "on their way." Bob had built a thatched roof over the box and cut windows into it. He had thereby changed the cabin into a passably comfortable staff room. One wall had a big poster of a boxing champion. Probably African or American.

Bob was relaxed but did not waste time. One of the missionary organizations in Gondo had received a radio message from Wok, the Western Regional Capital. A British community worker was seriously ill and needed to be got out. The road journey by Landrover might take anything up to eight days depending on the water level in various river crossings. Too long. Besides, there were few rest houses on the way; the invalid was too weak to camp in the bush, let alone be jolted about. They had decided to fly the man out, first to Gondo and if necessary to a hospital in Kenya.

"So where do I come in?" asked Martin. "I've got no medical skills."

"Money!" explained Bob. By luck one of the Lebanese trading companies operating out of Nairobi had a small plane down at the airport. Bob had spoken to the pilot. He was willing to make the trip before returning to Nairobi. But he wanted US$800 cash down. It was a deal on the side. "I've told him Britwords will pay. Only you need to leave within the hour if you are going to return before dark."

Martin still felt light-headed from his own illness and fast. While Bob filled him with robusta coffee and sweet, maggot enriched bread from a vendor in the school yard, he made a persuasive case in his brusque manner.

"All pull together. Help one another in a crisis. Call it a market survey. Wok is an important market town. Make a good first impression. It will be an investment. Take a bag of words in the hold. Free sample. Distribute. Loss leader. By the way," he concluded, "the pilot's English."

Bob was unable to go himself, he explained because he was supervising exams. He could not approach Big Pete because the Lebanese trader maintained Pete owed him money already. "And I doubt if we could prise him away from his new woman. White, so my boys tell me."

Bob had already sorted out flying permits, the plane was ready. It all sounded simple. At most it would take no more than a couple of hours in each direction and a short spell on the ground in Wok.

"You'll be back in time for supper," winked Bob.

"All right," said Martin rashly, feeling like a latter day Biggles. "I'll do it."

"I knew you would," smiled Bob "you're not a bad bloke."

The plane was tiny, hardly larger than a family saloon. It was parked in a makeshift shelter, like a carport, on the fringes of the airport where the fire engine stood: a fire engine without an engine, an appliance without water.

The pilot, a sweaty, overweight Englishman in his forties pulled the aircraft out with one hand, rather as if it were a sailing dinghy on a launching trolley. He took a last deep suck on his cigarette, extinguished the stub under his heel and filled the fuel tank from jerry cans they had brought with them.

"I suppose it is aviation fuel," he said sniffing it doubtfully. Martin laughed nervously and stashed a few bags of words in the hold, a kind of locker. Again he thought of sailing boats.

"Is there room for us all in here?"

"Yes, you sit beside me and we lay the body on the floor behind. It seats five at a pinch."

"Pinch is the word," said Bob.

Martin had a vague idea he should spin the propeller or something, but Desmond, as the red-headed Brit was called, told him to climb in and take the co-pilot's seat. Desmond wriggled in to his seat, put on some headphones, pressed a starter button and they taxied straight on to the runway. They took off immediately and very steeply. Desmond levelled out eventually, set the plane on autopilot and took off the headphones.

"I like to fly as high as possible," he said "to keep away from ground-to-air missiles. Rebels bagged two choppers last week, did you hear? Mind you, heat-seeking missiles should not really be attracted by light aircraft.

"I hope not," said Martin.

"No, besides, it's not cost-effective. This old kite is not worth as much as a missile."

"Well, human life comes into it as well. In fact, I suppose that's why we're doing this."

"Frankly," said Desmond, "I'm doing it for $800." He explained he did not often get the chance to fly these days. He was really the East Africa office manager, but they used him when they needed an extra pilot.

"I suppose you need to keep your hand in," said Martin nervously. They were flying over savannah now. Gondo lay behind them in the haze, distinguished by the jebel, the rocky outcrop, that overlooked it and the platinum coloured ribbon that was the Nile.

"Yes, mind you, I don't enjoy it much. Flying makes me nervous. Of course, being British I don't show it. Anyway, it would panic the passengers." He laughed, an odd little, hysterical laugh. Martin felt an alarm bell ringing inside his right temple. He could think of nothing to say. The pilot prattled on about life in Nairobi. He apparently had nothing to do but get pissed and play darts at the English Club. He was saving for a cottage in England with roses up the garden path, just like every second white man in Africa. Presumably he would play darts and get pissed there, too.

A little later they were due to pass over Ginbek, a town rumoured to be the centre of rebel activity. Also a potential market for British Words, so Martin had been informed, words of politics and violence, words like peace and freedom and democracy. Dangerous words in untrained hands.

"Too risky," said Desmond, lighting a cigarette. "Very difficult to find, bush towns. I doubt if we could even spot it from here." Martin peered down at the scrub and savannah, featureless save for two small rivers and a dirt road like a bit of orange string: it all looked much the same to Martin and he said...

"Did you hear about the plane that overshot Jamba with a load of missionaries a few months back? It landed in Zaire by mistake and the missionaries were arrested as spies."

Desmond appeared embarrassed. "So was the pilot," he said, "but they were released after a day or two." The conversation stopped. After a lull, however, Desmond said with forced joviality,

"I don't often get lost."

"I suppose not," reasoned Martin "You only die once." It was meant to be a joke but the pilot gulped and choked on his cigarette smoke.

"I have a system."

"Yes?"

"Positive error."

"Positive error?" repeated Martin.

"Yes. You see, I assume I will not be able to find the airstrip. So I aim for a feature, a road, a river and then I follow it in to town. Infallible."

It made sense to Martin. The landscape was immense and uniform. Trees, scrub, the vast plain, but not so much as a hill or a rock. The largest towns in Gondo seemed little more than villages. Most buildings were mud and thatch and blended with their surroundings. Only a few tin roofs and one or two larger buildings betrayed the presence of human settlement. You would have to fly almost overhead to notice the average town.

"Fortunately," continued Desmond, "Wok is on the River Wok, so we are bound to find it."

Martin looked at their sole navigational aid. It was a Michelin map of East Africa. Martin had the same edition in his Landrover. The roads, he knew, were all wrong, being the old, long, disintegrated colonial roads. The new, aid-funded roads had not been drawn in. But the rivers were accurate enough. Nevertheless Martin had expected something more sophisticated than this, a chart with grids or something.

"How long does the flight take?" he asked.

"About an hour an a half."

"Curious," he gagged. "We seem to have been in the air for nearly two." He wondered for a fleeting moment whether he was being kidnapped but one look at Desmond reassured him on that score. The man was sweating profusely and lighting another cigarette. Nothing calculated there. It would make a good story, though, something to write to Alice about. He wondered where she was. She had once spoken of joining him in Gondo. Since he had arrived he had not heard a squeak.

"Desmond," said Martin. "If we were lost, could we turn around and find Gondo?"

"No chance. If we don't know where we are, we can't take a bearing, you see."

"Yes."

"Some airports have radio beacons."

"But not Gondo?"

"'Fraid not."

The conversation was becoming alarming. Both men were relieved when they did actually see a river glinting below them.

"There you are. The Wok River. Positive error," winked Desmond. He cheered up immensely and took over from the autopilot. "We'll be in Wok in ten minutes."

Half an hour later they were still following the meandering river and there was no sign of Wok. Neither were there for fifty miles in either direction any signs of a road that might lead to Wok. The pilot had lit another cigarette and sweat was spreading across his face.

"We've got plenty of fuel anyway," he laughed. The remark was meant to be reassuring but since it was an admission they were lost, it had the opposite effect. Martin noted the undercurrent of hysteria again. "May I look at the map?" he asked.

"Certainly," Desmond said politely. Martin took it, turned it the right way up with an apology, explaining that he found it easier to read that way. He could not concentrate on it all the same. He knew he wanted to be sure there was only one river. Then he would know they were more or less in the right area. But the Wok River, like the mainstream of the White Nile, was not one river. It was more like a skein of wool. The main streams, all flowing towards the sea thousands of miles away, separated and rejoined one another, so it was impossible to say which was the real River Wok. On the map it was much simpler than on the ground. But one thing Martin did notice. The river was getting narrower and they were passing over some rapids. Martin remembered reading that in colonial days there had been a river service at least as far upstream as Wok, the southernmost navigable point.

"Excuse me," he said, his throat quite dry, "But where do you think we are?"

"Oh, about here I should think," said the pilot, pointing somewhere North of Wok. "Must have been a phenomenal headwind."

"You don't think we could be about here?" suggested Martin, pointing south. "I think we are flying upstream."

Desmond took this very well. "Quite right, quite right. Silly me. I turned the wrong way, didn't I?" And he banked the plane steeply to turn back the way they had come. "Positive error is fine. It is the negative ones that trip you up, ha ha!" He took back the map, turned it upside down and studied it again. "Yes, a road should converge from the left, then it leaves the river again at that big bend and then crosses it in Wok."

Half an hour and three big bends later they had found no road and the pilot was lighting his fifth cigarette. Remembering his remarks about darts Martin said, "I don't suppose we've got any beer aboard." Desmond did not appear to be listening. He was staring down intently at the river.

"I hope you're right about this," he accused Martin, "Can you see which way the river is flowing?"

"Doesn't seem to be moving at all," Martin replied. A purple flame seemed to have ignited inside his head. Hadn't Desmond admitted that if they did not know where they were, they could not even set a course to return to Gondo? Nairobi, Entebbe, Kampala were probably too far. They would come down in this vast expanse of Central Africa. No one would ever find them or learn what had become of them. Irrationally Martin was furious he had brought no sandwiches. Already he had fasted three days.

Then they saw a road. When the road left the river the pilot followed the road and Martin's heart sank as the river fell away from view. It had been their only source of hope this past hour.

"Trust me," said the pilot, nervously "The road will lead us back to the river in about ten minutes."

Neither of them spoke for those next ten minutes. Martin was not the praying kind, but his eyes burned like searchlights as he pierced the haze ahead for a glint that would reveal the languid river. The pilot took his last cigarette from the packet, a gesture to which Martin attached a morbid significance.

"The road must go somewhere," he told himself. "Perhaps we could land on it if need be."

"There's Wok!" announced Desmond. He ceremoniously folded the map and slapped it down on the floor as if playing his ace. "It had to be one way or the other."

That was when Martin started trembling. He saw a few tin roofs, a football stadium, the dirt landing strip and he started trembling all over with relief. He was not cut out for this kind of thing, he decided.

The pilot was very decent about it. "I thought you looked a bit worried," he said. "Really though, you can't go wrong. Not with my system."

"Positive error," Martin gulped as they circled to land. At the last minute the pilot suddenly forced the plane up again.

"Landing wheels," he apologized. "It's always better to put them down before you land." He circled once more and this time made a perfect landing on the rocky, red strip.

"Congratulations," said Martin. He was soaked through with sweat.

The pilot shrugged modestly. "It's nothing when you know how."

They taxied to the end of the airstrip but there was nothing there. So they turned and came back. Half way down the marram scar they saw a Land Rover racing towards them flashing its lights. It led them to a spur off the landing strip where there was a mud and thatch shelter. Martin's day's work had just begun.

"I'm not up to this," he thought again. "I'm just not up to it," but he opened the door and jumped down and it was a physical pleasure to feel mother earth beneath his feet, even if she was still swaying a bit. He shook hands with a burly, smiling priest. For a moment Martin could not make out why the priest was there. He didn't need to be buried now. They were safe.

After more than three hours in the air, Martin would have welcomed a few minutes to refresh himself. A hotel room would have been nice or someone's private bathroom where he could run cold water over his hands and wrists, or better still immerse his whole head and shoulders; then a few minutes rest over a cold beer somewhere out of the glare. He wanted to rehydrate his body, pull his nerves and himself back round a common centre. He swallowed his panic, repressed a rising nostalgia for his neon lit, fuggy office in London, and with a quick word of excuse staggered out to the tall grass for the luxury of a pee. In Wok there were no hotels and no one had running water. There was no time either, for self-indulgence. The sick community worker, whatever that was, had to be located, put aboard the aircraft and flown back to Gondo before the sun went down.

Father Augustine was a well-fed, confident man. Unhurried in manner, he seemed to have things well organized. He offered Desmond and Martin tolerably cool water from a flask in his Land Rover and offered to drive them to the expatriate's house. The pilot opted to stay by the plane.

"You can't leave a plane alone," he said, "You come back and find the propeller missing."

"You're right," frowned the priest. "With all this rebel activity you'll find the whole plane missing. These men will guard it."

Desmond decided to stay anyway and got out a camp bed which he erected in the shade under one of the wings of the aircraft. "I'll rest. We've only got an hour if we want to get back today."

Martin accompanied Father Augustine to his vehicle and climbed in. The priest said in a deep voice,

"It is a pity I shall not see much of you."

"Yes, I'd like to spend more time here myself."

"You may change your mind when you've seen the place," laughed the priest. "Anyway, thanks for coming to fetch the patient out."

Martin looked at the big, calm, black man and wondered if he always wore a gleaming white dog collar, or whether it was put on for the occasion. The long black cassock was worn thin, but remained immaculately pressed. However the feet that operated the pedals were bare.

"How is the 'patient'?"

"If I knew that I wouldn't have sent the message."

The young man had a tukul of his own in the compound adjoining the mud and thatch church. Entering the hut it took Martin a while to accustom his eyes to the gloom. It was slightly cooler inside than out, but airless and swimming with the sweet sour smell of sickness. He made out a young white man badly in need of a shave lying on his side on a mat on the floor. The invalid was covered by a rug. Beside his face was an enamel bowl into which he had recently vomited dark bile. He looked up at the men but could not raise his head when the priest introduced Martin.

"He has come to take you to Gondo," he said.

The invalid croaked what might equally have been thankful acquiescence or frightened protest. Even this small effort brought on a spasm of retching out of all proportion to the small trickle of thick liquid it produced. Martin had to leave the fetid room. The priest re-emerged behind him.

"I pray we are doing the right thing," he said, allowing himself a moment of doubt. "We cannot spare you a nurse to accompany him. We have put his few things into this rucksack. We'll get them carried on to the plane. These things often look much worse than they are."

Martin stared at the priest. This man had arranged the whole evacuation. This man was responsible for his being there. He was efficient, in control and, so it seemed to Martin, totally without compassion.

Father Augustine, incongruous in his shiny black robe which did not conceal the usual large stomach of the privileged, returned Martin's look and said frankly,

"Martin, I know what you are thinking. If you were here longer I'd tell you why I dislike that young man. He has been nothing but trouble since he arrived, but God decrees that we love him and we are both doing our best to save him from premature damnation."

The priest, thought Martin, was a big fish in a small pool. That and his religion gave him the authority, the confidence to speak like this. However unconfident Martin felt, he did not envy the priest his self-deluding certainty.

When they tried to move the invalid they realised he was a stretcher case. At Martin's suggestion they returned to the plane to relieve Desmond of his camp bed. They found the pilot pacing up and down, sweating and smoking a cigarette. The plane had a puncture. The landing strip had been too rough, too full of sharp stones.

"Count our blessings it wasn't a blow-out," said the agitated man. Could have turned the old kite over on her back. I've seen that happen."

The puncture, the lack of even the most rudimentary tool kit, and no spare wheel meant at least a day's delay. Martin was not sorry. Weak from his own recent illness, shaken by the flight and nauseous from the stench of the sick man's tukul, he was capable only of living from one moment to the next. And at that particular moment he saw an empty camp bed in the shade, lay down on it and went to sleep.

ALICE'S STORY. PART THREE

After several days in Nairobi I got onto a small plane bound
for Gondo. It had one pilot and no cabin crew. There were
seven or eight passengers. I was seated next to a big white
man dressed in tight shorts and singlet, both khaki. The
only reason to dress like that seemed to me so that he could
display his muscles. We got talking. I told him I was visiting
Martin Thomas.

He gave me a funny look so I asked if he knew him. He
said he did. He said Martin was all right. He asked me
whether I was Martin's wife.

"I'm a colleague," I said guardedly, whereupon he relaxed.

"So you're not married?" he concluded.

"No chance!" I said, trying to sound flippant. By some logic
I failed to grasp he suggested that if I spent the night with
him he would save me from marriage. Life was too short to
get tied down was his philosophy.

His rather clumsy attempts at a pass were interrupted by
a disturbance in the seat in front of us. Two Norwegians,
Church Aid workers, so Pete my companion told me, were
having an earnest discussion. One of them drew an empty
jam jar from his pocket.

"I can't believe it," chuckled Pete digging me in the ribs.
"He's having a piss."

We had waited an hour in a shed at Wilson Airport to
complete customs and immigration formalities. There were
no toilets there any more than there were on the plane. The
flight was three hours long. One of the Norwegians was as
new to this as I was. His colleague was obviously better
equipped. However it is difficult even for a man to pee
unnoticed into a jam jar inside a light aircraft. Quite apart
from the bouncing about from thermal to thermal there is
very little privacy.

The Norwegian finished his business, or as much as the jam jar would hold, and began to screw the lid on as nonchalantly as possible. At this point Pete, who had literally been holding his breath during the performance, leaned forwards, tapped the man on the shoulder and said in a loud voice,

"Excuse me, but do you Norwegians always drink your beer warm?"

The poor young Christian spilled half the jar over his still unzipped slacks. I almost wet my own knickers trying to stifle my laughter. Pete didn't try to stifle his and of course such mirth attracted everyone's attention. A merry flight.

On arrival Pete offered once more to put me up in his bed. I thanked him, quite unprudishly I hope, but explained that I hoped to be staying with my colleague. Pete seemed a bit worried by this. He said he thought Martin might have travelled up-country. I told him I supposed someone would let me in, a houseboy or something.

"Or something. Like a house-girl?" he said. "That's what worries me."

"Why?"

"I've seen too much life, Alice. That's all. And you're not just a colleague, don't give me that crap."

He dropped me off at the compound. Said if I needed him the gaffir knew where he lived. It was dark and late and I had to wake the gaffir, a fierce little night-watchman armed with a bow and arrows. Martin had told me about this in a letter. I followed the path round to the bungalow at the back of the office. It was in darkness. I knocked on the door and waited a long time before I knocked again, harder and longer. A lamp was lit. It was carried past a window. A woman's voice called, "Jacques, c'est toi?"

I thought I had got the wrong house. "Does Martin Thomas live here?" I shouted.

"Wait."

The door opened. A pretty girl with a triangular face like a Burmese cat appeared holding a hurricane lamp up at arm's length. Her hair was dishevelled. She was sleepy eyed and scared. I thought she was in a night-dress but it could have been a thin cotton frock thrown on quickly and unbuttoned. It was dark, the light jumped and flickered and I was confused.

"Is Martin here?" I inquired.

"He's in bed," she said. She had a French accent. I told her I wanted to see him.

"Not now," she said, shutting the door. "I'm sorry." And there I was, my first evening in Gondo shut out of what I had regarded as my house in pitch darkness.

I slept almost until mid-day next day. I woke up in a strange double bed. As events floated back I wished I had not woken up at all. I was not ready for this.

A very attractive but sullen girl heard me moving about and prepared me some food. She told me Pete would be back about three p.m. Making an effort to break the silence she said she hoped I had found her bed comfortable. Seeing my consternation she laughed, and admitted it was Pete's bed. Nevertheless, she inferred she had sometimes shared it with him.

"Where did he sleep last night?" I asked. She pointed to the sofa and I said that he must have his own bed back at once. She said that whether I was in it or not, if Pete wanted his bed back he would take it. She seemed amused, in control.

When Pete returned, however, she was submissive, fearful. He ordered her about without even looking at her. Fetch this, fetch that. She did his bidding silently.

It was confusing. The French speaking girl in Martin's house, this girl. What were these men up to? I said as much to Pete who growled, "Women are only good for one thing."

"Black and white?" I retorted.

He looked at me slowly and said, "Yes." I do not know why I was not insulted or angry. I think there was just enough banter in his tone to make him bearable. And I was an uninvited guest in his house, literally in his bed if it came to that. I should not have provoked him, but I could not help the challenge,

"Am I only good for one thing, then?"

"I don't even know if you're good for that. Want to show me?"

"No, I'm not ready for that yet," I confessed and all of a sudden I felt foolish. I wasn't used to playing this game. I thanked him for his hospitality in what I hoped was a disarming manner. I offered him his room back. He said I could stay as long as I liked and keep the room. I was just to give him the nod when I was ready.

"I hope that's not a condition."

He laughed and we relaxed. He seemed a lot surer of the outcome than I was.

I have often wondered why I did not try Martin again straightaway. That night I would have found him at home. Perhaps I did not want my unacknowledged suspicions justified, my hopes dashed. Perhaps I needed to re-build my self-confidence. In an infantile way I needed to get on an even footing. That night I did not keep Pete from his bed.

In the morning I returned to the Britwords compound. Pete had told me the office opened at seven thirty. I thought I would see Martin before then, even if he was at breakfast with his girl-friend.

Gondo is not a large town and early morning is a good time for a walk. As I approached the compound I caught up with a young couple. At the entrance to Britwords the man pecked the girl on the cheek and she walked into the yard as though she worked there. She went past the office, though, and walked up the path I had trodden some thirty hours earlier. It was the same girl who had opened the door. The girl who had told me Martin could not see me.

She had her own key. But why was the door locked? She heard me behind her, turned and smiled innocently.

"Hullo," she said.

"Bitch!" I thought, "How can you act so sweetly?"

She invited me in. I swallowed my pride and went into Martin's, into Britwords', our house.

"I'm Therese," she said.

"I'm Alice. We met the other night."

"I know. Martin is better now. But 'e 'as travelled," she said in her French accent. "You 'ave missed 'im hagain."

A slap in the face would have hurt less. I felt ashamed, angry, disappointed and suddenly physically weak. None of Martin's letters had prepared me for this. I was probably still more culture shocked than I would admit. Why should I make excuses? People behave differently removed from their own environments. Simply, I burst into tears. No, that's an understatement. I was shaken by an uncontrollable flood of sobbing and wailing, I was an upturned bottle blub-blubbing out all my self-disgust and self-pity.

It was a cathartic experience and, I now believe, it immunized me for what was to come. This account of my "adventure" is the closest I have since been to tears. If things had gone according to plan, Martin would have returned that evening and probably nothing out of the ordinary would have happened to either of us. He had only flown up to Wok for the day. But when he did not return by dark we both realised there would be at least another day's delay. Therese said there was nothing to worry about. Even when the day's delay stretched into two, three days such hold-ups, she assured me, were normal. But she, too, was anxious to see him, as I am about to recount.

Therese was a sweet girl, a child. We had a long talk that first day. She helped me move in. She continued to spend her days there. The last time I was able to comfort her. Let me explain. During the day she lived in Martin's spare room while her brother was out at work. She called him her brother at any rate. He seemed very possessive, but he was a polite, surprisingly gentle young man. They were trying to get their papers together to emigrate.

I think they were pleased Therese had been able to nurse Martin through his illness. They had been able to give something in return. Therese spoke of Martin, I felt, with great fondness.

I suppose he was a kind of a father figure. They were insistent that I shouldn't be put out, though I felt that I was the one doing the putting out.

It was not for long. Suddenly they were told they were to fly to a transit camp in Kenya. Therese was actually very upset when she got the news. It meant she might have to leave without seeing Martin. She would not be able to thank him.

Both of them decided they wanted to come and formally thank me that evening. I said it was not necessary. I had done nothing. But they insisted that through me Martin would hear of their true appreciation. One day, Jacques told me, when he was as rich as Martin, they could be real friends. For the moment it was a master servant relationship. I told him I was sure Martin did not think in those terms. Nevertheless, said Jacques, they had been dependent on him.

Well, they came to thank Martin, hoping to the last he might turn up. But he did not and I stood in for him. It was a weird ceremony in the sitting room of the little bungalow with its tin roof and cement floor. They had put on their best clothes for the occasion. They had bought presents, too. For Martin a very expensive French dictionary "because his business is words," explained Jacques. They gave me a small leather purse that would have cost nothing in Kenya but which here in Gondo was relatively expensive. It had not occurred to me to give them anything. I had not expected gifts and I felt inadequate. So I offered to accompany them to the airport in the morning and see them off. I asked precisely at what time they were leaving. They were evasive. "Well, it's not quite certain now," was all they would say. Then Therese burst into tears and gradually their predicament and their humiliation became clear.

The Office For Refugees had reserved tickets on the national airline. An official had given Jacques the money to pick them up at the airline's office. On the way Jacques had invited some friends out for a meal to say thank you and goodbye. Therese had wanted to buy presents for me and Martin. Before they knew it they had spent the money given them for tickets.

I told them not to worry. The sum they needed was not great. Britwords had closed but I tracked Big Pete down and asked him to lend me one hundred Niles, as the money was called. He was curious to know what I wanted it for but half feeling I was being conned myself I did not want to be talked out of this gesture. I had seen all my hopes dashed, if only as I then thought, temporarily. I did not want to see Therese's dream of Canada smashed for the lack of fifty pounds.

The couple were very grateful. Jacques seemed embarrassed at taking the money, especially after his speech to me about friendship and dependence. Therese asked me not to see them off. It would remind her of Martin; she still felt bad at not being able to say goodbye to Martin. I think we both wondered if anything had happened to him. Therese had stopped telling me everything would be all right. But neither of us voiced our fears.

All this helped me put my own predicament into perspective and to find my feet. But when I reported my deed to Pete he laughed at me scornfully. He said they had given me the presents to soften me up for the loan; he doubted whether they had even caught the flight.

I was angry, partly because I thought he might be right. After all, I hardly knew the couple, and I was still reacting emotionally rather than rationally.

"Well, that's easily checked," I said. "There must be a flight list."

But there was no flight list. The airline had taken a block booking from the Office For Refugees. No names were recorded. I was able to ascertain that all the tickets had been used, but as Pete pointed out, anyone might have used them, anyone he said pointedly who had bought them on the black market. After all, flights were infrequent, seats always in demand.

One thing was certain. Jacques and Therese were no longer at their hotel. They had left without paying their bill or so the manager said.

I didn't care. In a couple of days Martin would be back. To fill in time, Ndua the office manager of Britwords had arranged for me to visit his farm. "You must see something of our country," he said. Neither of us had the faintest idea just how much of it I was going to see.

CHAPTER SEVEN

When Martin awoke the sun was beginning to go down and a pleasant breeze was bending the grasses. The scene around him had changed. People were coming and going, a couple of men were tinkering with a metal object, part of which they were heating in a fire. An old field tent had been erected and women were pouring water into an empty petrol drum.

"Feeling better?" asked a deep voice that Martin recognised. It was Father Augustine, dressed now in slacks and a short-sleeved shirt that had seen better days. "We've set up camp for you. The only accommodation in town is the schoolroom and Desmond here did not want to leave his aircraft."

Desmond detached himself from a group of figures watching the tinkers. "Not only did we have a puncture. We'd bent the axle and part of the landing gear. Or someone else had before us, who knows? Anyway, Augustine and I think you need a drink."

"We certainly do," said the priest, in a much more relaxed mood, slapping his paunch. "I'm taking you to our pub."

The priest posted two guards, one at each end of the plane, and a third to watch over their camp as he called it, before driving the two white men into town. The main street in the late afternoon sun looked like a set from a Wild West movie with colonnades of lock-up shops, standing up two steps from the dirt road. But they were all closed, except for one which sold soap, tins of Norwegian sardines and plastic mugs. The priest drove them into a disused petrol filling station, the pumps' metal skeletons rusting in the forecourt. A dead donkey, bloated and flyblown, occupied the space where once cars had been raised on a ramp for lubrication and service. Augustine parked carefully beside the ruin marked office and led his new friends down a narrow path behind the service station. They soon came upon a square, brick building the size of a Portakabin on a building site. In the wall was a window with wooden shutters. The window ledge served as a bar and shop counter. Martin could see that the shelves inside were lined with little bottles of beer, all the same: Skol, 33 decilitres.

"Smuggled from Zaire," explained Desmond, impressed. The only other drink, in identical bottles, was a local concoction labelled sherry.

A young woman sat inside the window on a comfortable chair. She reminded Martin of the women who sell themselves in luridly lit windows in Amsterdam. This woman was only selling beer, and reluctant even to do that. Her problem appeared to be that the men were proposing to take away a crate or two of beer and the woman was afraid of losing her precious bottles, worth more to her than their contents. She was only prepared to open three bottles for them to drink as they stood in the dust of the pathway and negotiated. Martin drank his down in one long draught like a man in a pub competition downing a yard of ale. Surprised to find the bottle empty so quickly, he offered to buy twelve bottles cash down. This was a small fortune for the girl, but still she insisted they drink the beer there, bottle by bottle.

Father Augustine intervened. He spoke in the girl's ear and she nodded. Making sure none of her wares were within her customers' reach, she slipped out through a bead curtain in the back and returned almost immediately with a smiling man who welcomed the priest and shook hands with all of them. He told them to follow the fence until they reached a bamboo gate. Here he met them again and admitted them to an enclosed compound. Inside, children, cats, goats and assorted fowl scratched and crawled. Their hosts led them across this space into a thatched lean-to that made up the tiny back room to the shop. It was separated from it by the same curtain they had just seen from the other side.

The visitors just managed to squeeze around a wooden table that filled the space, balancing with some difficulty at first on rickety chairs. The man called through the curtain to the girl, exchanged a few words with the priest and left them to it. Before they had taken in their surroundings the girl emerged with three bottles of tepid beer and a spanner which she set out on the table with three glasses. It was a large spanner and even Augustine was nonplussed as to how to grip a beer top with it. The girl, realising her mistake, smiled for the first time and took the spanner away. She returned with an opener comprising three nails hammered strategically into a wooden handle, and opened their beer for them. All three men were silent for some minutes as they slaked their thirst, then Augustine announced,

"Gentlemen, you may relax. There is no longer any urgency."

"Well, there's nothing more we can do this evening, anyway," admitted Martin.

"I've not made myself clear," said Father Augustine. "The young man died this afternoon."

No one said anything. Martin emptied his bottle into a glass, Desmond stared into his. Augustine looked at them in amusement, wondering perhaps what response English hypocrisy would produce.

"Well, thank God for that," said Desmond.

"Why?" asked Martin.

"Well, as Augustine said, it takes the pressure off. It saves us a lot of palaver too. Not to mention the suffering of that poor bastard."

"I suppose we'll still have to take the body back."

"Back! Where? No one in Gondo will want it. There's no mortuary to keep it in."

"But..." began Martin.

Augustine interrupted him. He explained that bodies did not keep long in the heat, that in his experience repatriation of bodies was too long a process to be practicable. The only solution was to get the corpse in the ground. The matter would be reported to the relevant Consular officials. Any necessary certificates would be issued. Of course, Martin would witness the burial. He might also, if he cared, take delivery of the teacher's few private possessions.

"Sounds as though you have previous experience," said Desmond.

"Alas," sighed Augustine in agreement.

They ordered another round of beer and Martin asked if they had anything to eat. The girl walked across the compound and returned with a red plastic bucket. It was full of eggs.

"Hard-boiled," said the priest. "Help yourself."

"Any bread?" asked Martin.

"Only eggs," said the girl.

It grew dark as they shelled their eggs and drank their beer. Desmond the pilot became fidgety, twice almost began to speak but stopped, embarrassed. Finally he got together a sentence that might prepare the way for his announcement. "You know, Martin," he said a little too jauntily, "it's a bloody good thing I insisted on payment in advance."

"Why's that?" said Martin, relaxed by the beer, the eggs and the velvet darkness.

"Well, with this poor sod being dead I needn't fly back to Gondo. I might as well fly on direct to Wilson airport." And turning to Augustine whose face was scarcely visible he asked, "Reckon I could pick up one or two paying passengers hereabouts?"

Martin listened in panic and disbelief as pilot and priest discussed the change of plan, each no doubt calculating what was in it for them. "Aren't you forgetting one thing?" he said "I paid for a return trip."

"I don't remember that," said Desmond. "I took a risk to save a life."

"You took 800 dollars," accused Martin. "You must still have it on you or with you."

"It was a cheque," lied the pilot.

Martin had never had a fight in his life, never been mugged, but his exasperation with the shifty pilot and his panic at being stranded drove him now to what for him was an act of violence. He had also been drinking on a very empty stomach. He stood up and screamed. "That's not true! You were paid in cash. I got the money myself." He tried to grab the pilot but missed and sent bottles tumbling to the dirt floor.

"My friends," said the priest soothingly, "stop behaving like savages. It is all my fault."

Martin sat down, Desmond who had been cringing from an expected blow straightened up. The girl brought in an oil lamp whose naked flame tongued the thickening night.

"I asked for help. You both came ⁻ for whatever motivation. Unfortunately the patient has died and he no longer needs your help. Am I right?"

"Quite right," agreed Desmond.

"Martin?"

"Yes."

"Good. Now Desmond, you were paid 800 dollars for what was assumed to be a return trip."

"Or one day's work," added Desmond slyly, "which I've done."

"Who paid, by the way?" asked the priest.

"I did. My company did," said Martin.

Augustine was not to be hurried. He ordered more drinks, filled their glasses himself and ran over the facts again. He got the men talking calmly. Desmond admitted that here in Wok he was already on his way to Nairobi "As the crow flies, at any rate." Martin refrained from any sarcastic remark about how Desmond flew. Instead he admitted that if alternative means of transport to Gondo were available, even a souk lorry, he would prefer to take that. Small planes, he explained diplomatically, did not seem to agree with him.

Augustine let them talk it out and then he put forward his proposal. "Eight hundred U.S. dollars is rather steep for a short, single flight," he observed, "particularly as it is hardly out of Desmond's way. On the other hand when you clinched your deal you did not know you wouldn't be going back. I suggest that you, Desmond, return 200 dollars to our friend Martin. After all it was not exactly a joy ride. And that you keep 500 for yourself."

"You mean six," said Desmond.

"No five. I further suggest that 100 dollars goes to the church expenses."

"The church?"

"To put it frankly, to me." said Augustine. "Is it a deal?"

"I'll buy it," said Martin. "I wanted to visit Wok anyway. But how do I get back?"

"Just a minute," said Augustine. "Desmond, do you agree?"

"Well...."

"Tell you what. I'll guarantee to find you at least one other passenger who will pay a hundred dollars when he gets to Nairobi."

"Okay," laughed Desmond. "You're a wicked old devil, though."

"I hope not," said Augustine with a glint in his eye. "Well, we had better get you back to camp. Sorry supper was not very substantial, but I'll arrange for a good breakfast."

"Don't go to any trouble," said Martin with linguistic reflex from another continent.

"No trouble," said Augustine. "Not now I know your pockets are stuffed with dollars."

As first light seeped into the tent, it brought with it into the men's uneasy dreams the sound of scurrying activity, soft footfalls, low, calm voices. Desmond, plump as a puppy, stirred wondered whether his precious plane were being dismantled, but the heavy net of slumber reclaimed him for another hour.

What the quiet sounds and gentle dawn had failed to do, the scent of cooking and the rising temperature achieved. The men emerged from their tent to find smiling faces grouped over a big bowl of millet porridge. A large black kettle simmered on a charcoal stove. It contained an aromatic brew of tea, milk, sugar and cardamom all boiled up together. There was even water for the men to wash in.

"Five star service," said Desmond, waddling off unselfconsciously into the scrub to relieve himself.

Augustine drove up in time to share the porridge. It was heavy, filling fare and quite enough to be shared between the three of them and all the helpers. They formed a circle around the bowl, thrust their hands in up to the wrist, rolled the porridge into a ball and flipped it into their mouths. It reminded Martin of play dough and tasted worse. However it was sustaining stuff and washed down with sweet tea the breakfast was a real pleasure. Real because badly needed and acutely enjoyed, unlike a western pleasure pursued as a treat, an extra, a mere luxury. This, thought Martin to himself to his own surprise, this is the life. This is the way to kill panic.

"You like our food?" Augustine asked him.

"Delicious!" said Martin.

It took Desmond the whole day to get the repairs on the aircraft done to his satisfaction and to negotiate the price of a drum of aviation fuel. Martin meanwhile unloaded his two small crates of words and stored them in the church. He spent a couple of hours trying to make radio contact with Gondo to explain his delay. It was hopeless. All he got was static. It was not until the following morning that he finally contacted a radio operator at the Office for Refugees and asked him to pass a message on to Bob. Reception was unclear and the radio operator did not seem very bright.

"You know Bob at the High School?" asked Martin. He could not remember Bob's surname, but everyone knew him as Bob.

"No. This is Office for Refugees, please. Over," came the response.

"Roger. I have a message for Bob at the High School. Over."

"Yes sir. Over."

"Tell him the Englishman is dead. Have you got that, over?"

"Tell Teacher Bob the Englishman is dead, over."

"Roger. And that Martin is returning by road. Over."

"Roger is returning by road. Over."

"No, Martin is returning by road. Over."

"Very good, sir. Over."

"Thank you very much. Over and out."

Martin could think clearly no longer. Survival in this country was such a full time job that he sometimes forgot what he was there for. Similarly, he had put so much effort into making contact, passing his message that he perhaps had not paid enough attention to the clarity of that message. He stepped dripping with sweat from the mission radio room and wished he had a change of clothing. He blinked and straightened up. He saw Augustine's Landrover coming up the drive towards him, flashing its lights. It was good news. Good luck. A German road building team was driving through to Gondo to begin their leave. Two of them had leapt at the opportunity of a direct flight to Nairobi with Desmond. It would save them days if not weeks. The third had to return to Gondo with the vehicle and would be happy to have Martin's company on the journey. If it didn't rain he reckoned he could do it in four days.

While the Germans sorted themselves out Martin went round the few traders in the town with his crate of words. None of them showed much interest until they realised the samples were free.

"Tell me what sells," Martin said, "and I'll supply you more of them." So one old man chose nouns qualified with the adjective rural: rural extension work, rural bank, rural cooperation. Another one took a fancy to longer, single words like aquaculture, desertification, maximisation. The pharmacist took a job lot of health jargon, though he was sceptical about words like preventative measures and primary health care.

"Not good for business," he explained. "My job is to sell cures. If people take preventative measures who will I sell my cures to?"

Martin thought to himself, "You didn't have anything in stock to help that community worker." Aloud he urged, "But you can sell preventative measures just as well. Look, here's a good word. 'Prophylaxis'" He held it out in his hand. "Or another one that sells well is 'immunisation programme.' The package contains a minimum of twenty-five associated words. Guaranteed."

The pharmacist scratched his stomach. "Well, as it's free, give me two sets. Some Kawaja may be interested at least," he said.

Martin's strength returned with his sense of purpose, a few more words to give away, a journey to prepare for. Departure very soon. His panic left him and he felt calm, clear-headed at last. Instead of giving his last bag of words away, he traded them for a shirt and a pair of jeans. He returned to "camp" with the roll of clothes under his arm. He felt almost relaxed.

Walking is a kind of thinking and as he enjoyed feeling the strength back in his legs, it occurred to Martin that moods, even certain perceived virtues were simply physiological functions. Bravery, for example. You could not pretend to be brave, or decide to act bravely. However strong-minded you were, your body would go its own way. It would sweat when it was hot, shiver when it was cold and do both when it was afraid.

"God knows," thought Martin, "I'm trying to make a go of it. Trying to master my fears. But every so often my body sends another message, a warning or a protest. It is telling me I shouldn't be here."

There was no use pretending to himself or to anyone else. He was afraid. He had been afraid in the plane when he thought they were lost; he had been paralysed with anxiety at the thought of being stranded in Wok in only the clothes he stood up in. Yes it was not the fear he could not cope with: it was the effect fear had on him. Was he a coward or was he brave? He did not know. What he did realise was that the biggest obstacle to his success in the Republic was something quite unforeseen. The biggest obstacle would be his own health.

"What were you doing in Wok, eigentlich?" inquired the German, whose name was Rolf.

"It's a long story," replied Martin.

"It's a long journey," said Rolf, offering a packet of cigarettes.

Martin explained he had come to evacuate a community worker but that the young man had died before they had been able to move him.

"Another one!" remarked Rolf.

"What do you mean?"

The German slowed down to drive round some bad potholes.

The road was so broken up that he made a detour through the bush, joining the red marram trail fifty metres on. "A bit risky," he said. "This black cotton soil. You can sink up to your axles, ja?"

"I don't know."

"I am telling you. Never leave the road is my advice."

"You don't always follow your own advice, then?" said Martin, to humour the man. The journey did not look promising. The man smoked and he had a kind of jauntiness that Martin could not share. And yet he envied this man his self-sufficiency, his feeling of being at ease with the country, with his vehicle. A man who could look after himself. Nevertheless even he had welcomed the idea of a passenger for company.

"Who killed him?" asked the German.

"No one. He died."

"So he died. We all die. But not when we are twenty four years old."

"Lots of people die young out here," retorted Martin.

"He was poisoned. I would say he was poisoned. Who did it? The priest?"

"Why should Father Augustine do that?" asked Martin, shocked. "It was the mission that called me out. He wouldn't have radioed Gondo to announce a murder."

"What's he got to lose? Looks as though Father Augustine has done well out of the whole business."

"No, that's not fair."

Only an hour earlier Martin had taken leave of the priest, thanking him for his help, apologizing for missing the funeral.

"I know," Augustine had said in his deep, unhurried voice. "White men are always in such a hurry. They have to change the world."

"I'd like to have stopped for a chat. I was rather hoping we could have spent another evening together in the 'pub'."

"Well, what's stopping you?" Augustine had challenged with a twinkle in his eye. "No, I am only joking. You have to get back to Gondo. I understand."

"Do you?"

"Well, frankly, no. But I know you will not be persuaded to stay."

"This time. I'll come back."

"They all say that, too. Go, my son," said Augustine. "Don't feel guilty."

"Don't feel guilty," Martin repeated to himself aloud inside the German's vehicle.

"Witchcraft," said Rolf.

"I beg your pardon?"

"Here is my scenario. Your community worker arrives fresh from Europe. It is a honeymoon at first. He makes friends, he has many new experiences. He sees good things. He sees bad things. The bad things he wants to change. The people turn against him. They put a ju-ju on the interfering white man."

"But it was a Christian mission. Surely Christians do not believe in black magic?"

Rolf guffawed. "What kind of Christians do you know? Eh? These people are terrified of black magic. They don't even trust their own brothers." Distracted for a minute he drove into a loose rock with a jolt that almost knocked them off course.

"Even if that were so," said Martin, clutching at his seat belt, "ju-ju would not have affected the community worker. Surely you have to believe in it."

"A bit of poison prompts belief. At any rate, others will believe it."

"I think this is all rather far-fetched," said Martin. "The lad got malaria or hepatitis or something."

"But you don't know which."

"No."

"Well, I say he was poisoned," said Rolf and lit another cigarette using the lighter in the dashboard.

"So sure. So certain," thought Martin.

And yet the man's confidence was comforting, and the journey an apprenticeship in simple survival, in improvisation. Rolf showed Martin how to mend a puncture on the road using a hot patch. The most difficult task was removing the tyres from the wheel rim. The German demonstrated the simplest way of refilling the fuel tanks straight from the 40 litre drums that occupied most of the back of the vehicle. Martin learned that, provided you carried a little money, you need not go hungry. There was no need to stock up, except with clean water. Chickens, bush meat, fruit and vegetables could be found in villages. And although they passed no more than two vehicles a day, most of these being souk lorries laden with passengers and their goods, the occasional roadside tea-houses kept open.

Usually made of mud with rotting grass roofs, they were owned by Ugandan refugees who decorated their dull earth walls in their own patterns of whitewash and pebbles. Flowers had been planted outside one tea-house, an adornment not practised by local people.

The two men drew up outside one such halt, eased their bones out of their vehicle and walked stiffly in to the shade. They drank from enamel mugs a hot sweet tea that had been boiled up with the milk and sugar and cardamom in it. The smoke-blackened kettle wheezed over its burning log outside the hut, permanently topped up and inviting. Martin preferred this mixture to the throat constricting, very sweet red tea served at most wayside stalls.

The hut comprised two rooms and a counter. The few unwashed tables crawled with ants and the chairs required of their occupants a good sense of balance. Bread and doughnuts made with egg and flour were on sale at the counter. Both men, enjoying the stillness and gloom after the glare and clatter of the road, drank a second mug of tea in grateful silence. Rolf dunked a doughnut in his but could not chew his way through it all. He flung the remains to a thin, almost hairless dog. The dog carried it out into the dust outside and settled down to relish the treat slowly in the 100 degree heat.

As they sipped the hot, milky life-restoring liquid a very ragged man walked in. He put his spear, bow and a quiverful of arrows in the corner, removed a small coin from inside his ear and paid for a mug of tea. He slurped noisily, ignoring the two travellers. He evidently was not going to allow anything to mar his enjoyment.

"I'm tired," said Rolf "Why don't you drive the next stretch?" And so the two of them began to take turns, three hours driving, three hours dozing.

Martin's confidence flowed back like a tide as they progressed. He began to enjoy himself. The Landrover roared and rattled, plunged and danced relentlessly through this ragged country, monotonous in its vastness but beautiful in its particulars. When Rolf dozed Martin felt more relaxed than at any time since his arrival in the Republic. For three or four days there was nothing he could do, nothing for which he was responsible, other than keeping on the road and reducing the distance between himself and Gondo. He was in a time capsule between the grotesque attempt to rescue the English lad and the frustrations of his office. He could savour the present moment undisturbed by worry or the need to plan. In the heat and the haze, the dirt and the dust, between the blinding green trees through which the bright orange road unwound, in this haze of discomfort and noise, the odd sight impinged on Martin's consciousness. Things he would write home about. A man falling off a bicycle at the unexpected approach of a vehicle; another man cycling along, bow over one shoulder, with a slain warthog on the carrier of his bike; children waving, bare-breasted women staring, waving and smiling back if he waved to them; a twisting, shifting vertical rope of dust that skidded along the road in front of them and whisked off into the bush like a snake on a skateboard; an entirely naked mad-woman who marched towards the vehicle causing them to stop. While ignoring them she thrust past, a spring in her step, her powerful buttocks and thigh muscles pushing her on as if she were an electric toy; hunting parties with bows, arrows and spears, one man carrying a heavy hunting net on his shoulders; the catholic churches, some of mud and grass, some brick-walled and tin-roofed; children rushing out from roadside settlements holding up live chickens and ripe mangoes for sale. Sometimes they passed blackened, burnt-out clearings in the emerald vegetation.

After one spell of bumping and jolting and the noise of his teeth and mind rattling in his skull, he stopped the vehicle, switched off the engine and the stillness rang in his ears until it was penetrated by the singing of the birds. He ran his tongue over his lips, tried to talk and had to clear his dust-filled throat several times and spit. His sweaty clothes had attracted the red dust as a magnet does iron filings. His hair was orange.

"This is better than flying any day," he told Rolf, and spat through the open side window of the cab.

For three days they drove on, staying one night on the floor of a school, another camping out beside the vehicle and the third in a large empty house. Rolf had kept this as a surprise.

"Tonight we sleep and eat in comfort," said the German. It was another of those bungalows built originally by a road construction company and subsequently run as a Guest House. Now it was deserted but a caretaker was supposed to keep an eye on it, open it up to German aid workers and others in the development game who knew about it. If a traveller was white the caretaker let him in.

While Rolf went to find the old man and make arrangements for a meal, Martin walked into what had been the garden to stretch his legs. A big kaok tree held a feathery palm lovingly in its rustling branches. Ragged banana plants held out hands of ripe fruit and papayas, too, grew abundantly. Behind the unkempt garden lay a pineapple plantation beyond which rose a spring surrounded by a copse of mahogany and other trees remaining from the original dense jungle like a cluster of hairs round a wart on an otherwise clean-shaven face.

Attracted by movement in the treetops Martin wandered over to the copse. He was astonished and delighted to find a troupe of long-haired, black and white colobus monkeys, their tails hanging down like frayed bell ropes. The grace of their aerobatics cathartically released the aches in Martin's travel bruised body. The monkeys leapt twenty feet across space to grasp branches that bent under their weight in a sweeping, sixty degree arc until the creatures scampered upwards, inwards to the main trunk and the branch that had been their safety net rose back to its natural position. Martin strained his eyes watching the antics of the colony. He followed them round their island territory. Their survival, he surmised, was due entirely to the great height of the trees. They were beyond the range of arrows and catapults.

"Never survive the gun, though," said a familiar, staccato voice. "Five years maximum I give them."

"Bob!" exclaimed Martin, grasping the tubby teacher's hand. "What brings you here?"

Bob looked embarrassed. "You, actually."

Martin did not understand. "Are you staying in the German house?"

"I am now," replied the fat man, mopping his forehead with a large cloth. He was staring at Martin as if he were a ghost.

"Good. So you will have supper with us. What is it?"

"You don't know, do you?"

"What's happened?"

"Nothing fortunately. Oh God, Martin. Nothing." He broke into a bray of bitter laughter that frightened away half a dozen of the closest monkeys from their high perch.

"Look, Bob. I know I am a bit of a sight. We've only just arrived. I'm waiting for a wash."

"It's not that..." choked the white man, crimson with mirth and frustration.

Then Martin remembered his mission. His flight to Wok, the death of the young Englishman. It was Bob who had asked him to go. "You got my message. About the lad. He died."

"So it was that Englishman who died. It wasn't clear..."

"But I radioed," said Martin, gripping Bob's shoulder frantically as the awful truth surfaced, willing it back down.

"I know you radioed, you idiot, but..."

They were interrupted by the approach of a third man, very dark, glisteningly good-looking and comfortable in the heat. It was Isaiah, Bob's protégé, the same well built youth whom Martin had met on the day of his arrival in Gondo; whose bed he had slept in the first night or two. Isaiah was aware of his good looks and he walked with an easy swagger. But when he recognized Martin beneath his shroud of red dust, hair, clothes, face all the same red brown hue, when he saw this apparition remonstrating with Bob, Bob his master, his father and his friend, the fat man red with suffocation, Isaiah's mouth dropped open and he sank to his knees.

"Isaiah, what are you playing at?" blurted Bob, convulsed with laughter.

"Bob, can you see it?" moaned his black companion.

"See what?" he snapped, exasperated.

"It's witchcraft. Zande magic."

The penny dropped and Bob with it. He fell to the ground in a renewed fit of laughter. "What do you see, Isaiah?" he gasped.

Believing Bob to be under a spell, Isaiah became more alarmed still. "The ghost of Mr. Martin."

"Isaiah, isn't it?" said the dead man pleasantly. "I'm sorry if I am responsible for a misunderstanding." He held out his hand but Isaiah recoiled in disgust. Bob screamed in the exquisite pain of his mirth. Isaiah took up the cue, yelling his head off as he ran back to the house.

Martin watched in disbelief. Then his attention turned to Bob still rolling on the ground like a loose barrel in the back of a lorry.

"You mustn't be angry with him, Martin," he croaked. "It's not every day a man sees a ghost."

The radio operator who had received Martin's message had had a busy day. By the end of his shift he had forgotten completely about the message from Wok. It was not until the following morning when he opened his note pad that he noticed his omission and later still when he passed the message to Bob. He became confused when the irate and anxious teacher questioned him about which Englishman was dead. Bob had also heard a rumour, no doubt kindled by the non-return of the small plane, that Martin had been killed in an air crash. After trying in vain to contact the mission in Wok, and feeling guilty because he had sent Martin up there in the first place, he decided to drive up and find out the truth for himself.

He called into the office of Britwords and told the staff not to report Martin missing until he returned. "I'll bring him back dead or alive," he had promised, whereupon Martin's secretary Vashti set up a wailing fit, surely shrill enough to wake him from the dead if that was necessary.

"The irony is," Bob went on, "that you chose Zande country for your resurrection."

"Why?"

"The Azandes were a powerful kingdom," said the schoolteacher, recovering his calm as he recounted this snippet of local history. "They ruled a large area of central Africa. Now they are a passive, unmotivated race. They are terrified of snakes, magic and witchcraft. They don't live in villages. They live in family groups, so great is their fear of one another. The early colonialists called them the Nyam Nyam on account of their eating people chopped into small pieces."

"I don't get it," said Martin. "Why Nyam Nyam?"

"They would lick their lips over morsels of human flesh and say with much relish, 'Nyam Nyam'"

"Or yum yum. I see."

"Anyway, as you saw from Isaiah's reaction, something of their reputation lingers on in Zande country."

"I'm sorry I gave him such a shock."

"Do him good. Teach him it's all superstition."

"I hope so. I wonder if he will ever touch me again."

Bob gave Martin an odd look and joked, "I hope not."

In fact Isaiah quickly recovered his composure and that evening the four of them feasted on a goat stew which with Elephant Beer soon restored their spirits. It was a merry meal, Rolf playing host, Bob talking about the local customs, interrupted from time to time by Isaiah. Again a feeling of well being crept over Martin. If only he could take life as it came, enjoy these moments of friendship, of improvisation, relax more, it should be possible to cope with the rest of it.

Bob decided that having come this far he would call on a few schools to see if they were still functioning. Martin was now tempted to accompany him, but thought he should continue back to Gondo with Rolf.

"I've been away too long," he declared.

"I don't know about that," said Bob, "but you have got a visitor."

"Where from?"

"Didn't ask."

"How do you know then?"

"Went into your office to tell Ndua I was going to look for you. Ndua was not there. Vashti told me he'd taken a visitor out for the day."

"We weren't expecting any visitors," shrugged Martin.

"It's your auditor, no?" laughed Rolf, opening another beer. "They never tell no one when they come."

"I hope not," said Martin. "He'll probably be gone when I get back."

"She," said Bob. "Think Vashti said she."

"Then, tomorrow maybe we find out," said Rolf. "Tonight we drink, ja?" And he filled Martin's glass.

ALICE'S STORY. PART FOUR

"Pete, you've been very helpful to me."

"I have my reasons."

"That's obvious," I said. I was feeling more confident with him now.

"Is it that obvious?" He looked surprised.

"Yes! But let's forget that for a moment..."

"For the moment... so?"

"Look, I don't want to sit around here all day. Can't I do something? Something useful?"

"Do you mean that?"

I nodded and he rubbed his forehead on his big fist. He was beginning to take me seriously. "Well, there is... No."

"Go on."

"Well you could go to the bank for me. Cash a cheque."

I was disappointed. "You're joking," I said, but he wasn't.

"No. It's a major job. It takes all day."

"What to cash a cheque?"

"Pretty well. Will you do it?"

"All right."

"Look Alice. It's a frustrating job. Drives me up the wall. That's why I'm asking you to go. Think of it as a social occasion. That helps."

I realised what Pete had meant when I entered the bank. In Gondo people still use money, real money, wads and wads of it. There are no credit cards, you can't even pay for things by cheque. The only use for a cheque is to withdraw money from your own account in the bank. Which is what Pete had asked me to do for him.

The first impression of the bank was the smell of the money. I mean that quite literally. People carry cash. This means in a breast-pocket or under the folds of a galabiah. It is close, next to the skin. It is therefore always damp. The notes are seldom withdrawn. They are repeatedly soaked and stained with sweat, counted out on a dusty surface and folded into another clammy pocket.

Now, there may be rebels and civil war here, and there is plenty of petty pilfering, but there is no organized crime. And so little traffic that if you planned a bank raid your getaway car would be obvious from the start.

Despite the use of paper money there were no barriers between staff and customers apart from one long counter, which separated the rows of six clerks from the swarm of customers on my side. There was nothing to stop any one of us helping ourselves to a few thousand pounds. The bundles of money were stacked like loaves beside the clerks within easy reach of the public. The whole business of banking appeared to lie in the taking in or the handing out of these loaves. The clerks counted it with extraordinary speed and dexterity and the customers took it away, or in the case of traders, brought it in like any other commodity in plastic bags or cardboard grocery boxes as though the money was, well, like a loaf of bread or a sack of rice.

By the time I handed my cheque over, the piles of notes had diminished. My clerk looked at the cheque and told me they had run out of money. I nearly giggled at this but instead asked politely what I should do. He advised me to sit and wait. In time a trader would come in and deposit enough cash. I was a bit sceptical. Pete had written a cheque for five thousand Niles. As I sat there watching, I suddenly wondered how much five thousand Niles was in bulk terms. Five thousand notes or more. I thought of a paper back book with four or five hundred pages. About ten paperbacks, then!

I watched and waited. All the transactions were recorded by hand. There being no electricity the bank could not effectively be computerised. But there was no mechanical typewriter, either, except the one used for writing letters.

The book keeping, the ledgers, the statements were all being written by hand.

Behind the tellers at the long desk between us was a roomful of scribes and scribblers patiently penning numbers. They all wore white shirts and ties.

I noticed that any transaction took a devious route around most of them, a signature here, an initial there, a note from a section head and so on. I watched the progress of individual bits of business. It took about half an hour to pay money in, get it counted, recorded and a receipt issued. It took over an hour to draw any money out. In my case there was no money even to be drawn. This gave me the feeling that I was being forgotten, deliberately passed over.

I had carried out the first procedure. I had elbowed my way to the front, held my own against the pushy, Arab merchants and the politer, more yielding Africans; I had presented Pete's cheque; the teller had pinned a scrap of paper to it, written a number on it and his signature. He had given me another scrap of paper with his signature and, I supposed, the same number. That was when he had told me I had to wait for more money to be paid in. Since then a number of plastic bags had spilled bundles of fetid bank notes onto the worn, wooden counter. My number had not been called. I suddenly realised that its twin and the cheque were still with my first clerk. Because he was waiting for the money to come in, he had not passed the paperwork round the circuit. Instead of bobbing down with the current it was caught in an eddy on the first clerk's desk.

I was moist by now. The bank was an old, brick building, but with all those warm bodies milling about, the intense heat outside, it had got hot. The air was so humid I felt like a fish in an aquarium. I swam up to the desk and found my clerk who had told me to wait in the first place.

"Is there any money now?" I asked.

"Plenty money, Madam," he said and sent my cheque off with its piece of pink paper on its white-knuckle ride round the monetary track. The clerk must I think have forgotten about the cheque until I reminded him and felt guilty. Either that or he was trying to be helpful. For he left his position and his stacks of money, retrieved my cheque and took it round by hand for the necessary signatures, a journey of only a few minutes rather than hours. He then gave it to the man at the end of the front line whose job it seemed to be to pay the money out.

A whole mob waited round this counter, Arab merchants in their white galabiahs through which and under which they seemed permanently to be scratching their balls, Africans in tight trousers and shirts, all men, all clamouring for attention.

The cashier had cultivated an air of indifference, of unhurried calm. The customers might have been a pack of hounds waiting to be fed. He ignored them except to call out a number.

"Fifty nine!" he shouted. It was mine.

"Here!" I cried as if I had won a raffle.

"Fifty nine!" he shouted again. The crowd muttered impatiently, willing him to take another ticket. But this time my cry was heard, I waved my bit of pink paper and the crowd of men politely parted, sweaty faces creased into smiles. Not even an Arab set a hand upon me in the crush.

The cashier took my slip without even looking at me, counted the money into two piles, not half as big and impressive as I had hoped and I reached for it. However the process was not yet over. I had to record the cheque number and my address in a book. Only then did he push the money towards me as though it was dirty linen, which in a way it was, slowly picked up another slip and called out the next number.

I put my money into a plastic carrier bag and somewhat apprehensively stepped out into the glare of midday where I bumped into Pete.

"Just came by to see how you were doing. I'll take your place for a bit if you want to go out for a cold drink."

"It's okay, Pete," I told him proudly. "I've got the money."

"Jesus Christ!" he whistled. "That's quick."

"Two hours is quick?"

I felt pleased with myself but annoyed that I should want to please this big bully of a man. I had nothing to prove. But it had been thoughtful of him to offer to stand in for bit.

A couple of shady looking Lebanese drew up with a big bag of money. They greeted Pete like a long lost brother and he returned their bear hugs. He introduced me.

"Alice, this is Abdoul and Mohamed. Very important men. If you want it, they can get it. Gentlemen, this is Alice, a very fast worker and my new woman."

The men gave me a knowing look, running their eyes over my damp body. I raised my hand to hit Pete in the face, but for some reason I smiled. The bloody nerve of the man!

"I'm not his woman," I laughed. "Not yet. He's got to earn my respect first."

"Respect!" spat Pete. "Then you never will be."

The other men laughed and went on into the bank.

"Arms dealers," Pete explained. "Under cover of safari expeditions for rich Saudis. Does that shock you?"

"You'd like me to be shocked, Pete, wouldn't you?"

He chuckled. I found him infuriating, patronizing and so damned arrogant. I knew he liked annoying people so I tried to take no notice.

The trip out to Ndua's farm promised to be a pleasant contrast to my morning in the bank. Even Ndua seemed to come alive at the idea of escaping his administrative chores in the office. It was not far to the farm, he told me. He normally walked it if he had a day or two to spare, but for my sake he thought we should take the Britwords Landrover.

I could see why. He had loaded it with an iron bedstead, four home made wooden chairs, a sack of rice stamped EEC Emergency Food Aid and half a Nile perch. "Presents," he explained, handing me the keys.

It was clear I was expected to drive. Well, I'd driven my own small car in London for years and once I had driven a minibus for a church organisation that took old people on outings. At least in Gondo there was no traffic. Not many roads, either, I found.

For the first fifteen miles we bumped along a track that followed the Nile upstream. We passed through an area so densely packed with tukuls that the only open spaces for recreation and defecation seemed to be the road we were following. Little children squatted over their snaking stools like little black garden gnomes pivoted on tiny, twisted sticks. It was a squalid, colourful area full of goats and hens and pipe-smoking women, women fetching water and pounding food, men with nothing to do but sit or stare and play leisurely games of chance. I could scarcely keep my eyes on the track but Ndua did not even notice the scene. I did jolt him out of his doze when we dropped into a particularly deep pothole which almost brought his bed frame through the roof.

When we reached a small village on the outskirts of Gondo, Ndua pointed to a rough track that led off to the right, away from the settled area and the river into the dry, thorny scrub. After fifteen minutes of heaving and swaying in second gear he told me to stop driving but remain in the car. He himself clambered out. I was glad I had followed Pete's advice and despite the heat changed into my jeans and trainers. We were surrounded by thorn bush and spiky grass. There was no more track. Ndua began walking through the bush and signalled me to drive behind him. That was when I learned how useful the low ratio gears were. Far more control and I could, tractor-like, more easily proceed at walking pace. I wished I'd tried it earlier.

After ten minutes of this pedestrian navigation we came to a footpath. Ndua climbed aboard and we tried to follow this thin, sometimes indiscernible line. Ndua guided me now this side of a casuarina, that side of a rock, over a gully here, round a termite hill there. The ground was firm and in some places even rocky; we avoided the larger boulders and bulldozed the small bushes. We had to shut all the windows because the thorns as they scratched and whipped past would have torn our flesh and deposited all manner of insects on the seats and on us. Ndua and I streamed with sweat as the sun beat down on the roof and the scrub became thicker and thicker. On one occasion I glimpsed the big horns of a herd of cattle corralled in a thorn enclosure. On another a woman passed with a high load of sticks on her head. People from the capital now had to come this far out for their firewood, Ndua told me. It used to grow on the edges of the town.

The ground became rougher and when the Landrover grounded on a big stone like a boat on a beach I wondered whether we should really be subjecting Britwords' property to such a pounding. Ndua insisted it was not much further. I drove on, pushing down grass much higher than the vehicle. Visibility stopped at the end of the bonnet, yet Ndua seemed to know every blade, every twig every stone. We eventually stopped in a little clearing and staggered out of our sauna into the hot but fresher air. Ndua led the way along a narrow path past some beautiful desert roses that starred their rubbery, cactus-like plant pink and scarlet.

Ndua was almost playful, gallant, holding back prickly branches which were in effect his garden gate. We emerged into a clearing the size of a tennis court where tall millet plants stood warming their purple-seeded beads in the welcome breeze. Beyond the dura patch lay an area of about the same size again. Hard, dry earth beaten and swept. One large, square hut with thorn walls and a roof thatched with broad, dry leaves faced a small round tukul of the same materials across an unfenced compound. A smaller replica, well protected with thorns was evidently a chicken house, and a roof supported by four tall poles doubled as a platform for drying some fronds of the bead-like grains of dura which had already been cut. Around the edge of the cleared area grew several gourds for use as calabashes.

I was entranced and Ndua smiled broadly, watching me. Little chicks, some surely only days old, scurried everywhere. A thin, tick-covered dog slunk away at the sight of me. I must say I was quite relieved. It was a mangy skeleton of a dog. It seemed to rank lower even in its own esteem than the more useful hens and cocks and the sleek, self-confident goats. One enormous billy goat with a thick, black beard ignored our intrusion and chewed at a stalk in utter concentration. Two glossy kids eyed me warily.

The women, for I suddenly noticed them, two motionless women, waited until we spoke to them before greeting me with handshakes and smiles and Ndua more with respect than affection. One proceeded to winnow beans by tossing them in a small, flat plaited basket so that the husks blew away, the other was splitting grasses and canes, the canes for chair seats, the grasses to weave into the tall, soft baskets I had noticed in the market. This woman might have been thirty or forty years old and she sat pleased and silent, self-assured but self-effacing, dextrously continuing her handicraft. The first woman, at Ndua's command, hurried into the house.

Ndua led me to the shade of a neem tree growing in the centre of the compound. There I sat in a deck chair made of wood and goat skin which felt thick and stiff. The woman, I presume a wife of Ndua's, quickly emerged from the house with a battered old teapot from which Ndua poured one cup of gahwa, a strong, sweet coffee by the smell of it. While he sipped this noisily, I was offered a basket of peanuts. I shelled and ate a few and wondered if I would be given anything to drink. I rather hoped not. I had my own flask with me: it contained boiled and filtered water. I took a swig to wash down the peanuts. As I did so a group of men with guns burst into the compound.

Ndua was as surprised and shocked as me. Two men came up to us, two or three others ran into the huts, as if searching for someone. The women screamed but all the soldiers, as I thought they were, ignored them. Very soon all of them, and there were in fact only five, stood in a circle around Ndua and me.

"Who are these men?" I asked.

"Don't worry, it's a mistake," he said.

The leader shouted at Ndua. I didn't understand the conversation, but Britwords and Kawaja were repeated. Eventually the men turned to me, smiled and one of them said in good English,

"I am sorry. We do not want to frighten you. Please be so kind as to answer a few questions."

"Of course," I said. I was frightened, but he seemed to be a gentle, even a courteous man beneath the military exterior; and he was quite young. Younger than his comrades, I guessed.

He asked me my name and why I was here. I didn't know if he meant here at Ndua's farm or here in the Republic and I hesitated. Ndua intervened in English and said he had wanted to show me a bit of the country. The men looked at him suspiciously.

"Where is your director?" he demanded. "Mr Martin. Is he not the Director of Britwords?"

"Yes sir," said Ndua to this young man.

"Where is he hiding?"

"Nowhere, Sir."

I thought the soldier was going to strike Ndua. I said, "Martin Thomas is not here. He's gone away."

"He did not come with you today?"

"No!" we both said, and the penny dropped. These men had seen the Landrover with the Britword logo. For some reason they had wanted to talk to Martin. I had not yet realised that they had hoped to take him hostage.

"Where are you from?" the man asked me, much more friendly now. He even put his gun down on the table and squatted down on his haunches beside me.

"London," I said.

"You're English."

"Yes."

"What's your name?"

"Alice. And you?"

He paused, surprised at my question and wondering no doubt whether he could entrust me with this secret. "Moses Amok," he decided. "And before you say anything, I've heard all the jokes. I was at the LSE."

"Really! Did you have a Britwords Scholarship, then?"

He laughed bitterly. "No, I do not think the Government of the Nile Republic would have nominated me. Why does Britwords collaborate with such a regime?"

Ndua tried to say something but the man was interested only in me.

"And where is your husband?"

"I am not married."

"Why not?"

"Maybe I have not found the right man."

The young leader revealed this to his men in their language and they laughed.

"It's true!" I asserted.

"So you work, I suppose."

"Yes."

"What do you do?"

"I work in the London office of Britwords."

Moses Amok jumped vertically into the air from his crouching position. He whooped in delight. He hugged me. All the men became highly excited.

"Then please, I must request you to accompany us," he said.

"I'll come, too," said Ndua, unwillingly. He looked relieved when they made it clear it was only me they wanted.

"I think," I told him, "you had better let the office know what is happening."

Poor Ndua. He looked bewildered. He did not know any better than me what was really happening. Only that the excursion to his farm had gone badly wrong.

CHAPTER EIGHT

It took Rolf and Martin a day longer than expected to reach Gondo. Their vehicle was subject to searches at police posts where normally they would make a brief halt to sign a logbook.

Sometimes in this land bereft of public transport the driver might be asked to give a lift to a policeman or one of his cronies to the next village; more often in Rolf's experience the police, bored and drunk, didn't stir from their chairs in the shade but waved the motorist on. Now they were nervous, agitated. They questioned the two white men at length. It became clear at one stop that the policemen were not so much interested in Rolf and Martin as in what they had seen on the road, vehicles, people... Had they given anyone a lift?

"What's all this about?" asked Rolf.

"Rebel activity," explained a perspiring sergeant with a sigh. Clearly the effect of heaving his large body out of its accustomed lethargy was telling on him. He mopped his brow with a large cloth and for his own comfort ordered the two men to accompany him over to the shade of a tree. Rolf suggested they all have a drink and fetched some cans of beer from the Landrover. Seeing this another policeman joined them.

It appeared that a couple of land mines had been planted in the road. A hospital jeep had been blown up killing a team of paramedics.

"They were the wrong target," apologized the policeman.

"Who was the target, then?" asked Martin.

"The army of course," said the policeman in surprise. He assumed that everyone knew the army was almost an army of occupation. An Islamic, northern backed force. "It's beyond our control," he sighed, "but such crimes will only attract the army. They will say we are not doing our job."

"Are there more mines in the road?" asked Martin, his holiday mood rapidly evaporating.

The policeman asked them to take a goat and a basket of mangoes to the next police post. The goat seemed quite happy to be bundled into the back.

"Mind he doesn't eat my words," said Martin.

"You have words?" asked the policeman.

"Oh, just a small sackful left."

"What kind of words?" asked the big, sweaty man, mind dulled by alcohol and the heat.

"Let's see. 'Good governance', 'rule of law', 'citizens' charter', things like that..."

"Not interested," said the policeman. "Give them to the rebels. It's a good cause." And as they began to drive off the policeman added with a wink, "Be careful. In a few weeks it will not be safe for foreigners to travel on their own." He waved them off with a hearty laugh. The goat bleated back.

These unexpected delays so close to home, the threat of mines and repeated warnings about their own safety changed the mood. Rolf became tense and impatient and drove too fast. Alarmed, Martin suggested he take a turn at the wheel.

"Why you don't like my driving?"

When it became evident they were not going to make it to Gondo by nightfall they realised they would have to spend the night somewhere. Rolf favoured camping in the bush and Martin wanted to find a school or a church building. As they were arguing they saw a sign pointing up a track to "Sisters of Life Mission."

"Stop!" cried Martin. It was the mission Bob had recommended. He had a friend there, Sister Caroline.

"You want a night with the nuns?" laughed Rolf.

"If they'll have us, why not?"

"We will try," agreed the German, turning the wheel. "Catholics always make themselves comfortable, no?"

The track ended at a gate above which a notice welcomed travellers to the Mission of the Sisters of Life. Behind the gate a compound shaded by well established flowering trees and shrubs invited them in from the glare of the road. Rolf clapped his hands but no one appeared. He tried the gate, found it unlocked and swung it open. Martin moved over to the driver's seat and brought their vehicle in.

There was no one in the front office. The two travel-stained men walked around the back and stopped in abrupt confusion at the vision they both witnessed. Across a lawn of sharp, blindingly green grass four women, three bronzed white women and one glossy black woman sat together around a trestle table playing cards. One of the white women, skinny and in her forties was smoking. All of them wore bikinis and behind them glittered a small swimming pool.

"Get thee to a nunnery," Bob had said last night. "Very pleasant one on the road back to Gondo. Friends of mine, if ever you're in a fix..." There had been a smirk on his big, round face but it had not prepared them for this. No, there had to be some mistake.

"These are nuns?" exclaimed Rolf. "I think we took the wrong turning."

"I don't care what they are," said Martin, who was feeling progressively weaker. "I could do with a dip in that pool."

There was a flurry of activity among the women. They slapped down their cards in a hectic scramble and burst into laughter. The black woman threw back her head to give a guffaw of mirth. As she did so she sighted the men.

"Hey, visitors!" she announced in delight. Her three companions turned. The thin woman stood up, wrapped a small bathing towel round her waist and walked barefoot over the grass towards Rolf and Martin.

"Hi there! I'm Sister Caroline. Welcome to our lil' community."

"Thank you," said Martin, dusting himself down.

"How can we help you? Puncture? Breakdown is it?"

"Something like that," replied Rolf, half offended, "we could handle ourselves."

"I'm sure you could," smiled Caroline.

"We wondered if there was any possibility," Martin said, feeling really quite giddy now, "that you could put us up for the night. We're returning to Gondo and would continue at first light."

The woman looked them over and explained that she was not really running a motel. She had heard of the mine incident, however, and knew of the hazards of travelling at night these days.

"Come and meet the girls and we'll see what we can do," she said. She introduced her colleagues. They might have been any women around the pool of a city hotel.

"Sister Dawn," she said introducing the Black Sister. "She's from Missouri."

"Caroline has to say that in case you think I'm just a native! Hi boys!"

"Sisters Jessica and Mary-Lou."

They both smiled at the nun, apparently unaware of the contradiction between the title 'sister' and their really quite small bikinis.

Rolf and Martin, clumsy in their clothes introduced themselves self-consciously. Martin mentioned Bob had tipped them off about the mission.

"Oh well," decided Caroline, "if you are a friend of Bob's we will certainly have to put you up."

"That would be very kind," said Martin. She seemed a long way away. Something was buzzing in his head. Caroline gave him a quick look, which he intercepted. He pulled himself together.

"Lovely pool you have."

"It is a great temptation," confessed Caroline, lighting another cigarette.

"Help yourself," said Sister Dawn. "But do take a shower first. To wash the dust off," she added tactfully.

"Do you have swimming trunks?" Martin muttered to Rolf. Caroline overheard and said,

"Oh, don't worry about us. We won't hurt you."

"We are only nuns," said Sister Mary-Lou as she painted red nail varnish onto the toes of her left foot.

Amidst laughter Dawn pointed to a straw hut in the corner. "There's towels and trunks of all sorts in there. Go on, have a dip. We'll go in and prepare some tea."

"Mind the snake. There's sometimes a snake under the clothes basket," said Mary-Lou without taking her eyes off the nail she was covering with lacquer.

"I think we've discovered paradise," said Rolf, making his way over to the changing hut. "Serpent and all."

"Bob calls it our little Garden of Eden," smiled Caroline.

"He also calls Caroline, Eve," said Mary-Lou mischievously. "Have a nice swim."

The water, though not cool, refreshed the men and cleared Martin's head. By the time they had dried and changed, the nuns returned with a tray of tea and angel cakes, the latter a deliberate irony, Martin suspected. All except Sister Caroline wore ankle length skirts, soft shoes and long-sleeved blouses "to keep us from the mosquitoes." Caroline wore jeans and leather boots. She announced she was just driving into the village to collect some provisions; moments later they heard her roar off on a large, off-road motorbike.

"I hope she's not going shopping for us," said Rolf. "We have food in the Landrover. Well, beer we have."

"Beer?" said the nuns. "Elephant beer?"

"Yes actually."

"Then you provide the beer. We provide the rest."

"It's a deal. And I've got some good pawpaws and melons which need eating."

Drinking back his tea Martin looked at the three sisters and said, "It's hard to believe you are all nuns."

"Did you expect us to be toiling away in heavy black habits?" teased sister Jessica, blushing a little. She was the youngest, auburn-haired and comparatively shy.

"I suppose I did. But it's the way you behave like normal women."

"We are normal," said Dawn. "The only difference is, we have a calling. Our job is a vocation."

"Yes, I expect I have an old-fashioned notion," said Martin.

"Are you a Christian?" Mary-Lou asked him.

"There's a lot I find difficult to believe," he said.

There was a pause and she asked, "Well, do you play bridge?"

"Badly" confessed Martin."

"Oh, that's a pity," said Dawn, "because we are really pretty good."

"That wasn't bridge you were playing when we arrived."

"No, that's a game of our own."

"It looked fun. You teach me. I teach you some German games, yes?" suggested Rolf.

"We turn in pretty early, actually," said Jessica. "We get up early, too."

The conversation returned to what the nuns did. They were not an evangelical order, it appeared. They lived together and made a point of keeping fit and healthy so that they could withstand the demanding regime they subjected themselves to most of the time. They did make an effort to learn the languages, to fit in with the community, to mediate with the voluntary organizations. If the Canadians came to dig wells the Sisters of Life trained the villagers in maintaining the pumps and in healthy use of the facility. If the Germans set up clinics the Sisters of Life helped the locals to run them effectively. If the British brought in spare parts for vehicles and machinery, the Sisters of Life, Sister Caroline in particular, helped set up rural workshops in which to train villagers in the basics of fitting and welding and even a bit of machine tooling where the power was available.

Martin made a mental note of their activities in case he could supply them with suitable British Words. He had job lots labelled 'appropriate technology', 'rural health' and 'vaccination' and such like. He thought perhaps 'population control' might not sell well. But then, selling his words was the problem. No one, neither the people nor the charities nor the aid organizations had the money to purchase his words. He was beginning to question why Britwords had to make a profit. But he checked himself. To question such a fundamental principle was tantamount to heresy.

On her return Sister Caroline brought the latest news of the rebellion. Discontent was growing, she confirmed. She did not condemn it. It was unbearable that these people's lives should be subject to the alien culture of the North, she thought. But any civil unrest would make life difficult for the Sisterhood of Life. Already the government had clamped down on missionaries, refusing to renew their residence permits. The Sisterhood had got round it so far with a good conscience by registering individually as social workers, teachers, instructors and paramedics. But this deception only fuelled the suspicion of the central authorities that they were really all C.I.A. agents intent on destabilizing the country. "I fear," said the good sister, "that our days in the 'Garden of Eden' are limited."

These forebodings, although lightly delivered cast a shadow once more over Martin's own horizon. Soon after a pleasant supper he again felt very dizzy and excused himself. By morning he had too much of a headache to travel. Rolf was anxious to get on and Caroline, it was who came up with the solution. Rolf could resume his journey and she would intercept Bob whom she knew to be visiting a school run by a mutual acquaintance. She could reach it on her motorbike easily in half an hour. Martin grateful, apologetic and sick was in no state to argue. As Rolf drove off Martin managed to joke, "I hope you will not suspect Sister Caroline of poisoning me."

"Perhaps she will even save you," said Rolf. "So long and thanks for your company." But Martin did not hear. He had sunk into a pain-numbing slumber.

ALICE'S STORY. PART FIVE

They took me back to the Landrover first. "Follow that man, quick!" ordered Moses. He poked me in the ribs with his gun. "Run."

"Look," I protested, "there's no need for that." He slapped my face with his open hand. Hard. Span me round by the shoulders and pushed. "Run."

I followed the first man. He led us to the Landrover. The LSE Graduate looked at its contents. He ordered his men to unload the bedsteads and furniture that Ndua had tied on the roof and stowed in the back. The men hurled them out into the bush. Moses kept his gun pointed at me as though I were a dangerous animal. When his attention was briefly diverted I put my hand in my pocket, clasped it around the keys to the Landrover, withdrew my hand and flicked the keys behind me into the bush. I was terrified, my head was spinning with fear, my face still stinging from the blow. But some cold voice inside me said,

"We won't get far without the keys."

The men seemed pleased with the provisions. There was a brief discussion. One of them sat in the driving seat. The key was not in the ignition. Moses swaggered over to me. I flinched, thinking he was going to hit me again. But he bent down to retrieve the glittering metal bundle from behind my feet.

"I believe you have dropped something," he said. "We'll look after them for you." He lobbed the keys to one of his men who passed them to the one in the cab.

"Let's go," he said. To my surprise we continued on foot. The same man led, almost at a jog. Moses followed behind me. He was very close. Once he stepped on my heel and my shoe came off. I was too scared to stop. I just knelt to retrieve it and scrambled on a few metres. But the stones were too sharp.

Moses shouted an order. The vanguard stopped. I was allowed to replace my shoe. It was good to have a break. I was shaking as I tied the lace. Gladder than ever that I had jeans and shoes.

"Can we slow down a bit?" I pleaded.

"Not yet."

We pushed on. Some of the thorn bushes cut into my jeans, tore my flesh. I wondered about blood poisoning, infection. Worst of all, I worried about simply keeping going. I supposed, that with my waiting about in Nairobi and my four days in Gondo, that I was beginning to become acclimatized. But I had no creams to protect my skin from the sun. Nothing to ward the insects off. No soaps or shower gels, no bath to relax in at the end of the hike. All these things that I had taken for granted before had suddenly become luxuries. That we had no water was more than a lack of luxury. What frightened me most, especially that first afternoon, was thirst. My memory of the first three or four days march is of thirst. A throat-stopping, lip-cracking thirst. And I had set off that day with a litre of boiled and filtered water in my flask. A flask that had been left behind on the farm in the initial surprise. But on my forced march I was so intent on avoiding the longest thorns, the sharpest stones, on keeping my balance and keeping up that I had no time to worry about what was else going to happen to me.

After some hours, or perhaps it was only one, but it seemed interminable, the men followed a depression downwards. We came to a dry stream bed. Moses told me to sit under a tree. I sank down, sobbing in relief. My legs ached now and they were sore from the scratches of thorns that had cut through their denim covering.

"We will find water."

The men dug down with their hands. After about a metre one of them called for something. The other men searched along the riverbed and returned with a flat stone. They dug deeper and soon water started to seep into the black hole. Moses took a small calabash, half a gourd, from a side pocket in his trousers and filled it. He offered me some first. The soldiers watched me curiously. Thirsty as I was, inhibitions about disease, about contamination made me hesitate. Even big, blustering Pete filtered his drinking water. But this water came from deep down and there were no signs of human habitation around the source. I sipped a little. It was sweet. I gulped down the rest. The soldiers laughed. Moses refilled the calabash and drank a few mouthfuls himself. His men followed suit, kneeling at the hole and cupping the water in their hands. They were equally frugal. Throughout the days of my captivity I was constantly amazed how little these lean, tough men could live on. I never saw them take more than one meal a day. No wonder, then, that when such men become politicians they grow so fat. Being fat is a sign of success, of substance.

We set off again. My muscles had stiffened during the short halt. It was an effort to set them in motion again. The pace had slackened. Perhaps Moses had thought we were away from the danger zone; free from pursuit. I wondered how long it would take Ndua to get back to town and to raise the alarm. And if he did, who would react!

New problems arose. As we walked through the dusk and into early night, it was difficult to see the path. I stopped once or twice. At one point I burst into tears. Moses told me more kindly not to worry. To keep going.

"I can't keep going."

"Soon we will stop."

"And then what?" I wailed.

He told me not to worry. No one would hurt me. No one would want to hurt a woman.

"Why have you taken me then?" I said, trying to pull myself together.

"You are useful. Don't ask questions. Don't worry. No harm will come to you."

I was too wretched and weary to be much reassured but I suppose I felt some relief.

We smelt the smoke before we saw the fires. A small group, possibly a family, was cooking a meal. The cluster of huts was not unlike those on Ndua's farm. The people seemed to know Moses, though they were not exactly welcoming. He barked some orders at the women who were sitting round the simmering pot. The youngest, as far as I could tell in the firelight, slipped off into the darkness. She soon returned with a blanket that smelt of smoke and earth and human bodies.

"For the night," said Moses.

"Thank you."

We ate a porridge-like substance. I was given a hut to myself with a mat on the floor to sleep on. The blanket, I hoped, would keep the mosquitoes off. Before I went to bed there was something I needed to do. As I tried to slip behind the hut one of the soldiers gave a shout and levelled his gun. I explained to Moses what I was about.

"Don't run off," he said.

"Some chance," I retorted. "Where would I go?"

Nevertheless he was waiting for me when I reappeared and told me there would be a sentry outside my door all night. I hoped he would stay outside.

CHAPTER NINE

Bob and Isaiah came to the mission two days later. Martin would not have known if it had been the next day or the next week. He had slept over twenty hours. Once his fever had subsided he managed a meal. A dip in the Sisters' pool refreshed him and brought his strength back. "Just a heat stroke, really," he excused himself and felt better for the explanation.

Bob's old short wheelbase Landrover did not have much room for the three of them but they transferred some of the contents to the roof and Isaiah uncomplaining coiled his supple body up in the back, relinquishing the passenger seat.

"I don't deserve this," said Martin, waving goodbye to the Sisters.

"No, you don't," growled Bob. "You're a bloody liability."

"Perhaps one day I'll be able to return all your favours."

"I aim to keep out of trouble," said Bob, but a smile spread over his face. "Don't be a bloody fool. No one's blaming you for a touch of malaria. Besides, who sent you on this fool's errand?"

"Surely not the Lord. Aren't those Sisters a great bunch?"

"No sense, though. I've been trying to persuade them to move out. It's getting too dangerous. I must remember to give this fuel order to Big Pete. They're out of almost everything."

Bob dropped Martin at the Britwords compound in the late afternoon. The office had closed. Martin went straight to his house. He could not face the office and accumulated business until the morning. Besides the keys were with Ndua.

He noticed two mailbags in his front room, a delivery from Nairobi. These could wait, too. He wanted a shower, a change of clothes. He was not quite sure how long ago it was he had set off for the day in the clothes he was wearing. He had bought a second shirt and a pair of trousers in Wok. During his sickness the nuns had washed everything but it felt good to put on something different, to shave with his own tackle, to re-occupy the space he thought of now as his own. Darkness dropped like a shutter, he lit some lamps and remembered the mailbags. Before he could change his mind he heard a car go by, reverse and hoot at the compound gate. Cursing he went out and saw a pick-up.

"Bloody hell," yelled an unmistakable voice from the darkness. "It's Martin. Where the fuck have you been?"

"It's a long story..." Martin shouted back. He unlocked the gate and let Pete into the compound. They went into the house together.

"I saw a light," said the big man, dressed as usual in shorts and singlet despite the dark and the mosquitoes. "Thought it was an intruder."

"If it was, why did you hoot?"

"Scare him away."

Martin was surprised. "I'd have expected you to leap up on him from the darkness and beat him to pulp."

"No way," said Big Pete. "You've got me all wrong. I don't go looking for trouble. Intruders can be armed. I don't pick quarrels with armed men."

No, thought Martin, you're just a big blustering bully, really. He said, "Besides, they might have been bigger than you. Have a drink?"

To Martin's relief Pete laughed at the joke,

"What've you got man?"

"I don't know. I've not been back long."

"Yeh. The house smells musty. You need to open up some windows."

While Martin found some moderately cool beer and groundnuts Pete opened all the side doors onto the concrete veranda. The evening air was cooling and slightly less stuffy than inside. There was a hint of a breeze to come. Pete was watching Martin carefully,

"So you've just got back."

"Yes, Bob dropped me off a few hours ago."

"So he found you."

"We found each other."

Pete was unusually quiet. He ran a finger under the shoulder strap of his singlet, loosened the thick leather belt of his buttock hugging shorts, tried to make his large body comfortable in the wooden chair. Gentleness was not a quality Pete had much of but it appeared to Martin that he was making an effort to be considerate.

"I believe we have a friend in common, yeah?" he said, swigging at his beer can.

"Oh?"

"Alice Tupman."

"Alice! Where did you meet her?"

"Been stayin' with me, man."

"Where?"

"Here."

"Here! What do you mean?"

"With me. Where else?" Pete took another swig and watched while the penny dropped. Several pennies.

"Well," said Martin, finally, "she could have stayed here."

"Yes, she mentioned that you were colleagues."

"Colleagues. Is that what she said?"

Pete looked at him. "Yes," he said defensively, "colleagues."

"So what's this all about? Where is she?"

"That's what she said about you at first. After a night or two at my place she seemed to forget about her work."

"What work?"

"Same as you, I guess."

"I don't think she came here on business."

"Oh Christ!" said Big Pete. "You don't mean to say you were screwing her, too. Bloody women..."

142

"What have you done, Pete?"

"She was a great lass. She said you were colleagues."

"So we are. What do you mean, was?"

"She's only gone and got herself kidnapped."

Pete explained how Ndua had returned distraught to the office. The Landrover had been stolen, Alice had been abducted by gunmen. That same evening Radio Gondo had received an anonymous message that the Director of Britwords had been captured. No one had known whether this meant they had kidnapped Martin up-country or whether the rebels had mistaken Alice for the Director since she had been driving the official vehicle. Or perhaps even both.

"If only I had been here," said Martin. "Poor Alice. Why didn't she warn me she was coming?"

"Women are like that," said the expert. "No use blaming yourself."

"And where's Therese, come to that?"

"Therese and her lover boy? Oh yes, Alice was mixed up in that, too."

"Jacques is Therese's brother."

"Oh yeah!"

"Where are they?"

"Gone. Done a bunk. Or maybe they are in Canada." Pete tried to remember the story Alice had told him. Martin interrupted.

"She's definitely gone?"

"You should spend more time at home, old son. Both your birds have flown the nest."

"I was only away for a few days."

"That's women for you," observed Pete, philosophically.

All Pete could add was that Ndua had been taken away by the police for questioning, suspected of deliberately leading Alice into an ambush. Vashti, the secretary on Pete's advice had been trying to radio the Embassy in the neighbouring

Sudan, which had responsibility for the Republic of the Nile. However it appeared that no one manned their radio outside office hours. Meanwhile Pete himself had been going round his contacts. He had hoped to cut the rebels off before they got too far.

"When did this happen, then?"

"Yesterday. But they probably took bush tracks. The savannah would just swallow them up. Even if we had helicopters I doubt if we would find them. These guys know their territory like the prick in their hands."

"What will they do to her?"

"To her or with her?"

"What do you mean?"

"Well obviously they will want to exchange her for prisoners or for money..."

"Has there been a demand?"

"No news at all... but how the bastards will treat her, I can't say. A white woman." Pete crunched his beer can in his hand and got up. He offered to take Martin home for a meal but Martin declined. He had a few things to sort out, he explained.

"You can say that again!" laughed Big Pete. "But Martin, take it easy now. There's nowt you can do till the morning. Best make the most of tonight."

"Yes. Thanks for calling."

Martin watched Big Pete drive off into the night. Only one of his rear lights was working, he noticed mechanically. Better tell him about it when he next saw him. He shut the door. Turning back, his eye fell on the mailbags. "Might as well make a start," he thought. "Tomorrow will be a bit hectic."

He picked the nearest sack, untied the cord binding its mouth and tipped the contents on to a side table. There were several pouches containing office mail, the usual invoices and inventories, printouts on pyjama paper which, unfolded would have been sufficient to decorate his walls. Martin ceased to read this, since of the hundreds of sheets cataloguing the global performance of Britwords, only half a sheet referred to his post and to date no returns had been entered. He wondered if any other of the manipulators read the results from countries other than their own. Or was it, as he suspected, that HQ found it cheaper to send kilos of identical outpourings to everyone rather than spend expensive human resource time on sorting information country by country.

Weight for weight, however, the number of global circulars and questionnaires exceeded this green and white striped list of figures. Well, Martin reasoned, it was Britwords not Britnumbers.

If only some of the words had been unique and personal to him. All this correspondence for the sake of "good communication" and not a human note in it.

"English is a very desirable global commodity," wrote the Director-General in a policy statement. "Britwords must capitalize on this demand." Language as a commodity was what Britwords sold. There was no standard, no quality control, other than the assumption that British words were somehow more desirable and therefore better than American or Australian words. And words in foreign languages were not even considered.

Sometimes it was difficult to understand what the words he was offered might be used for. One circular acknowledged the problem and offered a series of "Human Resource Honing Workshops." Martin deciphered this as an invitation to attend a staff training weekend. A questionnaire was to be completed, stating preferred venue, although manipulators were not guaranteed places on workshops of their choice. Moreover while Britwords would pay accommodation, international flights had to be met from country trading surpluses. Since the courses offered were in Hong Kong, Rio de Janeiro and Brussels, Martin ruled out this opportunity of honing his skills. To travel to the nearest international airport could take a week. The round trip including the weekend course could take over a fortnight. He shuddered at the thought at such a long absence. Look at the damage his last few days out of Gondo had caused. To his relief he read that the closing date for applications to be received in the HQ was a month ago, oddly enough before the date on the circular itself.

Another circular asked him to complete a profile of his own staff and to produce a competency matrix. He was to list their real/ideal performance against behavioural indicators. He noted that no space had been allotted for cultural difference, deprivation, malnutrition and factors such as climate, poor infrastructure and so on. The norms were those that prevailed in the temperate climate of HQ.

His mailbag contained reminders for various other returns. These reminders, too, had been sent to everyone with the disclaimer that if they had replied the circular was to be ignored. If like Martin, other manipulators had sent in their situation analyses, their impact studies and their marketing plans, why did HQ feel the need to despatch all this mail? Or was it that more experienced directors ignored it all anyway and just got on with their work which was selling words.

Another letter from Corporate Policy Group seemed to give them all carte blanche. It told them more firmly to "assume ownership of their project" Manipulators were to be more "proactive". A questionnaire was enclosed exhorting them to complete yet another "SWOT analysis" setting out strengths, weaknesses, opportunities and Martin could not remember what the 'T' stood for. The message was that as long as you got results you could do what you liked.

There was, in contrast, comparatively little information on precisely what it was that Britwords had to offer. Martin glanced at one promotional leaflet for a word package headed, "Bandwagons." He read, "In order to activate the learning process it is imperative to consciencize women. Empowerment..." Martin gave up on the gobbledegook. Somehow, against his struggle to set up the office, to feed himself and to pay his staff, the welter of messages from HQ seemed an irrelevance. He was no longer even sure that what he was there to achieve for them had much relevance, either. Words here, English words, did not mean the same. When the regime called for "Piss and Stability" they meant they wanted domination of their own kind. When the leader of the freedom fighters spoke emotively of "Lustin' Peas," he meant fulfilment for the black inhabitants of this beautiful and potentially fertile land. For each faction the words "Freedom and Democracy" had a different ring. Sometimes Martin found it difficult to suggest what use either side could make of his word packages.

He recognized that Britwords' very purpose was to exploit what the Department of Trade and Industry regarded as the country's richest natural resources, more valuable than its resources of oil and gas: its words. The DTI regarded the stock as a renewable resource capable of unlimited exploitation. Britwords wished to encourage English as a language for commerce, for the dissemination of knowledge, as the language of entertainment. Domination by the word rather than by the sword. Britwords was encouraging countries to neglect their own literary and cultural fields and spray them with the poison of half understood British Words, words conveying ideas and concepts long discarded in Britain itself. Contaminants like 'fair play', 'social justice' and 'family values', currency no longer in circulation at home. Some of Martin's colleagues pretended to find this cross-fertilisation enriching, stimulating. Well, in the Republic of the Nile, the best Martin could report, and he recognized he had only been there a few months, was that all the seeds fell on stony ground.

Not that Martin thought the blame was entirely due to Britwords. His Director-General was right in a way. There was a demand for the English Language, for the product as he was exhorted to call it. But there were also demands on the English language which were weakening it, which blighted the crop. He thought of all the reports he had ploughed through, the heavy clay of international prose, written by experts more often than not in a language that was not their first language. These men and women, if they ever loved and laughed, if they had any passion, experienced it in their first, in their living language.

Martin did not blame them, either. He, too, was capable of producing reports in various other languages but he knew he would never achieve the elegance of a native speaker. In his own language, and had he not said his finest achievement of the year had been to write a poem, he doubted whether he could write an evaluation report or a project proposal in prose interesting to a lay reader. All he could aim at was clarity. So why should the international aid mercenaries whose time was costed by the hour, the shuttle diplomats, the politicians and officials of multilateral and multinational organizations concern themselves with the quality of a language they had been trained to use automatically, without any feeling? A language that for them had no personal connotation, no magic. A language without a childhood, without dreams. Even the professional wordsmiths, the foreigners who wrote in English for the international market, the contributors to Swissair's in-flight magazine or the creators of advertising copy were dull in comparison to native writers. The real thing, and occasionally Martin picked up a good report, an original article, a genuine account, glistened and gleamed, it shone out, it rang true. It gave pleasure. Not just the intellectual pleasure of its message, but a pleasure in the loving use of the medium: words. And yet so often now, those native writers were also to be found among the worst offenders, the politically correct anaesthetists of language, those who thought themselves progressive in trying to write a non-sexist language but who merely churned out trite emasculated sentences, the deadeners who tried to coin euphonistic and inoffensive expressions to master misfortune, illness or cruelty and whose clumsy circumlocutions caused more ugliness, confusion and fog. Martin could only imagine such people were severely visually handicapped, blind to the impact of the right word.

Martin sifted through the rest of the mail he had not intended to open. The other bag he felt could wait until the morning. But doing nothing increased his anxiety, allowed his uncertainty to grow. Surely there was something he could do about Alice. Surely there was some way he could at least report her missing. But he could not think of it. The mail came and went on a weekly charter flight; there were no telephone or fax lines and the radio link, as Pete had pointed out, was of no use when there was no one at the other end. He wondered what Bob would make of it all. He decided to go and see him. He put his shoes on, got out his torch. Then he thought better of it. It wasn't Bob's problem.

He went over his conversation with Big Pete. What had Pete meant, "after a night or two at my place she seemed to forget about her work." She could only have come to Gondo to visit him. If only she had written. He would have been there. None of this would have happened. There wasn't even a note in his house, not even a "Hi!" or a "Goodbye" or "Get in touch when you return." Not a word. She had evidently pretended she was on an official visit. But why had she moved in with Pete? It didn't make sense. Perhaps she had left an explanation in the office.

There were a few letters in Britword envelopes among the pile of official mail. Letters he had not opened. They were from Corporate Human Resource Group. Pay and Personnel matters, probably. He opened one up. It was from the Head of the Group.

"Dear Mr. Thomas,
We are concerned that we have received no news from you for over six weeks. We are unable to reach you on the telephone. We should be grateful if you would make contact at your earliest convenience to confirm your well-being.
Yours ever
Judith Wragge (Ms)
Head CHRG"

The letter was dated two months previously. He opened the other two letters. One was an earlier version of the same message reminding him that two months' reports were now overdue. The last letter acted like a torpedo inside his skull, dispelling the weariness and apathy brought on by the bulk of the mail. This letter was only a month old. It informed Martin about HQ's concern at his lack of performance. While allowance had to be made for inadequate communications and possible ill-health, his continued silence was causing serious concern. This letter was signed by the same officer, Ms Wragge, but it was the PS in different handwriting that sank him.

"I miss your letters, too," Alice had written. "There seems to have been a breakdown over the last month or two. I have hinted to Britwords that you must be all right without actually admitting to them that I had been receiving lovely long letters from you - well for the first few months at any rate. I hope mine have been getting through to you. If not, they're burning a big hole somewhere!! Can't wait until my leave in Gondo. Do please confirm you'll meet me. We will "carry on" where we left off, unless you've met some glorious ethnic creature you are not telling me about.

With love

Alice.

PPS I've not told Britwords I'm coming to Gondo. That's our secret."

Martin's brain was reeling. The kidnap, Therese's departure, the breakdown in communication with his head office and their assumption he was not doing his job, and now - this! This postscript on an official letter was the first he had heard from Alice since leaving England. Where were all her other letters, then? He tore at the second bag and dozens of airmail letters spilled on to the floor.

He dropped to his knees and sorted the mail where it lay. Most of it was from Alice. He piled the blue aerogrammes together in date order. There were other personal letters. One from his bank, two from insurance companies. There was even personalized junk mail offering free cars, free radio alarm clocks and a "time share in an exotic location."

Martin looked at the three piles he had made of unopened letters. His love letters, letters from family and friends and the heap of private business correspondence and unsolicited rubbish.

There was no immediate need to open any of them after so long a delay. He needed some air. He would clear his head in anticipation. For the second time that evening he picked up his torch. It was too late now to disturb Bob. He would just take a short walk along the road.

He stepped out gingerly probing the darkness for snakes. There was no one about. Only expatriates had generators and therefore light. Most people went to bed with the darkness, slept and rose with the dawn. After a while Martin found he could make his way well enough without the torch. The moon was full enough to show the way and to cut out shadows of the trees on the glistening road. Like a snowfall on a city back home, the moonlight brushed a veneer of purity over the scene.

The stillness was broken by the sound of an approaching motor. A vehicle was coming up behind him. Martin did not want to meet anyone he knew, didn't want to talk just then. He shrank into the shadows, hiding behind the trunk of one of the tall neem trees that in daytime shaded this stretch of road.

The pale flood from the headlights thickened into a deeper, more focussed yellow as the car drew near. As it passed Martin the lights were switched off, the engine cut and the vehicle coasted another hundred yards or so along the deserted road before drawing silently into the side. For a few seconds the brake lights stared angrily back at Martin.

Martin waited to see what would happen. There was something familiar about the Landrover, though of course there were scores of identical 4-wheel drive vehicles in town. Martin wondered why no one had got out. Perhaps the driver was not feeling well or was lost.... He decided to go and see.

Before he reached the scene he heard raised voices. A man's voice and a woman's. A scream that was cut off. Suddenly the nearside door burst open and a body was propelled out backwards, as if pushed. Almost before it thudded to the ground, the motor cleared its throat, the lights stabbed the night and the Landrover accelerated away as fast as a Landrover can.

Martin stood still, waiting for his eyes to readjust to the moonlight. Then he made out a dark heap on the ground where the body had fallen. He heard a moan and the figure stirred, stood up shakily. Martin was afraid of frightening the woman. He could make out now that the thin figure was that of a woman. Or at least, he could make out her frock. Her dark features and limbs merged with the night.

The woman dusted herself down while Martin held his breath. She silently tested her limbs, checking no injury was done. Then she spat, hawked noisily and spat again. To

Martin's horror she began walking towards him, a faceless wraith in the moonlight. She approached silently feeling the verge with her bare feet.

It was too late to signal his own presence. Martin froze, hoping she would not see or sense him. Praying she would not bump into him. On top of her violent ejection, the shock might finish her.

She paused very close to Martin, searching the ground. He could hear her breathing, hear the small sobbing sounds in her throat. Martin felt he were a ghost and had to restrain himself from comforting the girl, from coming to her aid. As though through an act of kindness he would kill her.

She was so close that he could smell her warmth and her distress. He could see that her frock had been torn in the fall or earlier. A faint breeze lifted a branch and a shaft of moonlight fell for two seconds on the woman's face. Martin suppressed a gasp. He had recognized the girl. It was Margaret. Margaret Obote, the Ugandan refugee who had said she would do anything he wanted.

This recognition triggered another. He remembered what it was that was familiar about the car. Unusually it had rear lights at roof as well as at bumper level. And the upper offside bulb was not working. He had noticed that when seeing off another visitor. That other visitor had been Big Pete earlier that evening. Margaret, his passenger, had clearly not been willing to do everything he wanted. Or perhaps she had and this was how he repaid her.

The girl found what she had been looking for. The footpath trodden through the scrub by refugees left the road near where they both were standing. It was the well used short cut along the river bank to the camp.

Before Martin could react, Margaret disappeared from sight. No use calling her. It was too late. Several days too late. And what could he do? He could hardly look after himself adequately.

It was every man for himself out here. And woman. Besides he had Alice's letters to open.

On his way home he wondered, nevertheless, what Margaret had done, or not done, to deserve such brutal treatment. Martin felt contaminated by association. And then something Pete had said about Alice came back to him.

"You were screwing her, too?" Had Pete used Alice in the same way, then? Was the whole kidnap a cover? No, it couldn't be. Not unless Ndua was in on it, too. But such subtlety was beyond Ndua's imagination. Martin tried to pull himself together. Told himself that he should not always think the worst of people.

But the night was soured. He had been looking forward to returning home, going to bed and reading through Alice's letters. Now the anticipation was dead. He was reluctant to open them at all. The letters had been written in innocence. Innocence and perhaps love. To unseal them now would be despoliation. Martin felt sullied. He did not think he would ever be able to read the letters now. Not in the spirit in which they had been written.

Alice's Story. Part Six

The guards were no trouble. It was the insects, you might say, that bugged me. Despite the mat I lay on, they seemed to come up through the earthern floor. Being quite dark inside the hut, I could not see what life-forms they were that were scurrying, buzzing, flitting, whining and scraping about the hut. I rolled the fetid blanket tightly round me and tried to sleep. Something flew into my hair and got stuck. I struggled to release my hand from the bedroll and plucked at the crusty insect. Despite these discomforts I soon fell into the sleep of exhaustion. It was still dark inside the tukul when I felt someone shaking my shoulder and ordering me to get up. I staggered outside. The fresh air was as good as a shower after my musty prison. In the grey, pre-dawn light I made out figures moving, heard the swish of a woman sweeping and gentle conversation.

Moses said we would walk on a few miles while it was still cool. Day broke as we set off. Despite my aches and pains I was intensely aware of the still beauty of the breaking dawn, of the newness of early day, of the bush sounds that only seemed to emphasize the vast stillness of the savannah.

The terrain changed imperceptibly. Thorn bush gave way to low trees. There was a little more shade and the track was less stony. We stopped in a copse, evidently a place familiar to Moses and his men. Two of them disappeared into a thicket for ten or fifteen minutes. I dozed, sweating now although it was still early. Probably no one was yet at work in their offices in Gondo. When the men reappeared they were carrying two large calabashes of liquid. It was the most delicious fruit juice I have ever tasted and there was as much as any of us wanted. The soldiers enjoyed it, too. It was the only time we exchanged smiles.

Moses was a lot more relaxed as well.

"I hope we did not frighten you too much yesterday," he said.

"What do you think?" I shrugged.

"It's nothing personal. Actually, you are helping us."

"Against my will," I pointed out.

"That's a detail," said the LSE graduate.

"What are you planning to do with me?"

"That's not for me to decide."

"So who is it for to decide?"

"Come on. We must move," he said.

We marched only for one more hour when we stopped in a village, if such a small cluster of tukuls can be called a village. But it seemed quite established. I noticed a well. Vegetables and papaya trees had been planted near the huts and were protected from the goats by thorn fences. Chickens scratched at the swept earth.

Everyone seemed to know Moses and his men. They welcomed him warmly. The adults studiously ignored me. Only the stares of the children convinced me of my own presence in the dream. On Moses' instructions two women eventually came up to me, smiled and led me away with them. Moses told me, "Go with them Greeneyes; they will attend to your wounds."

"Attend to my wounds!" It made me sound like a battle-scarred revolutionary. One of them.

We went to a stagnant pool with green scum on it. One woman wearing a thin skirt waded in thigh deep and mimed the motions of washing. I was supposed to follow her and bathe in it, bilharzia and modesty notwithstanding.

I removed my shoes, socks and jeans and took off my blouse. I waded quickly in. Mud oozed between my toes. I hoped no worms would enter me through my feet, that no bacteria would colonize my cuts and scratches. For all its lethal contents, real or assumed, the water closed around me like a balm. I ducked under, washed with a bricklike bar of soap one of the women handed me. When I got out contaminated, perhaps, but refreshed, the women forced me to sit down. Each grabbed one of my legs. They rubbed a sickly sweet-smelling ointment into my sores and blisters. The whiteness of my skin fascinated them. They rubbed at it suspiciously, cautiously at first as though treating dead flesh. When they realised it was the same warm stuff as their own they became comfortable with it. They placed their gnarled black hands on my thighs to show the contrast. We all laughed.

We rested, ate and sat around for the rest of the day. In the late afternoon we marched on. In the presence of the men, my two female minders were unwilling to say goodbye. But I felt a lot better for their attentions.

The next day or two, or three, it is difficult to remember, fell into a similar pattern. We walked long distances. I recall seeing a mountain appear on the horizon one morning and by nightfall we were camped in the mouth of a cave on the lower slopes. We did not speak much when we were on the march. We walked in single file and in my case, threading up and down these stony paths, or following the tracks the men pushed through the shoulder high grass demanded much of my attention and more of my stamina. Walking into the unknown day after day, on an empty stomach is a far cry from hiking in the English Lake District on a breakfast of bacon and eggs. And I had no elastoplast, no creams to protect blisters, no Kendal Cake or bars of chocolate to bite on for energy. It was a slog and a painful one, but as the rhythm developed and my anxiety receded, I also felt strongly privileged that I was enjoying a unique safari.

We did talk during our rest breaks. I learned a little about Moses but he remained very reserved. His men spoke no English and I suppose he did not want to provoke feelings among them that he was becoming too friendly with me. Neither, of course, did he want to discuss where we were going and what his plans were. I see now that he probably did not know. I am convinced he kidnapped me on his own initiative. It was not simply a case of mistaken identity. I do not think there had been any pre-arranged plan to kidnap any expatriate, let alone the Director of Britwords. Moses had probably been on a raid and I had, so to speak, fallen into his hands. Anyway, there we were, marching through the bush so that Moses could display his prize to some divisional commander to whom I was to be something of an embarrassment. Be that as it may, it did not make my experience any the less alarming at the time.

What did I learn about my taciturn captor? An uncle had paid for his studies in UK. He had expected to return to a post in the University of Gondo, to combine his teaching perhaps with some consultancies for the international organizations based in the town. However the central government was already taking control of this troublesome centre of learning. The Vice-Chancellor was removed and vacant posts filled with scholars returning from state approved schemes. Britwords, like the other organisations, worked through the government of the day and in its way contributed to what Moses saw as government repression. He was as unsympathetic to the aid donors as to Britwords.

"What we want is our freedom," he told me. "The Western countries are not helping us."

"What about freedom from disease, freedom from poverty, freedom to choose an education?" I protested, thinking of the work of the few charities in Gondo I had read something about.

"To cure a disease, first you have to cut out the cancer," he replied. "And what choice have we for education? Even I, MA Econ, LSE, what chance have I of teaching in my native place? None, because they..." he gestured towards the north, "want to impose their way of life, their religion and their laws on us. They want to stop us thinking. And you, your organisation Britwords, is supporting them." He had become so agitated that one of his men ran up, gun at the ready.

"I'm sorry," I said. I had no reply. The bitterness in his outburst stemmed from his own experience. He had returned full of confidence with his qualifications only to have his hopes dashed. Too poor even to get married, he had gone into the bush, joined up with the rebels, and here he was with what he hoped was a valuable captive.

Moses' frustrations were understandable. I will say one thing for him. He never took them out on me. He was hard, but under the circumstances he treated me with consideration. I wish I could say as much of the District Commander.

CHAPTER TEN

"Hullo! Anyone at home?" Martin recognized the squeaky voice but could not place it. A woman, white, slightly Northern British. He heard her clap her hands and call again. "Martin? Are you there?"

He went to meet her and found she had already come into his front room. She smiled, showing her crooked teeth.

"Delia. Hullo."

"Not very security conscious, are you? No, I'm joking. I know you don't want to see anyone, least of all me. I know what it's like when the one you love goes missing."

"Who spoke about love?"

"You told me when we first met that you were almost married. So I jumped to the conclusion that your colleague came here out of something more than a sense of duty..."

Martin did not know what to say. That Delia whom he hardly knew should jump to the conclusion that he was in love with Alice was one thing, that she should say it another and that she should say it now... Good thing she had not seen the pile of letters, still unread, under his pillow.

"Martin," she said firmly. "I've come to take you out."

"Out of what?"

"Out of your house, out of yourself."

"Delia, it's the middle of the night!"

"It's well past dawn. And I don't suppose you've slept much. You want to get her back. I know what it's like. So I'm taking you out for a walk. It'll do you good. We'll be back in a few hours, I promise." It seemed to Martin that she was about to add some sort of joke but decided to keep it to herself, eyes dancing behind her smeared glasses.

Having earlier that night, last night, sat staring at Alice's accumulated letters, undecided what to do with them, not opening them half out of superstition that to do so would somehow harm her further, Martin was still under the spell of recent events. His dismay at Alice's kidnapping was not a complete antidote to his elation at possessing the letters. They were a signal from the past, the safe world of their courtship, that he dared not read in his confused and confusing present. In this state Martin was unable to resist Delia's will. Her sympathetic smile and determination offered him an escape, swept him into action. Though tough and faded like a pair of well used jeans, Delia was essentially kind. Kind and strong. Above all she was company.

She drove him to the north of Gondo beyond the new airport towards the Luri river. She followed the traces of a colonial road which in former times had linked the markets of Gondo with a village which produced the fruit and vegetables of the season for its citizens. Martin was unaware it had ever been a road until Delia pointed out conical heaps of hard core here and there, outcrops of the original surface eroded now by decades of rains and neglect. Some bridges, too, remained across streams, but they were unusable because their approaches had been swept away. Delia drove instead through the dry riverbed.

"No one uses the road anymore you see," said Delia. "There are no vehicles to use it."

"But we still get fruit in the market."

"Yes, the women carry it on their heads. They leave at four in the morning to set up in the market by eight or nine."

As she spoke they passed a man pushing a bicycle through the bush. Slung across it, head almost in the dust on one side, tail trailing on the other, was a glassy eyed Nile perch. The valuable catch was five feet long.

"Several people in Gondo will be having fish for supper tonight," smiled Delia.

A few miles beyond the airport Delia drove up under an old mango tree. It was clear they could go no further in the Landrover. The five bridges that had once formed a causeway across a skein of small streams were still standing but there was no road to link them. The deep pools of water surrounded by swamp were a world in themselves. Large lily leaves tugged at their roots in the current and their flowers opened wide and white in the early sun; fish splashed and darted, some striped like zebras, others brilliant red and black. Beyond, the voice of the bush seemed to be calling out of the intense quiet. Nowhere the sound of an engine nor the irritation of recorded music.

Silently Delia and Martin picked their way across the bridges. The track ran straight for half a kilometre, waist high vegetation on both sides. In the distance they saw the line of trees that defined the main riverbank. Every so often women passed coming the other way towards Gondo. Delia greeted them in Arabic. Some of them shook hands, asking where the white couple were going. One asked Martin if he had come by car and he tried to explain he had left it a mile back beneath a tree. The woman seemed happy with his reply and walked on with a big basket of guavas on her head and a plastic bag of guavas in one hand. A young girl with a similar, though smaller burden stared at them.

As Delia and Martin neared the life-giving river the grass reached above their heads and smaller paths tunnelled off the main track. Delia led Martin down one of these towards the river. People they met showed no surprise at the encounter but often betrayed their curiosity in the questions they asked. They were always friendly, dignified and Martin did not feel unwelcome. Nevertheless when the path emerged into a clearing he did not like to intrude. He put an arm on Delia's shoulder to stop her. They both peered at the village scene from the opening of the tunnel as if looking back through a time machine.

The village consisted of a group of mud huts with straw roofs. Around the huts the ground had been cleared and beaten to form a smooth, snake free area. A tall, bare-breasted woman was leaning back against one hut smoking a long-stemmed pipe with an air of authority and tranquillity; outside other huts younger women knelt grinding the nuts for paste on a stone or pounding the grain with a heavy wooden mortar. A few chickens scratched about, small children played. The men were away. The whole area was shaded by old mango trees, planted perhaps by the same hand as had grown the shade trees along the former road where they left the Landrover. Other fruit trees grew round the periphery. Everything in sight was made from the mud, the grass, the trees and plants and the river clay of the immediate vicinity. If the village were to be abandoned, it would all return to the soil, even the porous pots, and after five years there would no longer be any trace of human settlement.

This particular cluster probably represented one family, the village itself extending in such groups a long way in both directions along the river. The peaceful, domestic scene contrasted sharply with the tumbledown huts of Gondo town squatting wretchedly in their own rubbish and excrement, exposed to the cruel sun, squalor and disease. Although they were poor and bored here, too, their grain stores, their little huts on stilts, were full. Only a few hours from town they had space, tranquillity and time in abundance.

Delia looked at Martin and asked, "Enough?"

"Yes."

"We must go back before it gets too hot."

Unseen they retreated. Before they regained the main track they passed an old woman black and wrinkled as a liquorice mole. She offered to sell them marissa, the local beer. They declined the offer.

"We carry no money," explained Delia.

The woman showed no disappointment and trundled on towards the village. The heat was accentuated as the morning breeze dropped. Behind the tall walls of grass they could hear snatches of conversation and knew it came from settlements such as they had just seen. Delia said that in a few months these huts would be the only landmarks in a burnt, dried-up and rocky landscape.

Suddenly and silently three tall men appeared in front of them. They were black as shadows, naked, and each carried a spear as tall as himself. Martin's reaction was of shock and fear which quickly turned to shame when the older man said,

"Kawaja, White Man, Good Afternoon. How are you?" It was morning but his smile was timeless. Martin took the man's dry hand in his and said,

"Hallo. I'm fine thank you. And you?"

"Kawaja!"

All three men shook hands ceremoniously with both Delia and Martin and went on their way.

"That'll give them something to gossip about," laughed Delia in her squeaky, comical way. Her light-headedness infected Martin. He felt relaxed in the presence of this self-assured woman.

"You seem very much at home here," he remarked.

"I suppose I am," she said.

"What do you teach at the university?"

"Oh, I don't teach any more. I work in the Vice Chancellor's office."

"As what?"

"Oh," she said vaguely, "a kind of unofficial registrar, I suppose. There is a real registrar but he is not often on seat. Anyway, even if I did still teach, we haven't had any students for two years. Can't feed them, you see."

"I wouldn't be able to sell the university my words, then."

"Not unless someone else paid for them."

When they got back to the Landrover the two women with the guavas were sitting by it, waiting for a lift into town. A crowd of about a dozen children had gathered. Two

164

of them were twelve or thirteen year old girls, the rest very small boys presumably in their charge. They looked at Martin with grave curiosity. As Delia unlocked the vehicle one of the smallest boys approached Martin and held out his hand. Martin shook it, saying, "Hallo there!" All the children burst into laughter and wanted to touch him. A bold one felt the hair on Martin's legs and giggled. His own Dad, no doubt, had smooth black legs like an exotic fashion model.

Martin helped the two women into the back with their loads and climbed in beside Delia. Delia started the engine. The explosion of noise in the quietness, the vastness of the plain, startled them.

"I wish I had brought some words along," said Martin.

"Why?"

"To give to those kids."

"You know," said Delia kindly, as she steered lurching round a thorn bush, "I don't think they need them. I think we could do with more of their words."

The heavy fragrance of the guavas filled the vehicle as they jolted back to town. Martin wondered what his colleagues were doing in London. In Head Office he had never questioned his work, nor the underlying value of the exports. He had meticulously worked out the costings and the logistics and filed reports. They measured success by the quantity of words they exported and the income so derived. Out here in The Republic of the Nile it all seemed somehow irrelevant. These people had good words of their own. Different words and songs. They still had song.

"Can these people survive?" he murmured.

"That," said Delia as they approached the new airport built for military reasons, "is what the civil war is all about. The government wants to impose alien laws. They wish to enslave these people. Re-enslave them."

The freshly excavated runway cut across the traditional tracks, a smooth orange scar in the scrub. Along it a cripple

165

was making his way back from town, swinging his body along with the aid of a tall stick. He looked like an ant walking along the edge of an endless table. Right across the plains between the town and the first scrublands a ribbon of people joined town and country. Some of them walked on deep into the savannah beyond.

Delia deposited their hitchhikers. Martin lifted the baskets of fruit on to their heads and was astonished at the weight. The women waved a cheerful goodbye. It was still only 9.30 when Delia dropped Martin off at his compound. He invited her in for breakfast but she had "things to do" at the university.

"Well, thanks for the outing."

"You look much better for it," she said and tooted as she drove away. He realised that not once had they spoken about Alice. He went back to his bedroom, removed the letters from under his pillow and tied them up with a piece of Britwords red tape. He resolved to open them only when he and Alice were reunited.

ALICE'S STORY. PART SEVEN

Gradually my feet toughened and my stomach accepted without complaint the porridgey food and unfiltered water. To my surprise I was beginning to cope more easily with the daily marches. Moses would still not be drawn on what plans he had. Although I sometimes caught them stealing a furtive glance at me, I established no rapport with the other men. When they handed me a fruit, or occasionally a bowl of merissa, a kind of beer, they never looked me in the face or acknowledged my thanks. Moses, I am sure, would have liked to talk more, but he had an example to set to his hard and silent men. In different circumstances we might have become friends.

One day, as we approached a large settlement he told me, "Here I must leave you."

"Why? What will happen?" I blurted.

"The Regional Commander will decide."

Only then did I realise that the daily marches had offered a kind of security, a routine, as though the very act of walking were a kind of therapy. I didn't know where I was going but I felt I was in safe hands. When it came to survival, at least, these men knew what they were about. And presumably we were heading somewhere!

That somewhere turned out to be Aguka, a former district capital and now the regional command of the liberation army. There was a formal camp. Some of the soldiers, the officers I suppose, wore uniforms of a kind, simple fatigues, leather belts, ragged shirts with epaulettes. Few had boots.

Moses became increasingly edgy. He told me to wait under a tree, guarded by two of his men. He went inside a mud hut whose outer walls had once been whitewashed. We heard shouting. Ten minutes later I caught a glimpse of three men emerging from the other side and disappearing deeper within the camp. Two of them seemed to be leading the third against his will. That third man might have been Moses. If it was, it was the last I ever saw of him.

My two guards stirred uneasily as we waited under the tree. Eighty per cent of life in the bush is waiting. If you are a hostage into the bargain it is one hundred per cent and every moment is filled with tension. If only I could live in the present, I told myself, what stories I would have to recount. But when the future is so uncertain it is difficult to enjoy the moment.

Eventually a uniformed man came to the entrance of the hut. The doorframe was in shadow. It was impossible to see his black face or the gestures he was making. He shouted angrily at my guards. One of them pulled me up roughly and pushed me towards the hut. This was the first physical contact I had had with any of them since I was abducted from Ndua's farm.

The man in the doorway watched me come across the baked earth towards him. "This way," he said, as I got near, turned his back and led the way into a small room that served as an office. He sat down behind a wooden school desk, much too small for him. Apart from his desk and chair and a rusty filing cabinet the room was bare. I stood on the earthen floor, facing him. Clearly he felt at a disadvantage with me towering over him and shouted past me. A lackey brought in a three-legged stool. "Sit down," ordered the officer, reducing me to an appropriate level below his. "Welcome to Aguka," he added, more comfortable now.

"Thank you," I said in surprise, and my smile evoked one from him in return.

"You speak Arabic?"

"No."

He looked disappointed. "Then I interrogate you," he said with a worried look, "in English."

He unfolded a piece of paper, a form, and took a biro from his shirt pocket. Holding the biro poised over the question he read, "Name?"

"Alice Tupman," I said. I began spelling it but I could see that he had written A.L.I.S. I spelled my second name instead, but he stopped me. He did not want his unfamiliarity with English names pointed out, particularly not by a female of the species.

"Address?"

"London," I said, to simplify matters.

He was pleased. "Good!" he said. "Profession?"

"P.S."

"P.S.," he repeated and stared at me hard. His eyes seemed to look in different directions and I did not know which one to look at. "You work for Britwords, yes?"

"Yes."

"So what is this P.S.?"

"I am a personal secretary in our personnel, that is to say human resources department."

"In Gondo?"

"In London."

"Then why you were in Gondo?"

"Visiting."

"Visiting Britwords?"

"Yes. No. Well, it was a sort of holiday."

The interview dragged painstakingly on. This man, whoever he was, had obviously attained his rank by persistence and doggedness. Even allowing for his limited English, he was not my idea of a revolutionary high-flier. He had probably been a clerk under the old regime. Slowly it dawned on me what was bugging him. For a start his interrogation was circumscribed by the form he was following. And secondly he thought, as they all must have done, that Moses had kidnapped the Head of Britwords. When finally I managed to convince him of the truth, he left the room to consult with his colleagues. On his return he informed me that I was under house arrest. I could not see what difference that made.

"When will I be freed?"

"The District Commander will decide."

"When?"

"When he returns to camp."

It was several days before I was brought back for a further interview. This time I was led into the main room, a "deceptively large" space as estate agents back home would have described it, with a high, thatched roof full of mould and cobwebs and creeping lizards. A fan on a long, steel rod hung down over a polished, conference table. There was no current to turn the fan or light the electric bulbs, but the basket-like structure of the roof kept it cool enough inside, sieving in just enough air and daylight. As my eyes adjusted to the gloom, I saw that a large man in a tight uniform was sitting at the far end of the table. Two other men sat, one on each side of him. One in civilian clothes was preparing to take notes.

The soldier who had brought me in saluted, announced me as Mrs. Alice and left. The fat man took no notice. His lackeys, taking their cue from him, also pretended I was not there. I sat at the table.

"Who told you to sit down?" roared the fat man. I remained seated. It was not bravado. I was simply paralysed with fright.

"Do you understand English?"

"Yes," I managed to say. My throat felt very dry.

"Then answer my question."

"No one has told me to do anything," I said. He looked hard at me. His plump cheeks glistened and his eyes looked like little currents inside the sweaty folds of flesh. He wore a tie and the collar of his shirt cut into his neck. His uniform did nothing to improve his temper.

"Remain seated," he ordered.

"Thank you."

"You are welcome to our camp."

I could not reply to this. I had not been made to feel particularly welcome. Perhaps this was unfair. My presence was an embarrassment to this ragtag army. All the same they had given me food and shelter. Their own conditions were no better.

"Are you enjoying your holiday?"

"It's been unusual," I muttered.

"Speak up." He obviously did not appreciate nuances of humour. I tried to explain that I had been captured before I had really found my feet.

"You have seen a lot of our country," he said, laughing heartily at what was his idea of a joke.

"She has already seen a lot," repeated the other officer to the man in civvies. I thought for a moment he was going to write it down.

"You work for Britwords."

"Yes, but..."

"Don't but me. I will do the butting." He nudged his subordinate who snorted with obedient laughter.

"Britwords is an official organization?" he asked.

"What do you mean by official?" I asked.

"Don't be cheeky to me, young woman," he exploded. The second officer wagged a finger at me.

"I..."

"Do you think I do not know what I am saying?"

I tried to answer his question. "I am sure Britwords is registered with your government."

"My government!" He almost foamed at the mouth. "I reject the government."

"Yes. I'm sorry. But those of us who are guests in your country have to work with the people in power."

"Who put them in power? Who keeps them in power? You white people are all the same. You come over here. You live in big houses. You drive around in air-conditioned cars, you drink duty free alcohol. What good does that do? Does that help the people? No, the only people you know are the people in power. That's why you keep them there, because they keep you here. Keep, keep. Have you got that?" he asked the secretary, rather pleased with his own rhetoric.

"'Keep, keep', yes sir," replied the scratchy scribbler.

"Britwords is a charity," I hazarded. "We have no duty free privileges."

"No beer? No whisky?" he said in disbelief.

"Only at the market price."

"Soon alcohol will not be on the market. The government disapproves of the sale of alcohol. What will you do then, Eh?"

I told him I knew very little about the politics and practicalities of his country. I was a newcomer when I was whisked away. The District Commander mopped his brow with one of those foulards that army officers sometimes wear round their necks and mouths, particularly in the desert.

"Why did you come?"

"I told you. For a holiday."

"Did she tell us? Have you got that written down?" he asked the secretary.

"No. Yes. Sir!" he said, still scribbling.

"What does your husband say to all that?"

"I am not married."

The commander looked shocked. He eyed me with curiosity.

"Why are you not married?"

"No one has asked me," I lied.

"What is wrong with you? Stand up."

"You don't understand."

"Stand up!" he thundered. I did as I was told. He made me turn round, walk to the door and return to my seat. I felt quite naked under his gaze, particularly as the men made remarks in low voices while I performed. "Why does no one want to marry you? Are you rich? Have you a dowry?"

"No. It's different in our country."

"Do not worry. You will be my wife," said the repulsive man. I hoped he was joking and kept silent. "Well," he threatened, "you do not want to marry me?"

"I should prefer my freedom," I said.

"So you refuse me?" He was still half joking, half menacing, but the mere idea of being turned down riled him. "You don't like me. I know. I am a black man. You do not like black men?"

"That's not true."

"Do you know any black men?"

"Of course I do. There are lots of black men in England."

This astonished him. "Where do they come from?"

"They are born there."

He took this in slowly and relaxed. "Then England cannot be as bad as I thought." He thumped his secretary on the back and the startled man laughed as he was expected to do. I decided to seize the opportunity,

"Are you going to let me go then?" I suggested. He thought this was an even better joke.

"She walks all this way to see us," he said to his men, wiping his fat face with his foulard, "and then she asks us to fly her home."

I said nothing. When their squeaking and chortling stopped, the second-in-command muttered something to his chief.

"Would Britwords pay to get you back?"

"A ransom, you mean?" During my days of marching the idea of a ransom had crossed my mind. I wondered who would pay it. I felt sure that Britwords, or the Treasury to whom they were answerable, would find a regulation prohibiting ransoms the payment of. "I doubt it," I said.

"What about an airfare? Expenses?"

Only then did it hit me that no one in Britwords knew I was in the country. I had told no one in London and if Martin had known he would have been at the airport to meet me. That left only Ndua and Vashti and they only had my word for it that I worked for the same "outfit" as they called Britwords. No one knew I was here and no one cared. I felt very sorry for myself all of a sudden and I broke down. This exasperated the District Commander who was already at a loss as what to do with me. He ordered me to leave the room. I felt sorry for Moses whose foolhardy act had landed them with this unwanted captive. I had the wild idea that he might be made to take me back, but the thought of any more walking was suddenly more than I could bear.

A few hours earlier I had been congratulating myself on how tough I had become. Now, being marched out of the gloomy hut into the full blast of the sun, I turned to jelly and collapsed.

When people since have questioned me about "my ordeal", they ask me how I was treated, sometimes adding "as a woman." What they mean is was I raped or otherwise molested. They are sometimes disappointed when I explain that in the circumstances I was well treated. "As a woman", probably better than their own chattels. However, after my confrontation with the District Commander, who probably found me too scrawny for his taste, I was to undergo an even more unnerving experience. By then, physically I was at my lowest ebb. I had been parted from the taciturn companions of my first march, there were no signs that anyone intended negotiating any terms for my release and simply to let me go in that wilderness was out of the question. I was weakened and demoralized. That is the only way I can explain my own behaviour. Submissive to the point of fatalism.

After my meeting with the Commander I was told that I would be sent to a safe village. After one more night in Aguka in a bug infested hut I was woken from a half sleep before dawn and given a bowl of sweet tea. Two men watched me drink it thankfully. The older man wore boxer shorts and the remains of a bush shirt. The shoulders were in ribbons but one intact breast pocket held his pipe and tobacco. The younger man wore a stained T-shirt and jeans that had moulded themselves to him. He also carried a gun. As soon as I had finished my bowl of tea the old man moved off. The young man with the rifle told me, "go", meaning follow the old man. He walked behind me and kept on prodding me in the bottom and saying "Go, go" as if I were a cow. When I could put up with the goading no longer, I stopped in my tracks and screamed at him. The old man turned around, growled something and for the rest of the morning the armed man kept his distance.

We reached a small village of straw huts before midday. The old man sent his companion on ahead and sat down on a rock beside me, indicating that we should both rest. From the waistband of his shorts he took out a knife and cut into the fibrous branch of a travellers palm. Tipping the stalk to his lips he drank the liquid it contained. In sign language I asked him to cut a drink for me, too. He did so with a chuckle. This was the first thing to pass my lips since the bowl of tea. The liquid had no taste, I supposed it was water stored by the tree, but it was refreshing.

When the other man returned he conferred with the older man and they looked at me. "Go go!" the younger man ordered. This appeared to be the extent of his English. The older man, now that he had established a rapport by giving me water, added, "Chief," and pointed to the tukuls. They led me to the largest hut and the younger man pushed me through the low door. He pressed two of his fingers between my buttocks as I bent through the opening and propelled me roughly forwards. Neither of my guides followed me in.

Inside there was room to stand upright. Four men squatted, nevertheless, on their haunches facing inward from the wall. I stood in the middle of the hut. No one asked me to sit. There was nowhere but the floor to sit on.

The men looked at me with curiosity and muttered amongst themselves. It was difficult to make out their features in the gloom. They appeared old and ragged and red-eyed. One of them had a nasty cough. Then one of them made a sign and gave an order which I did not understand.

"Take off your clothes, please," said one of the men. I refused. "They do not want to hurt you. They want to look at you only," said the man in good English. He was younger than the others.

The chief repeated his order more harshly. "I am afraid that if you do not undress they will do it for you."

I had very little to take off. I began with my shoes, or what was left of them. My jeans, too, were in tatters below the knees and split along one seam. I had nothing on underneath. I had thrown away my cotton panties in disgust and despair some days ago. I removed my jeans and stood in a shirt that just covered enough of me for modesty. They made me remove that as well. I slipped it over my head. They looked at me silently. The one who spoke English asked me to turn round. The man with the cough cleared his throat. They stared like farmers do in an English market when they are assessing the merits of a cow. They didn't raise their eyes above my waist. They murmured slowly without excitement or apparent lust. Then the chief wanted me to approach him. He ran a calloused hand over my thigh. My flat bottom puzzled him. He passed a remark as he stroked it that made the other men laugh and caused an outbreak of coughing in the afflicted man. But it was my pubic hair that interested him most. I was pushed from one to the other so they could all feel it.

I was beyond embarrassment and somehow I felt my fear, too, subside. I was an object, certainly a female object, of curiosity, but not, I thought, a sex object. The man who spoke English seemed more embarrassed than me, giving me only a cursory once over and a slap on the bottom, for which flippant gesture he was reprimanded. My alarm returned, though, when the fourth man squeezed my clitoris and made a thorough exploration. He inserted a finger into my vagina, which I might have informed him was technically rape in Britain. But in Britain similar things happen to foreigners at Heathrow, I told myself, under the name of intimate searches.

When they made me kneel on the floor I thought I really was for it. Particularly as they spread my knees apart and a hard hand from behind this time, explored my hidden places, or places that normally are hidden. I froze with terror and despite the heat I began to shiver.

"They will not hurt you," said the younger man again. "Try not to struggle."

"I wish I could believe you."

"None of us have removed our clothes," he pointed out.

I was expecting the final humiliation, to be rolled on my back or forced in some other way to perform sexually for the men. But the chief through his interpreter told me to get dressed and sit down. I fumbled with my jeans and sat cross-legged, trembling. The chief called an order and a calabash of water was passed through the door.

"You are thirsty. Drink."

I sipped the tepid water, knowing how valuable it was. I felt I had undergone an initiation rite and that I was now accepted. I could not stop shaking, nevertheless. The men spoke together for a few minutes and the English speaker told me,

"It is good. You will stay in our village. You will have the protection of the chief."

I remember either thinking or saying, "Some protection!" before I fainted.

CHAPTER ELEVEN

Martin walked into his office and found Vashti bound to her seat. Or so he imagined. She was wearing an impossibly tight and very short pink dress which impeded her efforts to wriggle out from behind her desk. In her struggle she knocked a large gun on to the floor, ignored it and pranced ululating around the room.

"I am glad to see you back, Boss. I thought they had got you, too." She was not sure whether to hug him or not. Martin held out a hand, shook hers and asked,

"What's that gun doing here?"

"Protection, Boss. I was the only one left. I reckoned they would come for me next."

Martin calmed his secretary down enough to learn that she had at last got a message through to the Embassy. "Only now I have to tell them that you have been released."

"Me? I was never kidnapped."

"You were missing."

"Oh no!"

"I've been running the office on my own. Do I get substitution pay?"

"Substitution for whom?"

"For you, for Ndua, for the packers, the driver... I could be rich!"

"You can't drive. Besides the car's missing, too. Look, I'm grateful to you, Vashti. When all this settles down I'll see what we can do. Just now I have a lot to catch up on."

"Yes Boss."

"And please call me Martin."

"Martin!" She flashed a delighted smile.

Martin did not make much progress before Bob turned up.

"Just heard the news. You're a travelling disaster area. Delia told me what happened. She'll get Alice back if anyone can."

"Delia? How?"

"Contacts. Intimate." Bob made a crude gesture.

"Delia?"

"Influential lady, Delia. Didn't I tell you? Well, I'm off."

"Where are you going?"

"Get Ndua released. Presumably he is innocent?"

Martin, who had forgotten that his office manager was still in police custody, insisted that that was his responsibility. Bob was not a tactful man. He looked Martin up and down with a sad smile and said, "Better if I do it on my own."

Offended, Martin said, "Might I ask why? Ndua is my employee."

"School. Police Chief's son in my class. Another son wants admission."

Martin shook his head. "I don't think we should play games like that."

"Proves my point. Better off without you. Ciao." Isaiah held open the door of his pick-up for the rotund white man, slammed it shut after him and leapt gracefully into the back himself. Tired and distraught as Martin was, he recognised that there were some good people about. He was almost beginning to feel at home.

"Come on, you've got a business to run," he told himself.

But Martin was not to be left in peace for long. He was distractedly sorting out the accumulation of mail and messages when Vashti entered without knocking to announce, "The British Ambassador."

A very hot young man followed her. He must have started the day looking quite smart. He wore a short-sleeved white shirt and striped tie, recently pressed navy blue trousers and black shoes whose highly polished toecaps were covered in a film of red dust. He was carrying a black attaché case with HMG embossed on the fastening. Not his own initials but those of Her Majesty's Government. Big, wet patches stained the armpits of his shirt and his face was pocked with beads of sweat.

Ignoring his own discomfort and the strangeness of his surroundings, he extended a moist hand to Martin with the words, "Good Morning. You are Mr. Thomas, I take it?"

"Yes."

"Good to see you. My name is Jack Hobbs." He handed over a card proclaiming the "ambassador" to be Second Secretary, Consular.

"That was quick," said Martin, impressed and called out to Vashti to bring their visitor a drink.

"How do you mean, quick?"

"Well, we only got the message through to the Embassy this morning."

"What message?"

It emerged that Jack Hobbs' visit was fortuitous. He had come down on a routine visit, partly to update his own records on expatriate Brits living in the Nile Republic. He also had some intelligence, as he put it, to pass on. "I tried to telephone but I could not get through."

"There are no functioning telephones in the Republic," said Martin. "Even the ministries have no phones."

"But they have numbers."

"Oh yes, everyone has telephone numbers. But the system has not worked since colonial times." Martin looked at this young man, hardly out of university and so imbued with the illusion of his own importance. "You must have left the Sudan very early."

"First light," he said, sipping a coca cola that Vashti had brought in with a curtsey. "You want to keep these in a fridge, you know. Much better cold. Yes, hired a Cessna, actually. Main difficulty was getting in from the airport. Not a bus in sight. Or a taxi."

Martin, remembering his own arrival, felt some sympathy for the young official. "There are no buses or taxis in Gondo. No fuel for that matter. That is why we cannot turn the fridge on. Not enough fuel to power the generator all day."

Hobbs was not listening. "So I had to walk in to town. Damn sticky place. Not even a decent hotel, I gather."

Mark stared at him in amazement. "Don't they brief you back at the Embassy?"

"There's a travel log, but no one has time to fill it in. Efficiency savings, you know."

"No one has been down here in my time, either," said Martin, "but I suppose I have not been here very long."

"I was told I might pick up a drum of avgas in Gondo."

"Avgas?"

"Aviation fuel. For my return flight. The pilot went to look for some."

Martin thought it unlikely that Gondo Trading had any actually in store, but he reckoned Big Pete would know where to look. "He would want cash."

"No problem. My pockets are stuffed with US dollars," boasted the young man. He was full of himself and his flight. It had been his first trip in a light aircraft. At last Martin raised the matter of the kidnapping.

"Jolly good thing I came then," said the young man, excitedly.

"What can you do?"

"I don't know. I'll write a report."

Martin took him over to the house to refresh himself. "Sorry about the mess," he said. "I've been on trek. Make yourself at home."

Returning to his office, he felt like an old timer. However it was difficult to get down to any routine work. He was half expecting a message, a ransom note, some news or other. He kept himself busy for the sake of it, to be occupied. At least he could liase with this Embassy bloke direct and make sure he got the full story. Martin supposed he should tell Hobbs about the man in Wok, the man who had died. If he had not agreed to fly up and help him, he would have been at home when Alice arrived. Then Alice would never have been kidnapped. Martin buried his head in his arms and fell asleep at his desk.

His sleep was short. Invigorated by a shower and a change of shirt, young Jack Hobbs was soon back. "I forgot to ask you," he said. "We need to organize a meeting."

"We?"

"Oh, didn't I explain. You are a warden."

"A what? Who says?" Hobbs explained that in remote areas where there is no consul a leading expatriate is chosen to be responsible for fellow countrymen in the area, and to report back to the Embassy. "You get an invite to the QBP, of course."

"QBP? Forgive me, I'm still not quite with you."

"Queen's Birthday Party."

"Oh," said Martin without much enthusiasm. "Well, it might be good for business, I suppose. But why did you choose me?"

"Well, Britwords is the most official sounding business in Gondo. It has a certain cachet."

"But Bob, and even Big Pete know everyone much better than me."

"It's not the person."

"I'm flattered. Anyway, what's the meeting for?"

"For all the expats, of course. If you have a moment, perhaps you'd cast an eye over this list. It may need bringing up to date." The Second Secretary Consular opened his attaché case and brought out a file. "We'll need a village hall, school or something, to accommodate them all."

"What's the meeting about?"

"Well, it's confidential, really, but you have to know sooner or later. I have come down to give you all a security briefing."

"I'd like to help..." began Martin.

"Good man," said Jack, enthusiastically.

"But I have a few problems at the moment. Not least, Alice. She's been taken hostage."

"You did mention that, yes. In fact, I was looking through my notes. It is a Miss Martin, apparently, who is missing."

"Martin! That's me."

"So it is. Martin Thomas. Well, I can tell them I've found you, then."

Martin stared at this young man in disbelief. The diplomat looked as pleased as punch.

"The person who was kidnapped is Alice Tupman. She is still missing."

"Not what it says here."

Into the middle of this farce drove Bob, tooting jubilantly. He swung his Landrover into the compound, drew up in a cloud of dust and lowered his large body from the cab. Walking round to the passenger door, he eased a figure from the seat. Martin's bruised and battered Office Manager emerged into the sunlight slowly like a buffalo released from a byre. Martin ran down to greet them both.

"Ndua. Are you all right?"

"No, he's not," said Bob. "Need two bottles. Scotch. Bail."

"I might have one," said Martin, dubiously.

"Somebody want Scotch?" said the Second Secretary, Consular, who had followed Martin into the compound. "I've got a plane load of it."

Bob looked in amusement at the crisply turned out young man. "Contraband?" he asked. "Who's your friend?"

"He's the ambassador," said Vashti, who seeing her office colleague stagger from the Landrover, had run out to help. "Aie, aie!" she wailed. "My brother, you look awful."

Between them Vashti and Martin got Ndua into the shade.

"I'm okay. But maybe today I take the day off. I'll report tomorrow." He sank down on to the veranda step.

"I'd drive you home, but the car's gone missing."

"I know. And Miss Alice."

"Do you know who took her? Did you recognize…"

"Oh no, not you, too, Martin," groaned Ndua, covering his face with his hands and starting at the pain of contact with his bruises. Martin noticed weals on the under-side of his arms, where he had evidently fended off blows.

As usual, Bob came to the rescue. He would drop Ndua off home, "borrow" some of the Embassy whisky, round up the expatriates and try to unearth, probably an apt expression in the circumstances, a drum of avgas for Jack's return flight.

"And you'll want to see Delia," he said to Hobbs.

"How did you know?" asked the young diplomat, on his guard.

"Everybody does," replied Bob, smugly.

In the sudden quiet after their departure, Martin was again struck by weariness. The sun was right overhead, the tin roof cracked in the heat. In the main office Vashti was humming again as she blithely sorted words into different sacks. Martin told her he was returning to the house to go through some personal papers. She was in charge.

"I'm always in charge," she replied, merrily dropping names into one sack and hurling abuse across the room into another. "You know what, your English words, they seem real heavy but a bag of them, it don't weigh too much."

"You may be right," said Martin and for the first time in many days a smile cracked his tense face.

The meeting called by the consular officer drew most of the Brits who were in Gondo and even a few from outside town who had heard on the bush telegraph that a free booze-up was in the offing. It was the first time Martin had seen them all together. Bob presided over his World Bank funded library which he had offered as the venue. Whenever anyone commented on the thatched container, more like a warehouse than a shelter for human beings, particularly in that climate, Bob said, "Equipment, furniture, badly needed. Second hand Air-conditioning? No? Books? Books you've read once?"

"Playboy, Mayfair any good to you?" asked Pete. "Or something even more educational maybe? Where's the beer?" Martin watched as he spotted Jack and went up to him. The big man in his tight fitting shorts and singlet gripped the civil servant's hand firmly.

"Good evening. I'm Pete. It's my fuel you're using to fly back."

"I'm most grateful. How would you like to be paid?"

"Now and in dollars!" said Pete, slapping him on the back. "Oh, you've spilled your drink." Abruptly forgetting his money he sauntered over to a young woman who was eyeing him up.

"We've not met."

"Mary," she smiled. "I've heard of you."

"I'm flattered."

"You wouldn't be," she said, "if you knew what I had heard." Pete looked her over as if he were buying livestock. She had a pleasant rather than pretty face. Her strength of character was evident in her open, slightly mocking expression. Her dark eyes matched her black hair, this evening piled in a bit of a stork's nest on her head. Pete ran his eyes over her full figure with its heavy breasts. In the humidity a ring of moisture was forming where her bare nipples pressed against an unironed, but clean sleeveless blouse. A thick leather belt accentuated her waist. A skimpy tie-died cotton skirt caressed her ample hips. She had the kind of curves that African men appreciated. There was a bit of a craze among some of the white women volunteers to

186

have babies by black men. Mary had gone more bush than most and was known as Black Mary.

"Well, let's not waste each other's time," Pete replied. "But Mary, if ever you fancy a white man for a change, I'll see if I can fit you in."

"Gee, thanks!" she said enthusiastically. For a second Pete looked disconcerted, unsure whether or not she was being sarcastic. But he recovered and swaggered over to a group of foresters.

Everyone was a trader or an aid worker of one sort or another. Volunteers, technical cooperation officers, some in forestry, others in health and yet others in agriculture. There were a few lecturers and teachers but Pete was the only real entrepreneur. None of his money came from the British taxpayer - or at least none of it directly came from aid or government sources. It was a sign of the continuing unrest, though, that most of the commercial community had left.

"I can't see Delia anyway," Martin remarked to Bob.

"No, she won't come."

"Why not?"

"Knows it all already."

"What?"

To answer his question Jack Hobbs sounded a pen against his glass of G. and T. for silence. If anyone heard the signal, none of them took any notice. The hum of conversation was becoming louder and shriller as more and more alcohol was consumed. Bob, ever the schoolmaster, stepped in as usual. He clapped his plump hands and called for quiet.

"Guest from the capital," he announced. "Wants to speak."

"Hooray!" came a single ironic shout.

"Thank you all for coming," began the Second Secretary Consular confidently. He did not doubt his own importance. "I expect you are all wondering why I called you here this evening."

"To tell us it's bloody dangerous 'ere," said a Welsh farming consultant.

"Well, actually, yes. In a nutshell," muttered the speaker.

"Then let's be 'aving our tickets one by one and you need say no more," said the little man they called Taffy, winking at his companions. They gave him a round of applause.

"In a nutshell!" said one of them in a slurred voice.

"Our analysis of the situation..." continued poor Hobbs.

"Oh they've analysed it, then," said a forester, nodding wisely.

"Found it to be ongoing and all," replied Taffy.

"Our analysis of the situation is that it is not yet too serious."

"Not yet?" exclaimed a volunteer who worked in one of the government ministries, helping with the accounts.

"Precisely," replied Jack, "but we should all take precautions."

"Speak for yourself, Laddie," said the Welshman.

"Shut up, Taffy. Let the boy have his say." This coming from the mouth of Big Pete, the rabble fell silent.

"Thanks, Pete. Now, the way we see it, there's a civil war brewing up."

"Never!" exclaimed Taffy in amazement, but Pete shot him a dark look.

"We are monitoring the situation closely. Clearly those of you in more isolated areas are at greater risk. I am thinking of VSOs in particular. The Embassy is in constant contact with your Field Officer, who is unfortunately not able to be with us this evening."

"He'll be all right then," said Black Mary, throwing a challenging look at Pete.

Hobbs ignored the sulky looking girl and said, "And I do not have to remind you that we have already had one kidnapping."

The young man prattled on, unaware of the incredulity to which his speech gave rise. No one in Gondo had ever thought of the distant Embassy as being of much relevance to them, or of much use generally. At best it was thought of as a remote uncle who turned up once a year to throw a Queen's Birthday Party. Sometimes 'he' helped people in trouble, renewed passports and registered births and deaths. The extent of this well-meaning uncle's ineptitude was brought fully home to them by Jack's words.

"Delia warned me it might be embarrassing," Bob confided to Martin. "Well, he's green but he'll learn. Nice looking lad."

Jack was informing everyone that they had to have an evacuation plan. Even if it were politically possible, there was no chance of flying them out. They were out of helicopter range of the capital or any neighbouring country's airport. Theoretically a Hercules might airlift them to safety, but a rebel army could block the single runway with a tree, a vehicle....

"Or a cow," said somebody, referring to a frequent hazard.

Martin wondered how Alice had so successfully been spirited away. No one had reported hearing a plane or helicopter, true enough. Neither had his Landrover been found. He supposed she had been driven through the bush.

Jack began talking about forming a convoy. One of the lecturers, an anthropologist whose UNESCO funded study of the cave paintings of the Toposa had been interrupted by the unrest, pointed out that all the roads out north to the capital or south to Kenya and Uganda, started on the other side of the Nile bridge. Now the bridge would be the first strategic target to be captured or destroyed, then the airport.

Jack cut off this incipient lecture. "Yes, our Military Attaché pointed out that very point at Monday's Prayers. He suggested a route westwards through Zaire."

"Zaire!" exclaimed the lecturer, aghast. "You can't be serious."

"It's not very far to the border."

"But beyond the border there's nothing. No roads. Six hundred miles of anarchy and wilderness." The academic sounded so horrified that everyone laughed, including Jack.

"Well, I don't want anyone to panic. As I said, it hasn't come to an evacuation yet."

"And if it does?"

"Well, now we have a contingency plan. And," he continued vaguely, "in the event of an emergency, someone will come down and co-ordinate things."

"How?"

"I do not want to go into detail. Well, thanks, everyone, for being so attentive. And I hope I have reassured you all."

Rather than the applause he expected everyone fell silent in disbelief. Few of them had worried about their security until this buffoon had made his speech. Now they realised they were on their own. From the back of the hall the low tones of Mary the volunteer summarized the collective verdict.

"What a wanker!"

As she walked out, all her prejudices confirmed, a wave of laughter and merriment overtook the gathering as they polished off the refreshments.

Big Pete stole out after the girl.

Martin regretted he had offered to put Jack Hobbs up for the night. It would mean sitting up talking, drinking. At any other time this might have been a welcome break in the monotony. Visitors were rare. But Martin was tired. Dead tired. He'd been in the bush at five that morning with Delia. He'd been on the go most of the day. He still had a mass of things to sort out. He was so tired his teeth ached with fatigue. So tired he was floating outside himself. He watched his weary body going through the motions. He wondered why it was. What was the use? He should guide it to bed, let it lie down, re-enter it and sleep and sleep until body and soul were re-united.

Eventually the crowd thinned out. Bob was already clearing up the bottles with the help of his boys. Jack thanked him for all he had done.

"Welcome," said Bob. "Don't mind if we keep the empties? Teaching aids."

"Of course," agreed Jack. "In fact I could probably send you down some display panels. Bobbies, red buses, black taxis, beef-eaters, some royals perhaps, if that would be of any use."

"Made of what?" asked Bob.

"Cardboard. Life size. The people, I mean. Obviously not the buses."

"The cardboard would be useful," said Bob.

On their way back to Martin's house, Jack was in good spirits, "Well, I think that went down very well." Martin did not know if he was referring to his speech or his offer to Bob. The horrible thought was entering his by now very much detached mind that perhaps the words he was trading were about as much use as Jack's cardboard cutouts to the Nile Republic. He shone his torch in front of them along the dusty path. Had to watch out for night adders in places where the day's warmth radiated back out of the rocks. The part of him conditioned by his English up-bringing was wondering how he could excuse himself from the forthcoming discussions. He ought to talk about Alice, but he would feel a lot fresher in the morning. Jack took the matter out of his hands.

"Look here, Martin. I don't wish to appear ungrateful, but I made a very early start and I am knackered."

"I understand."

"Would you mind if I went straight to bed?"

"Not at all. Perhaps we could have a chat in the morning."

All very civil, thought Martin in relief. While his guest used the bathroom, Martin collapsed into a chair in his main room. On the white-washed wall was an old print in a heavy black frame. It was a Victorian pantomime poster depicting Cinderella fleeing the ballroom at midnight at the moment she shed her shoe. The picture was coloured in bold reds and black. The girl filled the foreground, plunging down dark steps. Behind her was a glimpse of the glittering ballroom, but the whole was framed by the solid, black castle, silhouetted by a clear, yellow moon. If Martin moved his head slightly he could see through the pane of glass that protected the poster. As it was the frame hung there like a mirror in which was reflected his own room, containing his table, his chair and lamp, and beyond that the blackness of the insect-filled night. On the edge of the pool of light, pointing out towards the concrete verandah lay a leather sandal. He recognized it as Therese's sandal and wondered why she had discarded it. It reminded him poignantly of the fairy-tale image obscured by the present reflection, the image of that other country, his childhood, his culture, his ball and chain, and he felt forlorn and home sick and sick at heart. He went outside to pick up the sandal. He looked around for the other one, but could not find it. He went back in, locking the door behind him. Therese had gone to the ball. Where, he asked himself for the hundredth time that day, was Alice? Why had he come here and dragged her into this? He had written letters enticing her to a country which was mostly in his mind. Who did he really know here? Africans, he meant.

He had spent the evening drinking with a lot of expatriates. For the most part misfits in their own country who had found a role for themselves in the anarchic scene that was the Republic of the Nile. Volunteers or aid mercenaries, merchants or adventurers, all relatively rich compared with the local people and by virtue of their colour pretty much above the law, such of it there was. Some like Big Pete abused their privileges. Others like Black Mary pretended they had none. Integration was their creed. Some turned their backs entirely on the expatriate community, refusing the support offered by its economic apartheid.

Were they accepted by Africans? Some, like the young man in Wok, seem to have been rejected if not poisoned by the society they had gatecrashed. Others, more popular were adopted as mascots or milch cows. A girl made pregnant by a white man stood a better chance of the bride price. If a black man had a baby by an English volunteer, and the child was born in the UK, it would have a British passport, that magic wand to Western consumerism. Martin warned himself against cynicism. Some people moved unselfconsciously in both circles. Bob and Delia for example, were equally respected in both worlds. Though even they, perhaps, were not fully accepted in either. No, Martin reflected, he must not generalize from his own failure to relate. Perhaps he should invite Ndua and family home for tea or something. Did Ndua have a family? Would they feel flattered or embarrassed? He suspected they would prefer money. But that would increase the dependency, the alienation. Martin's head span.

ALICE'S STORY. PART EIGHT

You didn't believe that, did you? I hope you didn't. People don't behave like that. Armies maybe, gangs... not simple rural folk. Not unless they have been corrupted by video nasties or have themselves suffered degradation. Even in those times of civil war, people in the villages welcomed you because hospitality was part of their culture; or they drove you away because they had had bad experiences. It wasn't their war.

No, I played a cheap trick. I get so sick of being asked the same questions. As I said. But also it was in a way a reality.

I told you that after my encounter with the district commander, I collapsed inside the hut. The next thing I knew, now that I look back on it, the next real thing as I now see it, was a kindly black face, a young woman's face looking down on me. The face came and went until the day when I was curious enough to register that I was in a bed, a real bed. The face, I soon learned, belonged to Mary Deng, a nurse who was looking after me.

I'll tell you more about that later. The examination by the men in the hut, in a way it did happen. Between my interrogation and my waking up in Mary's care, I lived through that and other bizarre experiences. I relived many experiences from my past, too. One of them, which I returned to in disordered episodes, was from my very recent past.

Before leaving England I had gone down to the country to talk over my plans with my parents. I was intending then to be away only for three weeks, the period of my annual holidays. I knew they would be disappointed that I was not planning to spend any of those three weeks with them.

I loved staying there normally, bathed in uncritical love. But it sapped me dry at the same time. I think I mentioned that I could never save enough on my Britwords pay to buy a place of my own. That's one reason why I live with my sister. I'd hoped at first to build up a life of my own, a full, active life. Somehow the years slipped by and I became trapped in a comfortable enough routine, part of which was visiting Mum and Dad, sometimes at weekends and for longer stays during my holidays.

It was dangerous to stay too long. The house, the village were like a sponge that soaked up my energy and initiative. The temptation to remain and vegetate was great. I am not a career person. I did my job well but I had no psychological need to be out at work. Not like some people. I worked because I had to, or so I supposed. I envied my parents their retirement. Not that they vegetated. They were forever extending and modifying their house so that it had grown organically around them. It sprouted like an untrimmed bush. Mum and Dad led a busy social life, too. I was not a bit surprised to find them out, the house locked up.

In the dreams of my illness I recalled every detail of that moment. I stood in the back porch. The kitchen door was closed. I looked around the little, covered space. And when I recall the inventory now I see it in my head as I saw it in my dream, rather than as a memory of the original reality. I see everything. From the roof six baskets, one flat and hard, two round and soft and three varnished wicker ones in various stages of decay hung full of dried flowers. Suspended on rusty nails in the wall were two pairs of gardens shears, one broken and the other gathering rust. On a box that served as a table lay a broken sharpening stone, two empty plastic bottles, one for coca cola and the other for lemonade. A broom without a head and a broom head without a handle were propped beside the door, obviously awaiting attention. Beside them stood several pairs of muddy wellies in varying shades of green, grey and black and different sizes. One had a hole in the toe, another had a bicycle puncture patch around the instep. Beside a garden fork two plastic freezer containers brimmed with fresh vegetable peelings for the compost heap at the bottom of the garden. A very greasy plastic bucket was nearly full of dirty washing up water to pour on the garden. All their bathroom and household water was siphoned off in the summer to pour onto the thirsty clay soil.

The vegetable rack was full of unwashed potatoes dug painfully from the garden which was as crammed and rambling as the house. A heap of dirty towels awaited a rainy day when they would be used to dry Crowbar the Dachshund, so-called because of the way she used her snout to decapitate mole-hills, turn over stones. On another nail hung a bag of old tennis balls. It must have been ten years since I had put them there myself after a weekend game, little thinking that would be the last time I should play.

I wondered how long Mum and Dad would be. No doubt they were out with Crowbar. Their car was in the garage. I looked for the house key but it wasn't in its usual place under the pot plant. I poked about on top of the freezer. I found another box of potatoes, a torch with no battery, one leather glove, a used biro, a hearth brush and a length of green garden twine. The brush was full of cobwebs and dead flies and a layer of dust seemed to seal these objects to the freezer top as varnish seals still life into a canvass. They were untouched and immovable.

I tried the door handle and found the door unlocked. I stepped into the kitchen, itself an overspill of the porch or vice versa. Everything in this house spilled from the garage to the kitchen to the garden to the conservatory, and from room to room. The very act of walking about was like completing an obstacle course. The doorframes and some of the ceilings were very low. The floors were littered with pots, a coalscuttle and logs to be taken in, and dog bones. I was always telling Mum and Dad that one day they would fall over something and break their own bones.

The kitchen windowsill was filled with pots and jars of cuttings from plants as various as the common geranium to the more exotic tobacco and hemp. Some of these were covered in domes cut from the top half of plastic soft drink bottles. A wooden bowl of gourds picked from the garden for decoration still stood on the very spot where two seasons ago they had hurriedly been placed to dry. The worm eaten, but treated and dark-stained beam bristled with nails and hooks from which hung skewers, old pots and pans greasy and battered, one of which I remembered from my childhood because it was the one in which Mum had boiled hot milk for my drinking chocolate. Clusters of brushes, bottle brushes, dog brushes, washing-up brushes, a scrubbing brush and mops and dusters more appropriate to a display in the Tate Gallery than any working kitchen, grew like fungi on the walls. Food for the evening meal lay on the only clear working space, beef marinating in an earthenware bowl, runner beans to be sliced, a saucepan of peeled potatoes soaking in the salty water. This half-prepared meal was surrounded by paint brushes stuck in the sludge at the bottom of jam jars from which the white spirit had long evaporated, a whistling kettle, an electric kettle without a plug, a screwdriver and some fuse wire, and a pair of sunglasses; also a bottle of greenfly spray and a Chinese ginger jar full of feathers gathered on various walks.

A clear passage across the floor to the sink and the workspace had been left between more boots and shoes and sandals, dog bowls and dog basket, two bald tennis balls, a chewed bone, and a dusty Hoover from another generation. A car battery seemed to be growing an acid garden of its own, a coal scuttle without a handle and filled with pinecones nestled against a trug full of lavender. The door from the outer kitchen, or scullery as Mum called it, into the kitchen proper could only be partially opened because it was so hung with coats and satchels and rucksacks and gardening aprons and old towels that formed a buffer between it and the wall.

I squeezed through. In real life I used to take all this for granted. In my dreams, because I returned to the scene several times, all the higgledy piggledy detail, this jumble of memory and muddle, the debris and penates of an unhurried, unworried life-style, was immensely reassuring. I suppose in contrast with the uncluttered but insecure situation I was in, my roots if you like, were nourishing me.

I do remember looking critically but fondly around me because I knew I was going away for a while. I did not realise those observations were being imprinted on my memory. The electric cooker was encrusted with burnt food, the battered and abused coffee percolator was equally blackened. Like the kitchen sink and the working spaces the oven was framed with implements old and new. There were three teapots on a shelf, a Chinese one, a conventional brown one and an ornate, flowery pot used for visitors. A copper indoor watering can perched behind the rear hob, a stopped clock, an egg-timer empty of sand and a small oil lamp, all splashed with fat, were balanced on top of the oven. Above the smoke extractor and beyond most people's reach were stacked plates and dishes, bottles and containers, a hop bine gathering dust and grease. To the right another sink contained a bowl of washing and the usual household detergents, green soaps, slimy cloths and plugs separated from their chains. There were a number of fitted cupboards around the wall which I knew were so crammed with baking tins, wire sieves, pans, glass and crockery and even bags of food that they spewed forth on anyone curious enough to open a door. But in my dreams it was as if each of these objects held me down, anchored me to life.

After my journey I was thirsty. I knew that when Mum and Dad and Crowbar returned from their walk, Mum would brew a big pot of tea. I decided to have a single mug to be getting on with. I filled the whistling kettle, put it on the hob, took a mug from the draining board and a tea bag from the caddy by the geraniums in the scullery. I did this automatically. Mum and Dad were forever bumping into each other in the kitchen performing similar routines, be it washing dirty dishes, making tea or coffee and so on. It would never have occurred to them to house the kettle, tea bags, mugs and spoons in the same area, let alone in the same kitchen. Things found their place by chance in this most unergonomic of households.

My search for milk was trickier still. I opened the fridge in the walk-in cupboard Mum calls the pantry and Dad the larder. A couple of jars of fish paste, some tomatoes and a grapefruit rolled out. There was no milk in the fridge, only bits of old food and a saucer of dried lemon, doubtless sliced for last night's G. and T. I juggled the contents back in and pushed the door hastily shut. "No system," I muttered and went back to the big fridge in the porch. On opening the back door I encountered Crowbar who barked twice, once in alarm, the second time in recognition and who charged affectionately into my knees.

"Dere's a clezzer gel," said a woman's voice. "She's found her sister!"

All this, of course, I have pieced together from scraps and remnants of those feverish dreams, supported by my normal memory of events.

Between the dreams and hallucinations, many of which involved marching through the bush, I was awoken out of my fever. Headaches, aches in my joints, a strong sensation that my skin was on fire. All that. Malaria, Mary said it was. Everything is malaria in Africa, in the same way as everything from a snuffle to bronchitis is 'flu' in England.

I also remembered, again in shreds rather than as a whole parchment, the texts of some of Martin's letters to me word for word. One in particular, which in a sense was his dream for us, was his description of his garden. I read it as a metaphor for what he hoped to create in Africa, the order we would impose on this wild and wonderful country between us. It was not ambitious. Ambition, as I knew from his reports, was not in Martin's nature. It was not "My African Farm" but "My African Garden." It was the last letter I got before leaving. Not only could I see it and read word for word in my dreams, but I saw, I visualised the actual garden. My dream was a film with Martin's words the commentary.

"It is mid-August and has been cool and relatively wet for a month. The garden which was a stony desert when I arrived in January is now a green battlefield and breeding ground for millipedes and centipedes, frogs and skinks and lizards, the largest being four foot long, every kind of beetle and insect imaginable, birds in profusion and cats and rats. At night, snakes and scorpions and mosquitoes take over like guerrillas and moths crowd around the lights. This savage, predatory wildlife goes on in my carefully planted garden which quickly became a jungle with the rain. It is amazing that any plant life survives at all. About one in ten of the seeds I planted survive, the rest being devoured by ants before they surface. Grasshoppers, ranging from small, green nursery rhyme chaps to matchbox sized locusts devour a plant a day. No leaf, not even the giant teak leaves survive unblemished for more than a day. Most beetles, it seems, are eating when they are not mating, and their mating gives them an appetite for more food. There are some spectacular insects, one grasshopper that is psychedelically coloured beyond the dream of the most hardened addict, the leaf insects that are more real than Woolworth's plastic leaves and certainly more perfect than any chewed leaf in the garden, the stick insects and the mantises which move more slowly than the hands of a clock, the sheep insects in wolf's clothing, including one disguised as a ferocious spider but which has only six legs...

"But I meant to tell you about the garden. I am eating my own tomatoes grown from English seeds which have metamorphosed into shoulder high plants. They need nets to support them. These plants produce good tomatoes, but although I water them daily, rain or no rain, one plant withers each day from the heat and dies. My cucumber and pumpkins and watermelons are doing better. Unfortunately a little beetle gets into each egg-sized fruit and produces its family so when you cut open the full grown melon you find it already eaten up from within.

"The native plants, okra, maize, ground nuts and sweet potatoes do well but are devoured even more avidly by the insects. Eggplants and peppers produce well but the bananas do not like the soil and the best papayas are male and do not fruit. There are some citrus trees and guavas here already and they should bear a fair crop.

"Because of the mortality rate among the plants there is no system in the garden, no neat rows of anything. I planted things in good straight English rows but in each only a few have come up. So the garden is a random collection of peppers, cucumbers, cabbages, pumpkins, tomatoes, beans - and the beans are French, African and Christian Aid beans. Only the groundnuts all seem to have come up and they have yielded no space to intruders.

"A similar disarray prevails among the flowers. One unkempt bush has all the time I have been here put out dense red flowers which the black and yellow beetles mutilate the first day they are in bud. Other flowers grow amazingly tall, produce a brief bloom and are forgotten, only to be replaced the next week by their own offspring. One little ground creeping plant opens its carpet of mauve and black flowers only between nine and ten in the morning and then under the sun closes up to become unnoticeable, almost invisible for the rest of the day.

"The weeds are the hardiest and the brightest of the flowers, wild flowers rather than weeds, except for their aggressiveness and tenacity. The grass is not like an English lawn, rather a tangled, prickly mat of stalks, weeds and leaves which produce an overall effect of green and provide cover for the ants and the lizards which feed on them.

"My garden, which would not have come into existence at all without my care, has grown up nevertheless entirely beyond and despite my control into a small, teeming world of its own. I cannot help drawing a parallel with my newly planted office and the life I am trying to establish in the interests of Britwords. Words, like seeds, sometimes fall on stony ground. But I keep on broadcasting cheerfully."

Believe it or not this all sounded wildly exotic to me when I read it in London. Another summer was waning, another summer of my unexciting life. I wanted to be among the ravenous insects, the wild tangle of writhing plants; I wanted to be part of that vital struggle for survival. I did not bargain for the survival course I got!

And reading about the garden now, after sleeping with far more exotic and obnoxious bugs, not to mention rodents, having hiked across a wilderness, Martin's description seems somehow naive, tame... But it was his enthusiasm that touched me then as it did later.

As my strength returned I began to be more and more aware of Mary. Mary Deng was my nurse. I think she enjoyed my company, too. She did not have many people to talk to. She was very dark and very thin and kept her hair cut short like a schoolgirl. She had a fine face, thin Nilotic lips with a long, chiselled nose. She had a small, sickly baby that sometimes snuffled, its own nose as yet unformed, at her inadequate breast. Her first born, she told me, had died. She was worried about this one. Despite her rudimentary training she did not know why it had no appetite. Poverty, I suspected, was the disease and I was an additional burden. But at least I was company, better company than some of the soldiers.

Mary spoke some English. She told me she had got pregnant by a schoolteacher in Gondo when she had been a student nurse. He was a good man and wanted to marry her but teachers were poorly paid and in recent years often not paid at all. He could not afford the bride price. Mary moved in with him anyway. This upset her parents who had expected a better return on their investment. When her husband slipped away to join the resistance she followed him. He took her to his village where the baby was born and died. Her husband was often away. But he did well in the movement and they moved on to this town which was a district garrison, as far as I could understand. She was recruited to look after the sick and sometimes injured rebels. For a while she had worked alongside a white man, a volunteer doctor, who taught her more than she had learned on her training course. It also improved her English. When after six months the volunteer was withdrawn, Mary found herself in charge of the medical centre. When I asked what medical centre, she opened her palm. It was the room I was occupying.

"Don't you need the beds?"

"Not yet," she said. "It is quiet. But when the offensive begins..."

"When will that be?"

But she refused to discuss war or politics. Perhaps she did not know much. She didn't know where her husband was.

There was one thing I had to ask.

"When will they let me go?"

"When you are strong enough."

"Tomorrow?"

She laughed and told me to be patient. Then, as if having second thoughts she gripped my hand and whispered in my ear,

"When you go, I will come with you."

"That would be nice."

"You are not a prisoner. They tell me you are our guest." My heart leapt. So they did really intend releasing me.

"Yes, I am the prisoner," she said. "I will come with you to England."

A few days later, as though to test my strength, Mary told me we were going to a rain dance. She had cleared it with the commander on condition a soldier accompanied us for our own safety. We were allocated a young man called Benson. He came from the village and was happy to be released for the ritual. He told me proudly that it was a great privilege for a kawaja to attend. I thanked him, as though he had issued the invitation and he smiled delightedly.

The idea was to walk. They told me the village was only a few furlongs away. In more prosperous times it would have become a suburb. But its inhabitants were all still local and adhered to their own traditions. They held the rain dance every seven years, so I was lucky, Mary said.

I do not know how many furlongs I lasted but it was clear I was not going to be able to walk all the way. I no longer felt ill, but I lacked energy and the sun seemed hotter and more blood sucking than usual.

"I'll have to go back," I said. "But you and Benson go on if you want."

"You must come," Benson said. "If I leave you, you will escape."

"I am not a prisoner," I said.

"She's a guest," Mary said. "And where would she escape to?"

Our problem was solved when a pick-up truck came along. In this case, literally a pick-up. It was serving as a bus to bring people into the village. I needed all my strength to grip on to the tailgate as we lurched along the boulder strewn track to the village.

When we arrived a small crowd had already gathered on a patch of cleared ground outside the single mud block that was the primary school. The chief and two of his elders sat together on a wooden school bench. They looked like a mixture of Laurel, Hardy and the tramps in Waiting for Godot. The chief wore a very old tweed jacket and black, English shoes. His feet were bare and the shoes no longer contained laces, but he had obviously dressed up for the occasion. One of the elders wore a black bowler hat. The other held a rolled umbrella, not the large parasol of ceremony, but the sort left on trains by stressed commuters in London.

I was introduced to this incongruous trio, who took very little notice of me. I supposed this had something to do with their dignity. We were given seats, hard school chairs but welcome nonetheless, under the shade of an ancient mango tree. Benson fetched us some drink. It came in 7-up bottles with chipped tops but I cannot tell you what the liquid contained.

I was happy to sit, to feel the breeze on my legs and face and to listen to the village sounds. The smells of thatch and goats and dust and of clothing worn a long time wafted across from time to time. My adventure had started from a scene like this, the clearing in the bush near Gondo which was Ndua's farm.

When the dance occurred it came as a revelation and a disappointment. I suppose I associated dance with the stage, with lights, with some sense of direction and purpose. I was used to dance as entertainment. Here too, I had expected some kind of spectacle, something special. But of course, when we see a stage performance even of African dance, everything is sanitized, choreographed and edited.

Salient parts are polished and rehearsed. The dancers are young, trained and vigorous.

The village dancers were not much to look at. Their figures were malnourished and they had scabs on their legs. Their trappings of animal fur and skins were mangy and tattered. They did not seem to dance with much enthusiasm. They executed a lethargic and complicated mime show and routine, more for themselves than with any sense of display. They ignored the hundred or so people watching them. When they shuffled off there was no applause, but everyone seemed satisfied. Where I had seen only appearances, the local people had derived meaning. They had understood the ritual that had been trodden out before their eyes.

"Did you enjoy it?" Benson asked me.

"It was very interesting," I said. "Is it all over now?"

"Well, the men have to go hunting now."

"But the rain dance?"

"The rain dance has finished."

"For another seven years," said Mary. "Aiee!"

Catching her mood of wistfulness and wonder I said, "Where shall we all be then?" I felt let down by what I had seen, but at the same time I had learned something. I could see nothing changing. Not here. Not for the better.

CHAPTER TWELVE

Taffy, the agricultural expert was due to go on furlough, as these old time experts still called their leave. Notwithstanding his earlier barracking, he approached Jack for a lift to the capital from where he could catch an international flight home. During his absence he was happy to leave his Landrover in Martin's custody.

"Would you mind if I used it as a runabout, just in town?" Martin asked.

"Go where you like in it. But Martin, don't give this one away, eh?"

Jack Hobbs had intended to make an early start in the morning. "We'll take off at dawn and follow the Nile," he had said.

"Sounds poetic," Martin had remarked.

"What do you mean?" responded Hobbs, offended. "It's practical."

"If you want to be practical, remember to fly high enough to avoid heat-seeking missiles. The rebels have camps along the Nile." It was a long time since Martin had written a poem. Love letters of a sort, yes, but no poetry. Not about Africa. Here it seemed somehow irrelevant. Raw experience left little space for the life of the imagination. Though come to think of it, Britwords did have a few sacks of it, of poetry.

"You know where they go for their holidays?" Taffy had said, starting out of an alcoholic reverie and disturbing Martin's own musings.

"Who?"

"The black men."

"I don't suppose they take holidays, much, do they?" replied Hobbs in his polite, cocktail circuit manner. "Few of them have much employment to take a holiday from."

Such reasoning was beyond Taffy's power at this time of night. He looked at the official. "They do. They do take holidays. They climb back up the bloody trees!" He exploded in racist mirth. Martin and the young official exchanged a look.

"See you in the morning," were Martin's last words.

Taffy was supposed to have picked Martin and Hobbs up at the Britwords compound first thing. They were all to have driven out to the plane together, collecting the pilot at the Lebanese Club on the way. Martin would see them off and keep the Landrover.

Dawn came but Taffy didn't. Hobbs was irritated.

"I do not propose waiting for him," he decided as the air warmed up and his third cup of coffee began to draw out the sweat.

"Short of walking back," Martin pointed out, "you have little choice."

"I walked here," Hobbs reminded him.

"The office will be open soon. I'll send out word then," Martin promised vaguely.

The delay gave them time to discuss Alice's disappearance. Martin gained little comfort from official assurances that the Embassy would do 'everything-in-its-power'. The Embassy was not even in the same country, though Hobbs claimed to have 'an effective liaison' with his opposite number in their mission in Khartoum.

"It will probably resolve itself this end," he said, "when they realise they have got the wrong person."

"If they demand a ransom," Martin asked, "will the Embassy be able to help?"

"I can't say. The rebels are as likely to want publicity as much as money. Perhaps when I get back we shall know more. We'll keep in touch."

"Easier said than done."

"In the circumstances," said Hobbs, "I think I should fly down again. It's easy enough. Just a question of budget. This charter cost £3000. That's more than my annual travel budget. But in the circumstances..."

"Shouldn't you talk to someone in the government here?" asked Martin.

"In an ideal world, perhaps. It's lack of resources, you see. Anyway, I am sure you know them pretty well by now. It's what you're here for, really, isn't it?" This hint, this implied criticism passed over Martin's head. The diplomat did not pursue his observation. The delay was making him increasingly fidgety. In the event Taffy was only an hour late.

"Hope I've not kept you," he said. "Feeling a bit rough this morning. Ah, coffee!"

They gave him the rest of the coffee and set off.

"I hope no one has stolen your plane," said Taffy. "Did you have the pilot sleep in it, or what?"

"No," said Hobbs, "I presume it is in a hangar."

Despite the Welshman's gloomy forebodings, the Lebanese pilot was found chatting with his compatriots in a relaxed manner. They had already prepared the plane for the flight. It was with a sense of relief that Martin watched them take off and disappear over the only landmark in that flat landscape, Jebel Kajur, the mountain that dominated Gondo, its airport and the roads out west. Martin had walked up the jebel in the early days, before his English energy and habits had been quite eroded by a different climate. He had written a lyrical letter to Alice about his one man, one day excursion. He told how he had discovered hidden crevices shaded by huge trees, had seen baboons disappearing behind boulders, watched a python scratch a scaly track over the smooth, rocky path almost at his feet. Big Pete had told him on his return that he was crazy to climb the jebel without a gun. Hyenas lived up there and came down to scavenge in the outskirts of Gondo at night. Now, gun or not, it was far more dangerous to penetrate such a strategic feature. Jebel Kajur was firmly in the hands of the rebels. The quarry at the foot of the hill had become one of their first camps. The wild idea suddenly occurred to Martin that perhaps that was where they were holding Alice. Perhaps his Landrover was also there.

Then flew down a monstrous crow, or rather a distant rumble became a roar, a shadow raced over the ground and a huge, silver grey plane circled in low over the town. Martin braced himself for the release of cluster bombs, then he realised with relief that it was the Silver Lady, the old Hercules that flew in supplies from Uganda to the traders and aid personnel. The operators, ex-mercenaries, specialized in getting freight to difficult places and remote outposts like Gondo. No doubt among the medicines and bags of rice, bibles and car parts, perhaps even in them, were concealed smuggled goods. Guns and bibles in, ivory and gemstones out, no questions asked.

In practical terms, the arrival of the Hercules meant that everyone of necessity rushed to the airport, every Landrover, Toyota, souk lorry and tractor was mobilised. It reminded Martin of a rural fire service in Britain. When the siren went, the volunteer firemen would drop what they were doing, jump into the first available means of transport and hurtle full pelt towards the fire station.

For his part, Martin was already at the airport in his borrowed Landrover. He was soon joined by people in other vehicles, smart 4-wheel drive makes from all the aid agencies there was an acronym for, UNHCR, WHO, UNDP, USAID, VSO and so forth; older privately owned pick-ups for the traders; ancient lorries for anyone with heavier loads. All clustered around the plane which stopped at the end of the runway, lowered its ramps to the ground and immediately began to disgorge the contents of the hold. For a moment Martin pictured the plane as a great, ungainly goose squatting to lay its golden eggs.

"Martin. Don't dither. Grab what's ours." It was Bob. "All thieves here," he explained, bulldozing his large body through the crates and packages, sacks and parcels that grew like a trail of excrement beneath the tailplane.

Inside the hold men were still frantically rolling crates out, hurling them down the ramp to tumble dangerously and spill among the white vultures. One big, plywood packing case burst open at the top of the ramp and large tyres, like sparks from a catherine wheel, cascaded through the crowd, breaking open other crates in their career. Bags of grain snagged on bits of machinery and spilled their contents, paper sacks of flour labelled Canadian Aid burst on impact with the tarmac and turned a small group of aid workers into instant banshees under the coating of white dust.

The sun climbed, relentlessly heating the tarmac and the men who toiled like ants around the plane. They were almost lost in the shimmering heat haze and the bright light reflecting from the grey fuselage of the Silver Lady.

"What's the hurry?" Martin asked breathlessly.

"They do not want to get trapped. The rebels will have seen them come in. The crew will want to take off before they become a target," explained a Norwegian Church Aid official.

"But it's mostly aid for their people."

"Mostly, yes," agreed the Norwegian. "Nevertheless it's a good target. Big and slow moving."

His words were lost in the roar of an engine being started, the exhaust from which was hotter even than the warm morning air. It singed the hair off Martin's legs, sent cardboard and ply flying to meet the kites and high-circling marabou storks. A whirlwind of dust and heat blinded the gathering. Before the last crates were thrown out all four engines were roaring and Martin had the presence of mind to drive Taffy's Landrover clear of the full blast. Many of the crates were left rocking in the full thrust from the plane's motors which flung the metal bonnet of a souk lorry far across the plain. The instant its hydraulic doors closed, the aircraft juddered forward. Shaken and numb with deafness the aid workers were left to identify their pickings.

The excitement of the plane's arrival and departure was followed by a tedious and tiring ritual. As each person identified his or his organization's goodies, be they supplies or equipment, he had to gather it all in one place and get the customs officers' permission to load up and drive off.

The customs men received their packing lists from the pilot only when the plane arrived. Two thin, poorly nourished officials, they relished standing in the heat as little as the white men. There was no plane wing to shelter under now, nothing above them but the cruel sun and beneath them the tarmac heating up like toast under a grill. But they relished their power. They had the waybills and lists under their arms, they were popular and in demand. Many organizations had greased their palms, others were less organized. Martin had been initiated by Bob but on this occasion had been taken by surprise and had nothing to offer the officials. Unlike those receiving supplies of beer or whisky, he could not offer them "a sample". Britwords had sent him a bag of mail, two sacks of words, which were of little interest to the men and three crates the size of a small car.

"Open!" a curious official ordered. Isaiah, armed with a crowbar and wire cutters from Bob's Landrover set to work wrestling with the steel bands and forcing open the nailed boxes. Everyone gathered round, some admiring Isaiah's strength and skill, others to see what was inside. Isaiah freed one side panel and forced it down. Then the other. Soon all could see the astonishing contents: a large lounge chair in a heavy floral pattern that would not have been out of place in the front lounge of an outer London suburban semi. An ironic cheer went up from the bystanders. Martin hid his head inside his elbow in embarrassment.

"I do believe you've got yourself the makings of a three-piece suite there," said Big Pete. "Come on lads, let's help him load it up."

"Wait!" said the customs man. "There is duty to be paid."

"It's O.K., Gibril," said Bob. "See you tonight. Drink?" The official understood and trusted Bob.

There were further cheers when Pete and Bob drove across the tarmac with an armchair each followed by Martin with a huge sofa strapped onto his roof, protruding several feet in front and behind Taffy's Landrover. Britwords was getting some more publicity. The sight would be described, the anecdote repeated, wherever men drank that night and for many months to come.

As he drove home, Martin felt tired and giddy. His head span, not only with heat and exhaustion but with the now familiar feeling that he did not control events. Rather, events controlled him. He could not keep going at this pace. Where did Pete and Bob and the others get their stamina from?

They were all, Pete and Bob, and Bob's boys and sundry other helpers in quite a party mood as they untied his furniture from the tops of their respective vehicles, unloaded various accessories such as castors, covers and bits of spare webbing. Martin staggered into his kitchen for a drink of tepid water. He had run out of gas and the fridge was no longer working. He told Isaiah they should all help themselves to whatever they could find. The choice was between warm cans of beer or tea. Martin knew what he wanted. He lit two burners of his kerosene stove and put on a kettle and a saucepan of water to boil.

He should have been helping unload. It was, after all, his furniture. But no one seemed to be missing him. He slumped into a metal-legged chair and watched the kettle begin to hiss round its wet base.

Some of the letters that Jack Hobbs had brought down for him still lay tied up with Embassy pink tape on the windowsill. He undid the ribbon. Love letters from the Ambassador, he thought ironically. The first one was a circular from his HQ informing him that a corporate culture consultant would be visiting all Britwords offices. The idea was that the house style, the furniture and perhaps even the appearance of the overseas residences should be instantly recognizable. The idea was to impose a global uniformity. "Like a bloody airline", thought Martin. "Recognizable to whom?" Reading on he noted that the conscientization campaign was to be conducted in two waves. The Republic of the Nile fell in the second, he was pleased to note. No action necessary until next year. The circular ended with a request to salesmen and women to send in their E-mail addresses on a postcard. Martin had no E-mail. He had no E, no electricity. If he had E-mail, he would not need to send a post card. Or did they mean an electronic post card? It was difficult to keep up with the jargon. Anyway, things did not seem to mean the same out here.

He glanced at the kettle. Not much sign of progress there. Absent-mindedly he opened a personal letter. It was a birthday card from his godmother, months old and forwarded from his home address in England.

He had hardly seen his godmother since his teens when she lived near his parents, but she had religiously sent him two cards a year, one at Christmas and another for his birthday ever since, usually with a laconic note.

"On Thursday I am going to dinner with the Morrissons. No doubt we shall hear all about Janet's second divorce. Such a good thing you escaped her clutches!"

Janet. He had not seen Janet for twenty years, not thought about her for fifteen. He saw her now, a child in his mind's eye.

A tall, Dutch barn behind a large, rather stock-brokerish country house. The barn is full of hay. A dark-haired, frolicsome, giggly twelve year old rolls out of the hay at his feet. Martin is only twelve years old himself. Strange. Her elder sister whose name Martin has forgotten is showing him around the home farm. She is ashamed of the tumbling little tomboy. Martin remembers vividly the flushed, excited, desirable child. He remembers she smelled of child not of woman. It is nevertheless the first time a girl has impressed him. She scampers wildly off almost immediately in a renewed fit of giggles.

Was it that year or later he began writing letters to her convent school? Letters that spoke of horse riding and house matches, but which were essentially love letters. He learned the cruelty of women when describing a bad fall. One summer evening Martin was carelessly cantering his nervous horse under the long shadows at the edge of a wood, intoxicated by the solitude and the freedom, by the beauty and stillness, when the horse shied at a paper bag in a blackberry bush and he sailed out of the saddle, landing on his back on the hard earth. He thought he would never breathe again, then wondered if he would ever walk. He recovered within half an hour but was stiff and sore for a week. He wrote to Janet expecting sympathy. He should instead have written to his mother, the only other woman he knew, for Janet's reply, though perhaps meant light-heartedly, shook him more than the fall. She had shown his letter to her friends, they had all had a good laugh, and the sting in the tale was, "I had imagined you to be a better rider than that."

Those were the years of firework parties, given by their fathers for fathers younger than Martin was now, and who enjoyed the explosions in the darkness, the hot flames of the fire and the cold winds over the fields far more than the terrified children. Martin hated bangs, crowds. He was frightened of the dark. Janet thrived on it. Even then she had a circle of admirers, self-assured children from a class to which he did not belong.

The hops and barn dances and the formal ballroom dances of his teens were punctuated by the same yearning and misery as the bonfire nights. Martin was spotty and self-conscious and Janet was always with another boy. Once he got her for the last dance, the only time the lights were turned out. At least, she promised to dance with him but he spoiled it all by spilling hot soup, or punch, anyway something that stained, all down her white, frilly blouse and black velvet skirt. They both missed the last dance and Janet went home in tears.

The letters continued. He remembered a photograph sent from a finishing school, taken side on, very posed, to show breasts, then very much in fashion and duly appreciated. He proudly showed the picture to his school friends and carried it in his wallet for many years.

They must have been in their late teens but not old enough to drive, for Martin remembered a Christmas being driven home in the dark and sitting in the back of the car beside her. He was not half as bold as in his letters but he forced himself to take her hand. That was his first, real, electrical contact with a girl and bliss, like ecstatic pins and needles ran up his body in the inexorable way the needle of a fuel gauge mounts when you turn on the ignition in a car. She allowed him to hold her hand. He was too paralysed with shock to know what else to do. The end of the journey was a relief.

The following term their letters took on a different note. The rude acronyms on the back SWALK (sealed with a loving kiss) and the daring BURMA (Be undressed and ready my angel) no doubt tempted the nuns to open and to confiscate Martin's letters. In any case the correspondence ceased abruptly.

He had probably possessed her more fully, come closer to her at any rate, during their enforced term-time separation than was ever possible during the holidays. At the point to points he was just the village boy sitting under a hedge with a dog and a red oxo tin of sandwiches; Janet was a competitor, sometimes successful. He could not congratulate her. He could not approach the dressy, horse riding class. His own riding was informal, solitary, on borrowed or hired hacks. Sometimes, if no one was looking she smiled at him.

Then suddenly she was engaged. Martin was by then at university, socialist and sarcastic, mocking the marquee and the morning dress. His own was hired from Moss Bros. Janet was the beautiful bride, dark and glittering in a white dress, and pregnant. When she drove away she had changed into an elegant chocolate two-piece. She looked very smart. That was the only time Martin kissed her. He had learned by then that for many of the other men who kissed the bride, it was not the first time. Or the last. Martin vented his feelings by despising the yeoman Janet had married.

She was twenty. That was over twenty years ago. Each of them had therefore lived their lives over again and Martin had no idea how she had spent hers. On her second divorce, was she? Martin had not heard about the first! He wondered if she had children and whether they went to a convent and rode horses. Had anything in her part of England changed? Was she in England? He could not imagine Janet middle-aged. It was shocking to think of her as the same age as himself. He folded the letter which had taken so long to reach him and which contained this heavy time warp within it.

The kettle was screaming, the water drumming in the saucepan. There was no sound of activity in the lounge. Pete, Bob and his boys had disappeared. They had not looked in again for their tea or beer.

Martin attempted to stand up, but his legs would not obey the signal. He made another effort, reached out to turn off the kerosene. The saucepan ceased its agitation, the kettle sighed and quietened down. Martin staggered through into his living room where his new furniture sat self-consciously on the concrete floor as incongruously as corseted ladies in a chicken run.

Martin collapsed on to the new-smelling sofa. It was good to lie down. The respite was brief. As he made himself comfortable, thinking of the sofa as a life raft that was just floating by, a knife of pain shot up the back of his neck and jabbed him behind the left eye. He was aware of a commotion, a hubbub, but was unable to distinguish whether it was inside or outside his head. The pain in his skull was bringing on the nausea he had been experiencing intermittently since his flight to Wok. And truth to tell, much earlier.

What lay at the root of it was fear. Fear like the smell that lingers in a room after someone has been sick on the carpet and never quite goes away. What was he afraid of? Of acts of violence? Of mines in the road? Of being kidnapped? Of punitive raids by the national army? Yes, all of this. All these things built up a tension that clung to his shoulders, heavy as a wet cloak. But Martin's real fear was more pressing even than this. More real. Martin's fear came with the realisation that he could not cope. And this was the fear that attacked the back of the knees and made the legs so weak, this was the fear that attacked he appetite and made the head spin, the fear that gnawed inside at the will as though it were a physical attribute. And in defence against this induced incapacity, he was angrily beginning to question the point of what he was doing anyway. Why subject himself to all this hassle. You had to believe in what you were doing and he had lost his faith. It was not he, Martin that was no good. It was the system!

Look at the others. Delia, whatever she did, was utterly committed. She was part of the landscape, eroded by the elements perhaps, but serene. Bob was devoted to his teaching and the boys he helped. He was a strict taskmaster but his acts of generosity were boundless. Martin knew that a large part of his salary went to pay the fees of those students who had no other resources. Bob was the kind of man who did what he thought right regardless. A man of principle.

Big Pete, too, seemed happy, even though that happiness was based largely on the gratification of his most basic needs. It probably helped to be a man of action. You were not plagued by thoughts, by doubts. You did not emanate the sickly smell of fear like a soiled carpet.

Martin wished he were not here. It was not that he longed for home or anywhere else. Nothing nostalgic about it. He just wished violently that he had not come to Gondo.

The noise grew louder. Bobbing into consciousness, Martin realised the noise was not inside but outside his head. People were shouting on the other side of the compound.

The sound swelled when Ndua opened the door, blundering in like a hunted buffalo.

"Wake up, Boss. We are surrounded."

"Ah, Ndua. How are you feeling today?" asked Martin, still prostrate. Ndua was too agitated to take in such pleasantries.

"Boss, you've got to get away."

Martin put a hand to his head. He imagined his skull to be visibly expanding and contracting with the pain. "Get away? What do you mean?"

"There's a mob. They say you are a spy."

"What on earth are you talking about? Where is everyone?"

"In the office. The whole compound is surrounded."

"Not all of it," said Pete, rushing in. "Sorry folks," he apologized. "I must get back and protect my stores. See you." He gathered a few papers he had left and fled through the verandah door, running down the side of the house. He also took with him one of Martin's coir mats. He had worked out that the end of Martin's bungalow was close to the compound perimeter fence. The clump of neem trees was quite thick. Pete threw the mat over the barbed wire and pulled himself over, running into the bush in irregular lines like a scared hare.

Martin sat up and asked, "What the hell is going on?"

"You had better follow him, Boss."

Martin looked at the six foot fence with his coir mat hanging on top. He hardly had the strength to stand up, let alone scramble over the fence. Even if he did, then what?

"No, Ndua. Leadership is what we want here. I am going to the office." Ndua did not argue.

"This country!" he said, shaking his head.

As Martin crossed the few hundred yards from his bungalow to the office he understood that the noise was coming from beyond the compound. It was just what he needed, a mob. He felt too sick to be afraid. If they wanted to break into the compound nothing would stop them. The gate was held closed with a chain and padlock. The rabble could burst it open or simply climb over it. What they would then do he could not imagine. Break down the house? Loot it? There was precious little to take. Little that they would want. A three-piece suite was an unlikely trophy.

He slipped into the office unobserved through the unlocked back door. Entering the main office like a sleepwalker he was amazed at the reception he got. Vashti in particular was delighted to see him.

"What are we going to do?" she asked.

"Sit and wait," I suppose. Martin was shaking, not with fear, but from the struggle with his body, the struggle not to

220

vomit the pain out of his head, from the effort simply to talk, to enquire, to advise. He wanted to lay his head down but there was no surface soft enough to place his throbbing, burning eggshell of a skull.

"Wait for what?" Vashti asked.

Suddenly Martin realised that she was frightened, that they were all frightened. That Bob, at a loss for once, sat at Ndua's desk biting his fingernails. He caught Martin's eye with a look of resignation. "They think Britwords is working for the government. They think we are all spies."

"Balls!"

"Tell them that."

"I will."

"There's worse. They've got Isaiah."

Martin looked at his staff, his friends and some of the helpers who half an hour ago had been unloading the three-piece suite. Beyond the veil of blinding pain was a group of people, good people, trapped and fearful. This made him angry. Not with the staff, not really with the mob. He was angry that he could not be left to master his own sickening, complaining body. Once he got his health back...

"Very well. I'll tell them to give Isaiah back and go away," he said. "I want a bit of peace and quiet for once," he shouted. No one tried to hold him back.

He was very weak. He had to stand a few seconds clutching the edges of the table while the blackness cleared. His shirt was soaked through. He knew he smelled bad.

He tottered towards the front door. It was locked and barred. He removed the bars and undid the locks. No one helped him. He picked up a bush hat he noticed hanging on a nail. He weakly pushed open the door. The bright light pierced him like a dagger in the face. He pulled the broad-brimmed hat down over his eyes and willed himself towards the compound gate.

The distance was not twenty five paces but it took him almost a minute, shuffling, struggling to hold back a retching fit, willing the pain in his head to ease, to give him some clarity of thought.

There were only about fifty people at the gate. Hardly a mob. They had no banners, no uniforms. A ragged bunch of troublemakers, of looters....

"Hullo, my friends," he called. There was no response. They were disconcerted at the approach of this gaunt, solitary white man tottering weakly towards them like a spirit. Martin looked at a red-eyed man who seemed to be their leader. The man lowered a sub-machine gun at him. "Yes," thought Martin calmly. "This is how it must happen. An end to my pain. Let it be quick. A burst of gunfire, a peppering of agony that will be absorbed, overwhelmed by this horrible sickness, this body already on a rack, then nothing, nothing...."

The temptation of oblivion was strong but the instinct for survival must also have been ticking over.

"You are making a lot of noise," he said. "What do you want?"

"Down with the English. Down with Britwords!"

"I could not agree more," said Martin, shaking a fist in the air. "Wait a minute. I will open the gate."

He began to fumble with the padlock that held the chain, ignoring the weapon still pointed at him.

"Move back, then," he said in a cheery voice, "these gates open outwards. I always said it was inconvenient, but there you go."

He realised that few of them spoke English but sign language prevailed. They drew back. Martin walked through and held out both hands to the man with red eyes.

"Where is your petition? Britwords, you know, is not officially part of government, but if you like I will pass on your petition."

The man with the gun looked startled. What was this crazy white man talking about? What did he want? Mesmerised, he handed over his gun.

"Gentlemen," said Martin, refusing the weapon, "I don't want your guns. Give me your words or give me your silence."

Since no one understood him, Martin saw that a stalemate was likely. A gesture was called for, so he accepted the weapon that their bemused, probably doped leader still inexplicably held out, and raised it aloft himself with some difficulty.

"Friends! I do not know how to fire a gun like this. It is no use to me. But if you wish to give it to me as a gift, I accept." He bowed to the leader and felt again the clanging in his head, the blackness creep over him.

The group began to mutter. The leader interpreted. "You tell Britwords we not like. They must not help bad people's government."

"I certainly will," Martin replied.

"We do not want aid to our government."

"I understand," said Martin, nodding slowly so as to contain the pain. This lent him an air of sagacity. "Since I personally can offer you nothing but this small service, perhaps you would be so kind as to take this weapon away." He returned the gun, which was becoming too heavy for him to bear. The red-eyed man accepted the gift. Then he held out his hand. The two of them shook hands solemnly.

"Goodbye. Nice meeting you," said Martin. He pulled the gate shut behind him and began to shuffle towards his office.

The crowd started to disperse. Half-way back, Martin sensed a disturbance behind him, a few cries. "This is it. A knife in the back." He felt the sting of a slap on the shoulder that would have sent him flying had not a pair of strong, black arms held him.

"Mr. Martin. You said one day you would save my life."

"Isaiah!" He had actually forgotten about Isaiah.

"They let me go. Thanks to you."

"I'm so glad. Perhaps you can tell me what it was all about."

"You saved my life."

Martin wished he had done so intentionally. But a life was a life. And it was so complicated. He saw his office door swing open and Vashti, Ndua and Bob hurrying towards him. Before they reached the bottom of the steps darkness encircled him.

During the two or three days it took Martin to recover from this second collapse, news of his exploit got around and he became a hero. The confrontation between a sick man at the end of his tether and a confused bunch of hungry agitators was transformed into quite another story. Martin was mythologized. He became Gordon on the steps, he became the captain who was prepared to go down with his ship. He was labelled as the English eccentric. One moment he imported three-piece suites into darkest Africa for his personal comfort. The next he was ready to lay down his life for his staff and his friends. He had talked a mob into seeing reason. Martin was a brave man.

No one was more embarrassed than Martin when he realised he had achieved this new status. For a start, the story was untrue. He had been out of his mind and exhausted when he had confronted the men at the gates. And they were a ragged bunch, roused by an agent provocateur and intoxicants. Martin was not a brave man. Far from it. Desperate, perhaps.

Regaining strength alone in his bungalow, he had the time to see a pattern in these recurring bouts of "malaria". He did not think it was physiological at all, though it was just as well everyone else blamed the hated mosquito. It stemmed from a deeper-seated malaise.

He could now recognize the symptoms. An attack always started in the same way. A dull headache that interfered with his concentration, that reined in initiative and enthusiasm, that shut down the supply of energy to the will and quelled all joy. Unheeded this turned into a giddily spinning rotor blade that whirred like a coffee mill in the middle of his skull. It ground down thought, creativity, free action. If Martin fought these symptoms, if he struggled on to a destination or persisted in finishing a piece of work, the pain intensified, setting off nausea and churning up his stomach. Essentially he was incapacitated. He had to lie down, to live this physical thing through, let this beast of pain and fear burrow its way through his body to the point of destruction.

He was afraid. He had had no idea that the biggest obstacle to his success in the Republic would be his own health. In London he had never taken a day's sick leave. And here, because he had been blinded by pain, those around him who understood nothing of his daily battle with himself, were hailing him a hero.

He tried to explain this to Delia when she visited, bringing mangos and dates.

"You think too much, that's your trouble," she laughed in her squeaky way. "You've got too much imagination."

"You're saying it's all in the mind?"

"Quite a lot of it," she agreed, scratching a scab on her leg.

"My point is that the mind has nothing to do with acts of courage. These things are not premeditated. You see a child drowning. Either you jump in yourself or you run for help. It's not a calculation."

"Or you ignore it. Yes, I agree, but there are other totally premeditated examples of courage. People that join a cause, women and men in the bush who join the rebels, for example, they know full well what the hardships and consequences are."

"Perhaps they have no choice."

"Is that a political judgement?"

"No. I am sure there are many courageous men and women who choose a line of action in accordance with their principles and stick to it." Indeed, Martin suspected Delia was such a person. And there were the nuns he had stayed with and many of his colleagues in the relief organizations.

"But what about so-called men of action?" he asked. "Are they brave? Or do they act on impulse? If they do, does an unthinking act make them any the less brave? Take Big Pete, for example. He wouldn't understand what we are talking about. He just goes out and does things."

"Like running away?" Delia asked, acerbically. "I think you've cut him down to size, actually."

"Me! What have I done?"

"The story goes that Big Pete was in your office at the time of the famous disturbance and bolted liked a frightened rabbit."

Martin remembered Pete running down his verandah and leaping the fence. "No, he went back to defend his store."

"Is that what he said?"

"Look, Pete is not a coward. He acts, doesn't he? In Leeds he might hit a policeman, in a pub he might pick a fight."

"Or beat up a prostitute. He's a bully"

"Granted, but that does not make him a coward. Here in Gondo if he wants to go hunting he goes hunting and sod the consequences. He doesn't agonize about the dangers. Perhaps he is stupid rather than brave. But he's not the nervous type."

"Okay," smiled Delia, "I'll give him the benefit of the doubt. But bravery is not only about physical feats, you know. It's about resilience, stickability. Getting on with what you believe in despite your worries and anxieties. I mean, what beliefs does a man like Pete have? What worries?"

Martin wondered what beliefs he himself had. He paused before replying. "I can only think of one thing!"

"Is it sexual?" chuckled Delia. Martin laughed and Delia told him he was looking a lot better. "By the way," she added, "I've got a bit of news about your friend Alice."

"Is she all right?"

"They won't harm her, if that's what you mean."

"Where is she?"

"Marching East towards Kidipi the last I heard." Delia explained that the whole kidnapping was a mistaken initiative by a young rebel. The leadership was embarrassed and would try to effect her release. It would take time.

"How do you know this?"

"Friends," said Delia. "By the way, is Alice brave?"

"I don't know," said Martin, to his surprise. "I suppose that is something she is finding out for herself."

As soon as he said this he regretted it. It sounded so callous. In truth he knew little about Alice. The real Alice. He was beginning to think that Alice, the girl he loved, was also all in the mind. Everything in Gondo was so real. Perhaps this was indeed the "real world" that people at home talked about. A world where things happened so fast, where so much effort went simply into survival, that no time was left over for the imagination, no time for poetry.

CHAPTER THIRTEEN

"Boss, I mean Martin, what are you lookin' so worried about?" Vashti asked. His secretary's ability to live for the moment always amazed Martin. Her country was falling apart, one colleague had been kidnapped, another beaten up by police and there had been the incident at the gates. To Vashti all those things had been and gone. For almost a week now there had been calm. Calm in the office, calm in Gondo. Her boss was well. Ndua had also recovered. They were on top of the job. There were even some welcome clouds in the sky to protect them a little from the heat. All the imagery was wrong, thought Martin, in a country where a nice day was a cloudy one and where sunshine and blue skies spelled discomfort. Darkness and shade were a positive relief. No sane person walked on the sunny side of the street. Nevertheless, he could still say of Vashti that she had a sunny disposition without any overtone of menace.

"Martin..."

"I was just thinking."

"Thinkin' 'bout that girl, Alice, I know," teased his secretary, not without a touch of jealousy.

Martin turned to her. "Vashti, put yourself in my shoes."

Vashti, whose smooth, black legs were bare from the hem of her very short skirt to her pink-painted toenails, glanced at Martin's desert boots and laughed.

"I don't mean..."

"I know what you mean."

"Vashti, forget my personal feelings for Alice..."

"I don't even know what your personal feelings are, Martin," she said coyly, tugging at her skirt which revealed perhaps rather too much.

"I am responsible. As Manipulator I am responsible, as a colleague, as a friend, as a compatriot. I am responsible for that woman."

Vashti stared at Martin as if he had gone off his head. "I don't see how you can be. You didn't know she would come running out to you in Gondo. You don't even know where she is. Probably married to a chief by now." She laughed hoarsely. It was not her concern, but she saw from Martin's expression that she had gone too far. "Don't worry. She'll turn up."

"Perhaps. Dead or alive. In the meantime I should be doing something to help."

"What can you do? Go play hide-and-seek in the bush?"

"If there was someone I could at least negotiate with."

"When they want something they will tell you."

Martin gave up. He had begun a letter to Alice's parents, but since there was no immediate prospect of getting any mail out, he had not completed it. In any case Jack Hobbs had promised to contact Alice's "next-of-kin". At least from the Sudan they could communicate with the outside world. "All channels", too, were open for news of Alice. News of Alice's kidnapping had not made much of a stir in the media, a sign perhaps that it had been a mistake. The rebels sought no adverse publicity. They were trying to present themselves as the legitimate alternative to an oppressive regime. The kidnap could only harm their case. Delia's reported sighting of Alice had at least spared Martin from venturing into Jebel Kajur, the mountain stronghold, in search of his girlfriend. Everyone kept telling him to remain patient. That the rebels were reasonable people.

Most of the expatriates working in the Republic believed that. They were sympathetic to the rebels. Though like anyone else they were at risk from acts of sabotage, they never felt targeted as a group. The rebels' quarrel was with their own government. News of the first atrocity, therefore, shocked the small foreign community deeply.

Martin was one of the first to learn about it. He walked over to Bob's house one evening before dusk, proudly bearing a water melon from the patch of ground he called his garden. Bob was usually to be found in his courtyard sipping tea under the shade of the tall plantains about this time. But to Martin's surprise the voice that called from the shadows. "Well, if it isn't our hero!" belonged to Big Pete. He held a can of beer in his fist. Two empty, crumpled cans lay on the ground beneath the table.

"I'd rather you didn't..." began Martin.

"Too modest... No, I'm sorry. It's easy to take the piss."

"Where's Bob?"

"Sit down. Beer? Isaiah!" he called. "Bring the man a beer."

Martin did not like the way Pete treated Bob's boys like servants. Certainly they waited on Bob, but that was different. Bob was a father figure, albeit a stern one, and their patron.

"I can get it myself," said Martin. "Though I'd prefer a tea."

"Suit yourself. Only I do not think you'd better go inside just at the moment."

"Why not? Has something happened?"

"Martin, have you noticed that whenever we meet I have bad news for you?"

"No, not always. But I take your point. My God, has something happened to Bob?"

"Not really. He's just a bit upset. He's being sick right now."

"Well, can't we do something?"

"Just sit down, man. And I'll tell you, too. Martin pulled a chair up to the tin-topped table and listened. Pete still needed to talk himself. He was edgy, shocked. The story did not come out in the right order.

"You know the Sisters of Life?"

"Yes."

"Well, they're Sisters of Death now."

"What do you mean?"

"Dead. Massacred. The lot of them. Village burned down."

Martin heard himself asking, who, why, and a host of other questions. His rational self. Emotionally he was trying to get to grips with the news. Sister Caroline on her motorbike, the card games around the pool. Jessica who had shyly brought soup and fruit to his bedside for two days.

"Who would want to kill them?"

"I don't believe it. Not the locals," said a voice. Bob came out of the house. His normally ruddy face was drained of colour, his eyes were red. He had been pressing back tears with his knuckles.

Gradually Martin pieced together the sequence of events. Following the delivery of supplies by the Hercules, Pete had got together the order for the nuns: rice, medicines and a spare part for Caroline's motor bike. He also found the fuel they badly needed. Having loaded his truck, Pete discovered none of his drivers were willing to venture out along the road to Wok. There had been too many rumours of attacks on police posts and on travellers.

"So I decided to take it up myself," said Pete. "I had to show them there was nothing to be scared of. Besides," he added sheepishly, "I had my reputation to think of. Thanks to Martin here."

"That's right," said Bob, trying to be buoyant, to rise above the tragedy, "blame it on Martin."

"Oh, I do," said the Big Man, continuing his narrative with a wink. He had begun to get worried when he approached the first police barrier. Normally he would chat with the men on duty, give them a bottle of something, buy a cup of sweet tea from the roadside vendor. But there was no one there. No police, no vendors. No tea, no mangoes, no chickens. Nothing. The town, or at least the huts along the road were also deserted. The population seemed to have melted into the bush. There was only one other checkpoint before the turn off to the nuns. After a further hour's nervous drive, Pete found this had been razed completely.

Any sensible person, Pete bragged, would have turned back. The roads could all have been mined, the rebels could have been lying in wait. Pete was, after all, carrying a precious cargo.

"But I was so close. And the thought of those all those sex-starved nuns waiting for me... Well, what man could resist the temptation?" he sniggered.

He saw the smoke first. In a do or die attempt he drove right into the compound as fast as his load and the rutted track would allow. The gate was lying on the ground, the bougainvillea scorched and the buildings entirely gone. Burnt out. Gutted. Presumably anything of any value had been looted first. There were no motorcycles. This made him hope that the nuns had got away in time. Until he went round the back and found their bodies.

"Whoever did it had enjoyed themselves," said Pete. "I mean, the women hadn't just been shot. Many of them were naked. They had been stripped. Mutilated. A lot of the bodies were in the pool. The water was red. The parts of their bodies that floated above the surface were covered in flies. Like black dressings. I went up to the nearest corpse. Splashed water on its face to drive them away. The flies. The face was familiar. Despite its fixed expression, big, scared eyes, a breast gashed off, I recognized her. It was sexy little Jessica doing her last strip tease for Pete. I started to pull her out. I had the crazy idea the bodies should all be buried or burned or something. But the flies, the smell...." Pete gagged despite his jokey way of putting things. "I let go of her stiff arm, she rolled over and sank out of sight below the thick water. I've seen a lot of things, Martin, in this bloody country, but this was disgusting."

Disgusted he undoubtedly was, but Pete relished telling the story. This was the second time in half an hour. He studied Martin's face to see what effect his words were having. Over the next few days and beers he would embellish the story.

Bob, who knew the nuns, their work and their compound so well, moaned and let out a huge bellow of a sob. But he controlled himself. Martin was frozen numb. The three of them sat several minutes in silence. It was the closest they came to prayer.

The news spread rapidly. Accounts of other massacres followed, told by the survivors who straggled in to Gondo bearing little else but their harrowing stories. Villages torched, a whole team of German zoologists killed in their camp, bridges destroyed. The media picked up the stories very quickly. It was almost as though they had been fed them in advance. The BBC African Service carried a full account, starting with the kidnapping of Alice, described as a "backpacker". They broadcast an interview with a government spokesman who said the army would move to round up the "perpetrators of these heinous crimes." It was the government onslaught on the terrorists, or rather on the people of the Nile, that was to force the evacuation of expatriates.

Before the Embassy managed to get its message across, Delia called on Martin, this time after dark. "I don't want either side to think Britwords is involved in this," she said, "on either side."

"What do you mean?"

"Weren't you accused of spying by the rentamob?"

"Yes."

"Well, of course, the government put them up to that. Most of the mischief is caused by the government or their agents. Indeed, all of it. You will have noticed in the BBC's report that no connection was made between Alice and Britwords. That was at the Embassy's request, no doubt."

Delia spoke with such an assumption of authority that Martin hesitated to question her. To play for time he offered her a drink.

"A beer will be fine," she said. "And I'll try out your famous sofa."

"You say the mischief has been caused by the government," Martin said, sitting down beside her.

"Do you mean to say that the Sisters of Life..."

"Were martyred by government soldiers? Of course they were. You can't imagine local people doing that kind of thing, can you? Particularly not the Christians." Delia flushed with anger.

"Well..."

"That's what the regime wants everyone to think, of course. They have two items on their agenda."

"They?"

"The Government. Well, the military. It's not quite the same thing of course. The military is stuffed full of personnel from countries to the North, as you know. The Islamic movements want an excuse to invade the Southern countries. That's why they are infiltrating the militia and government here and stirring the army on to raid defenceless targets. All the atrocities will be blamed on the terrorists. This will justify an invasion in the eyes of the world."

"Can you invade your own country?"

"It will only be their own, i.e. Islamic country, when they have wiped out all the local people. As you have seen, even quite close to Gondo, most people are peace loving rural folk. Different tribes, of course. But they realise their only chance of survival is to join together to resist the genocide. The more extreme, the more politicised of them want to overthrow the current regime and make a fresh start."

"Is that what you want?"

"My views have nothing to do with it," protested Delia. "Like you I am merely a kawaja, a foreigner."

"You said the government had two items on their agenda. What is the second one?"

"Well, it's related to the first, really. They want to drive the expatriates out, scare them off. They do not want witnesses. In particular they want to get rid of the missionaries, whether they call themselves social workers, health auxiliaries or Sisters of Life." Delia was speaking calmly, patiently, as though to a child. But she allowed herself one outburst of emotion. "It is a great shame, and I mean shame, what they are doing here. I love this country."

"Delia, you did not come here to give me a lesson in politics, did you?"

"You can't ignore the politics, Martin. But no. I came here to warn you. The army's next target will be Gondo."

"But they already have a garrison here."

"Yes, I know. But that is way out of town and not very strong. That could be taken by the rebels any day. No, I mean a real bombardment and occupation and all that that entails." She looked at Martin through her smeary glasses. The way she cocked her head made her look like a scruffy parrot.

"Why tell me?"

"Aren't you our warden?"

"Warden?"

"Responsible for the evacuation of British and Commonwealth citizens."

"Oh, yes. On paper, I suppose I shall be. But whatshisname, Jack Hobbs said he would tell me what it entailed on his next visit. Promised walkie-talkies and so on, if I remember rightly."

"You'll need more than walkie-talkies. Anyway there is no time to wait for young Hobbs to visit. My advice is to get them all out quick."

"I can't do that."

"You will have no choice."

"I can't run away and leave Alice behind."

"Leave Alice to me."

"You?"

"You're right. I did not just come to deliver a lecture. I came to say goodbye. I am going away for a while myself."

Martin looked at her in disbelief and with admiration. What made this scrawny woman so tough? What resources did she draw upon that he so obviously lacked even for the simplest tasks?

"It's not an act of bravery," she added hastily, remembering their earlier heart to heart. "I really have no choice... I don't want to end up in the Nile, or worse still, in their barracks." She pulled a wry, vulnerable face.

"I take it you won't be leaving the country, though."

"I think I can be more useful here."

"So why do you think I can walk out on Alice any more than you can desert your friends."

In her patient, humorous manner Delia gave Martin several reasons. For a start, like it or not, he was responsible for co-ordinating the evacuation. Secondly, he would not help Alice by remaining in Gondo. When she was released it would be most unlikely that she would be returned to Gondo. And thirdly, Delia repeated that if anyone could help, she could.

"If the army does invade, it's not going to help negotiations, is it?"

"What negotiations!"

"If the army attacks the rebels and if the rebels are holding Alice, I shouldn't think they would worry what happened to her. If she gets killed they can blame the rebels. Pass it off as just another atrocity."

"There you go again, Martin. I told you you think too much. You need to use that imagination constructively."

"I think we ought to call in the Red Cross."

"That's already in hand," said Delia, enigmatically.

Jack Hobbs did not get down to Gondo again. The military banned civilian flights. The Embassy, unable to get a message to Martin direct, recommended over the BBC that expatriates in Gondo contact their warden to arrange an early departure. They were advised to drive South. All the signs pointed to a major escalation of the Civil War.

"Well, Ndua," said Martin, "Looks like you've got yourself a promotion." His office manager showed no pleasure at the prospect of being left in charge. In his view the staff of all foreign organizations would be at special risk.

"I think I have another problem on my hands," Martin said to himself, trying to suppress the panic. "I take it I am the warden." This seemed to be the general consensus. Those who had heard the bulletin spread the news to others. Everyone rallied round.

There was no difficulty in assembling vehicles and enough fuel was found to take them to the nearest border. Since they were guaranteed safe passage across the bridge, there was no longer any question of taking the beer smugglers' track to Zaire, and to six hundred miles of wilderness and anarchy. They could simply follow the main road out through Uganda. In colonial times this had been a tarmacadam highway. Officials had driven their Humbers down to Makerere for the weekend. Now it was a rutted dirt road made worse by the heavy lorries that in the dry season and in periods of calm brought in everybody's supplies from East Africa and beyond. Although most bridges were down, the rivers were dry and Big Pete assured Martin that the convoy could manage the journey in a day, "easy".

The real difficulties were practical: what to take, what to leave. Some people expected to be back within a few weeks if the rebels took over. Others predicted that an Islamic force would not want them back at all if it won. And if it lost, Sudan or Libya might well intervene.

Martin had few possessions. He put his clothes and some bedding in a tin trunk, tucked in the bundle of unopened letters from Alice and left the house, its equipment and the three-piece suite in the hands of his staff. He instructed them to keep hold of it if possible...

"I'll be back as soon as I can," he said without much conviction.

"Oh, Boss," wailed Vashti, putting her arms round him, "why are you leavin' us to die?"

"Because we are only black men," said Ndua. "We don't count."

This plea and Ndua's unexpected rebuke stung Martin. There was no use explaining that the white men were effectively being expelled. He knew they were also running away. Unlike their African colleagues they had somewhere to run to. That was the difference. No point, either, in explaining that the Republic of the Nile was their country, that this mess was their mess. Staff in international aid offices, in voluntary and Christian organisations were particularly vulnerable. They were worried the army would find them guilty by association, single them out for punishment. And there was nothing their organisations could do for them, other than patronisingly to ask them to "mind the shop."

Some of the expatriates had personal attachments to local people. Most of them realised that without the proper papers it would be impossible to take a partner out with them. This was a let-out for many men, among them Big Pete: changing their woman was little more than an inconvenience. For others the dilemma was more acute. Father Patrick, for example, a highly respected missionary and social worker would not leave without his housekeeper. He could not bring himself to admit that for the last six years they had lived together as man and wife, though everyone knew it. He decided to stay behind. The last anyone saw of him, he was leaving "on a pastoral mission" to his housekeeper's village.

Bob was more forthright. He insisted on taking two of his boys with him. He intended to enrol them on a course of studies in UK and thereby get them into the country initially as students. If necessary he was prepared to adopt them. "They are already my sons," he protested. Martin did not argue.

There were several hastily arranged convoys. The Americans left first and took no one else with them.

"We'll blaze the trail," they said.

Martin's group comprised Brits and Commonwealth citizens. Everyone called it Martin's group by default. His reputation, however undeserved, lent him credibility. In fact, most of them were far more experienced than he was at trekking and in some cases at evacuations.

"The thing is," one of the foresters said, "to collect all the eggs you can lay your hands on, hard boil them, put them in a cool box in their shells and they'll see you through for weeks."

"I hope it won't be weeks!" frowned Martin. This talk of eggs reminded him of something.

"I never go on trek without a box of them," said the forester, "just in case, eh?" Martin smiled. Of course! The drinking place in Wok. That was it. Where he had cracked eggs and drunk smuggled beer. It had been one of the few occasions when he had felt at peace.

They left at dawn on the second day. This was to allow time for any of the volunteers and aid workers from outside Gondo to join the convoy if they wished. Being dispersed, many of them had alternative escape routes. Some people decided it was safer to remain where they were, rather than to congregate in the town. After all, it was Gondo that was the target. While the foreigners were planning their departure, a large proportion of the urban population also slipped silently away into the bush to regain their villages or perhaps their fighting units.

There were no more than a dozen vehicles in Martin's convoy. The only rule was to stay loosely together. At the bridge out of town, Pete, who had taken the lead waited until Martin had crossed in the rear. They agreed to follow this procedure at all the checkpoints along the way, but in between the vehicles spread out as traffic normally does. The whole exodus was more like a weekend excursion than an organized evacuation.

Everyone seemed to be enjoying the enforced holiday except Martin. He had taken up the rearguard to justify his position as warden. He felt responsible and guilty at the same time. He had not exactly assumed a leadership role. Bob had helped with the coordination, Big Pete had rounded up spares and supplies, everyone had contributed to food for the journey. Now Martin, leading from behind and still driving Taffy's Landrover could at least ensure no one got left behind. Except, of course, those they had not been able to contact. And Alice.

At least Taffy would be pleased that his precious Landrover had been saved. Martin had also taken a trunk of what he judged to be Taffy's most treasured possessions - some framed photos, clothes, binoculars, a darts set and a few technical journals. This had left room for two spare wheels, back-up parts and tools in case anyone in the convoy had a mechanical break-down, a 44 gallon drum of fuel, four large plastic containers of filtered drinking water and his passenger. This was Morris, the second of the boys Bob was going to educate.

Martin knew Morris on a casual basis, having seen him at Bob's house and exchanged pleasantries with him. He was a quiet lad, usually overshadowed by his muscular, more pushy "brother" Isaiah. Morris, though of slighter build, was equally striking to look at. His skin was very black, a shining healthy black. He had Nilotic features, a thin nose and eyes as bright and brown as washed pebbles. He bore himself proudly and with quiet assurance. When he smiled, which he did often, his white teeth advertised a message of fun and vitality. He was very excited. This was his first trip abroad and he was treating the journey as the beginning of a great adventure.

Rounding a corner about noon, the two men, Martin and his passenger, reacted very differently to the sight ahead. Several of the vehicles had come to a stop, corralled on a patch of cleared land. A column of smoke arose from inside the circle. Martin's stomach lurched. He immediately suspected a mine or a violent hold-up. He had half a mind to turn round and keep out of sight. He braked hard.

Morris, on the other hand, let out a yelp of delight.

"They've done it! I knew they would." He stuck his head out of the open window and sniffed.

"What is it?" asked Martin, fearfully.

"Drive close," urged Morris. "You can smell it."

Martin continued cautiously. Some of the others saw him and raised a cheer. Still Martin was perplexed. But Morris laughed, jumped out of the Landrover and ran up to the find Bob and Isaiah.

"About time!" said a perspiring Bob, wiping his face with a charcoal smudged handkerchief. "Give us a hand with the sausages."

Now things began to make sense to Martin. He understood why, after a furtive conversation with Big Pete, Bob had sped off ahead at the last checkpoint. He had wanted to set up a barbecue! He and Isaiah must have worked fast. They were already handing out Danish sausages, grilled bacon, beer and mangoes.

"Wanted a party before we left," he told his friends, "but no time. Atmosphere unconducive." He beamed at them, mopped his brow which became black with charcoal.

"Why the camouflage?" asked Big Pete, throwing a beer can into the bush.

"I don't think we should delay too long," said Martin with a worried look, and he went to pick up the can. "And we should not leave litter." Those that noticed his gesture at all gave him an ironic clap. Most people were too busy enjoying the solidarity and the sausages to share his anxiety. Bob came up to him and said, "Relax. Live for the moment."

"Yeah, man!" added Pete. "Where are the dancing girls?"

"You're incorrigible, Pete," said Martin.

"Trouble is, you're not," retorted the Big Man, flexing a bicep as he took a swipe at an insect that had settled on his sleeveless arm.

Gradually Martin succumbed to the party atmosphere. Gondo and all the tension of the last few days now lay behind them. It was only three hours' drive to the border.

My strength returned. So did my impatience. I could not find out what was going on.

"We are negotiating," they told me.

"What is there to negotiate? Why can't you just let me go?"

The officer to whom I was speaking looked at me coldly.

"Go where?"

I did not understand. I realised, of course, I could not just wander off on my own. Though I confess I did seriously consider it. I did not know they were trying to get me out of the country. They wanted me out of the way, out of their hands, but they did not want the government to get any of the credit for it.

"You will be handed over to the Red Cross."

"When?"

"Soon."

Soon was not to be. Not for me. But soon two other things happened. During a day of unusual activity in the camp Mary came running into my room, excited and tearful. She told me about the raids on Gondo. Rebel forces had destroyed some strategic installations. She spoke those words, "strategic installations" without understanding them.

"Radio station, ministry buildings, port, airport, that kind of thing," I explained, wondering if the Britwords compound had been hit.

"They fired mortars into the army barracks. Next time they will capture it." She stopped abruptly as if struck by a bullet herself.

"Oh Alice," she cried in real pain

"What is it, Mary?"

"They want me to go to war with them. Many people have been hurt."

I stared at her. To lose her now. This gentle girl. I do not know whether she had saved my life, but she had cared for me when I most needed it. I had become dependent on her calm, quiet presence. Besides, how could she take her child to the front line?

"When will you go?"

"Now. Now!"

A motorcycle stopped outside. The rider spoke to Mary. She hung her head. If I had felt guilty at putting myself first, she relieved my feelings by sobbing,

"I wanted to go with you. I wanted to go to your country."

"Perhaps you will, one day."

"One day!"

"Mary, thank you for all you have done." We hugged one another. "And good luck. Perhaps you will find your husband." She gave a brief smile and then shrieked,

"But what about you?"

"That's what I'd like to know." I almost felt I were being left behind in the bustle and the shouting. But the messenger on the motorbike returned and told me to make myself ready to leave at once.

"What is the hurry?" I asked.

"We fear an air raid," said the man. "Reprisals."

"Where are we going?"

"You ask too many questions. Are you a spy?"

"Oh God, not that again," I thought, and shut up.

At once in Africa, even in an emergency, means in a few hours or in a few days. True, Mary had left, but she was on a mission, she and her baby. In my case I had nothing to get ready and apparently nowhere to go. I returned to my room. My worn out jeans, washed and folded, lay on the trainers that had carried me across miles of scrub and savannah. How many more miles would we have to share? As I tried to make sense of what was happening there was a knock on the door and a white woman walked in.

"You are Alice Tupman, I hope," she said.

I looked at this gaunt, short-sighted woman with thick glasses and straggly hair. She wore army trousers far too big and a torn blouse. She had English walking boots such as ramblers wear, or used to, big heavy jobs with leather laces. On her back she carried a small, nylon rucksack in faded pink.

"Good God!" I exclaimed.

"No, just Delia. But I try to be good."

"Oh!" was all I could manage and she seemed a little embarrassed.

"How do you like it here?" she asked me. We might have been at an Embassy reception or strangers meeting in the bar at a holiday resort.

"It's very pleasant," I replied. We both laughed at the stupidity of our platitudes.

"Look, I've come to take you across the border. And I've brought you a few home comforts."

She swung the rucksack off her back and put it on the ground, undoing the plastic buckles. She pulled back a toggle to release the cord that gripped the throat of the bag and opened it out. I cannot imagine why this bizarrely dressed woman stooping over a rucksack in the gloom of a straw hut should have reminded me of Santa Claus, but when she presented me with my gifts I felt it really was Christmas. Delia handed me two pairs of sensible Marks and Spencers knickers, folded but not wrapped, a packet of tampons and a big, blue tin of nivea cream.

"I thought you would need something like this by now."

"It's exactly what I wanted," I said, still trapped in cliché by total surprise. But to show I really meant it, I embraced her, unfolded one of the pairs of knickers and slipped them on under my loose house robe, or cloth as Mary Deng called it. "I haven't worn underwear for weeks."

245

"I couldn't manage more," she said. "I wanted to bring you a Mars bar or something, but chocolate melts. I did just squeeze this in."

She handed me over a small jar of Marmite. I could not believe it. I unscrewed the top and stuck my forefinger deep into the pot. I sucked the rich, brown substance from my finger with relish. I licked my lips and took another dip.

Delia laughed. "Looks scrumptious."

I held out the jar. "Have some."

She hooked out a taste of the marmite on her little finger and licked at it tentatively with a cat's tongue. "I've survived on this stuff, you know.... but there's plenty of time to exchange stories. We've got a bit of a journey ahead of us."

"Not another long march?"

"Well, the first bit's easy. Ever been in a helicopter?"

It was a noisy, old-fashioned helicopter. Too noisy to talk. We scudded along very low and made two stops on the way. In both places people seemed to know either the helicopter or Delia or both. Apart from the pilot, whom she treated like an old friend, there was no one else on board. When she alighted, Delia was received like a first lady, but she reacted quietly and modestly.

After weeks of moving at no more than walking pace, and many days of those weeks spent sitting and waiting, the speed and movement threw me into a whirl of confused excitement. I could not bring my thoughts together. I could not formulate the questions I wanted to ask this serene, tough Englishwoman.

Gradually I learned she had been assisting negotiations and that she was to hand me over to the Red Cross. For various political reasons this could not be done within the Republic of the Nile. While the British Government wanted my release, they could not risk offending the military regime.

"They believe they are maintaining a balance in the region," Delia told me wryly. I nodded, but all I understood was that I was a nuisance to all concerned. My own government was no more enthusiastic about rescuing me than were my captors about detaining me. Much of their energy, I have since learned, was spent initially in denying that I had been kidnapped at all and subsequently in suppressing speculation that I might be released.

Delia told me that the rebels received assistance from Ethiopia but that that regime was not the flavour of the month in the British Foreign Office. Ethiopia had neither oil nor money to buy weapons, and therefore were classed as Baddies. The Republic of the Nile though more repressive, often to the point of genocide, wanted to buy British armaments. In addition it required expertise in opening up its new oil fields. The Republic was therefore ranked on the side of the Goodies. Britwords was to be one of the beneficiaries. A big contract for technological words and civil engineering jargon was in the offing, funded by the Overseas Aid Administration. All in all, to negotiate my release either with the rebels or with the Ethiopians might jeopardise many opportunities for trade and what was known as "British interests." Delia had understood this and had been instrumental in making arrangements with the Red Cross so that my release would not be 'blamed on' the British Government. But we still had to get into Ethiopia before these details became known to the Nilean army. They were sticking to their proposals for liberating me (dead or alive) themselves by bombing the rebel territory into submission. Even the British Embassy balked at this and were playing for time, perhaps the only natural diplomatic skill they still possessed. "But I'm being cynical," Delia said. "The less you know the better. Accusations of spying etc." She winked.

This explanation took place at the second stop. Delia had handed some packets to a group of ragged but respectful officers. Instructions, I guessed, some essential supplies, private messages. And, I suspected, as she took the small packages from her bottomless, pink rucksack, personal gifts. These wild-looking men appeared touched when she handed them over with a quiet word in their ear. The men wanted us to join them and drink tea, but we had to press on.

At the last stop Delia conferred urgently with the officer who met us. The pilot went off with him and two soldiers, two more men were posted to guard the helicopter and Delia and I were escorted to a hut in the village. Such accommodation had become so much part of my life that that I did not even look about me. I automatically set about making the bare interior comfortable for the two of us. We now had a bedroll each and a lamp. Food, Delia told me, would be provided.

"The helicopter will be returning. Our seats will be replaced by consignments of medicines and armaments." I hoped illogically my place would be filled with the medicines.

"I am afraid I will not be able to introduce you to the Colonel," she added, more to herself than to me.

"What's that?"

"No, I had half hoped Colonel M'Bang might be here, but of course, he has to keep on the move."

"I do not suppose he'd be interested in me," I said, shuddering at the thought of any more interviews with military top brass, Goodies, Baddies or otherwise! Delia started to say something but thought better of it. Instead she brewed tea quietly. After the commotion of the journey I had almost fallen into a doze when she handed me a big mug of the sweet lifesaver.

"Lovely!" I said. I had no idea what lay ahead, but I was enjoying myself. Delia, too, relaxed again as we sipped the tea. "Were you ever a Girl Guide?" she asked me.

"No, but I think I should have liked to have been one. Were you?"

"I tried it. But I found it a bit tame," she giggled, surprising herself with this admission.

I asked her how she got mixed up with the rebels.

"Quite by accident, really." She removed her glasses and wiped them with a piece of her shirt that had loosened itself from around her scrawny waist. It had been a very gradual process. After working at the then prestigious University of Makerere in Uganda, she and a few friends, British and African, had come to Gondo to try to establish a similar University in the new Republic. Like Makerere it was to be affiliated to the University of London. Delia was unblinkered by religion. She saw a Western style University as a valuable counter balance to the Islamic Universities to the North, and a chance for the black people of the Republic to get as good an education as their "Arab" brothers. But just as their first batch of students graduated, a series of coups shook the country. The regime that took control looked less favourably on a fledgling institution imbued with the spirit of enquiry. They found a use for some of the graduates, however, particularly the engineers and technicians, the agriculturalists. But some students called for free speech and democracy and human rights. The regime attempted to sack the neo-colonialist lecturers who had been implanting such subversive ideas in the mind of "The Youth." The students went on the first of many strikes. The Vice-Chancellor supported his staff and students. He was arrested and imprisoned.

"Poor Abraham! The ordeal quite changed him. From LSE to Leader of a Rebel Army in five years. Yes, he is the same

Colonel M'Bang I had hoped to introduce you to. And a very old friend."

Delia told me how many of the expatriate staff had left as their contracts expired. The university was closed down anyway, but Delia managed to stay on as a kind of administrative caretaker. The Embassy topped up her salary because they found her a useful source of intelligence. She only told them what she felt they should know. In return they would help with visas and formalities. Delia still cherished the dream of re-opening the university.

"I know I'm crazy," she said. "But I could not settle back in England. It's so grey and parochial, don't you think?"

"It's not always grey," I said. "Parochial, yes." And I told her about my last visit to my parents. Before I left we had watched a flotilla of hot air balloons pass over the house. I had tried to describe them to Martin in a letter.

At first there was only one. It bobbed up out of the valley ten or a dozen fields away. It rose slowly in the still, cool air of a perfect summer's evening. As it rose it drifted towards us, bouncing slightly as though the air had springs.

Despite the size of the blue and red striped balloon, you could tell from the basket suspended beneath it that it was still some distance away. It was not possible to make out the people inside the basket, though already their voices carried across the quiet landscape.

Every so often there was a spurt of flame and a second later the hiss of the heat reached our ears. It made Crowbar's hackles rise. As the balloon lifted above the subtle green and purple shadows of the valley backdrop and stuck itself on to the clear blue sky, two, three more balloons hove into view. They bobbed in surprise to match our surprise and delight, as we realised a whole batch of them, like bubbles blown by a child in one breath, must be preparing to leave the flat meadow down by the river for an evening voyage through the sunset.

Soon several tear shaped balloons, all different colours and patterns enlarged themselves as we watched until we could make out the tiny figures peering out of their baskets.

However the eye was captured not by the insignificant human load, but by the presence of the vast balloons themselves, eerie, silent, like grinning, cruel clowns; strange craft, themselves beings from another world. There was also something festive about them. One striped in vertical mauves and silvers was like an upturned bauble that should by rights have been hanging on a Christmas tree.

The first balloon, a multi-coloured crocus, had now risen very high and encountered a current that was taking it in a big sweep away from us. The other group was still low and coming towards us. One of them seemed to be having trouble gaining height and the human figures were scurrying about sending urgent bursts of flame into the belly of their Christmas balloon. The rasping of this released gas sent Crowbar scuttling for cover and set a number of other dogs across the valley barking as they noticed the sinister craft in the sky.

As the balloons passed over we could see that they were in fact moving quite fast. Like rotund dragons they gasped and breathed fire as they bobbed along on their otherwise silent and dignified course.

As imperceptibly as the balloons had stolen up on us, the sky had faded to a light pink. With the change of light the space galleons rose and wheeled and receded, until disappearing behind the trees on the other side of the garden, they sailed away into the young night.

Delia listened without interruption as I tried to recall, less eloquently than in my letter, the flight of the balloons. When I had finished she remarked,

"They obviously made a great impression on you. Is that what you remember most about UK?"

"Not quite," I said. "I had met a man. That - he - is the reason why I am here."

Delia winked and looked at me with a toothy grin. "That man would not be Martin Thomas, would he?"

"Yes. Do you know him?"

"We've met, yes."

CHAPTER FOURTEEN

It was a drizzly November afternoon in Bloomsbury. The dampness seemed to have sucked all the light out of the remnants of the stillborn day. Led through the cavernous, concrete building with its slow moving lifts and shabby corridors, Martin brushed shoulders with students who were drifting about their business unaware that in the basement a guest lecture was about to take place.

Obediently he took his seat in the front row of the neon lit lecture theatre. He drew his notes from an inside pocket and unfolded them on his lap while his audience, members of the African Commonwealth Society and their guests, settled comfortably down after their good lunch. He noticed that Jefferson, Controller of Human Resource Material and staff from the African Department of Britwords had been invited, along with some Foreign Office under-secretaries and a couple of African diplomats.

There was a lull in the cosy post-prandial murmuring and taking her cue from the expectant hush, a middle-aged woman rose from the front row. She attempted to stride to the podium, hampered somewhat by a thick, floppy jumper that covered her thighs and most of her knee-length batik skirt. The jumper was so loose that as she moved it slipped to reveal all of one shoulder, her throat and neck. She stood almost astride the lectern like a witch ready for take off. Her white legs were bare except for the flip-flops on her feet. She brushed back her wiry, grey hair, clutched at the wayward pullover to try and centralise it, cleared her throat and waited for the audience to fall silent.

"It is heart-warming to see so many of you here," she began. "And to welcome so many new faces. I am not surprised. Many eminent speakers have addressed our gatherings, but few with an account so fresh, so immediate as that which we are about to enjoy."

"Hear! Hear!" said a purple-nosed old gentleman in the second row, before he fell asleep.

"All of us are no doubt aware of the valuable work carried out in Africa by Britwords. But it is not often that they capture the public imagination."

"That could have been better expressed," muttered Jefferson to the colleague on his right.

"Vera means well. Do you think Thomas is up to the occasion, though?"

"Too late to back out now. Shhh."

The speaker was continuing, "Martin Thomas, I am sure he will not mind my saying so, was not seen as one of Britwords' high-fliers." Jefferson buried his tired face in his hands. What was this woman going to say next?

"Rather," she continued, "he was one of those reliable and conscientious stalwarts whom all too often many organisations take for granted. But in an inspired move, so typical of Britwords leadership, Martin was offered the opportunity to escape from his rut and to take on the challenge of running their most remote office. He was posted to a place which a month ago, Joe Public, if you will forgive my condescension, would have had difficulty placing on the map of Africa. Today Martin Thomas is a household name. Not content with saving the lives of his office staff when under attack from a frenzied mob, he successfully led the evacuation of a small but dedicated band of aid workers through bandit infested territory.

"At lunch, Martin told me he had not yet come to terms with these events, indeed he said he was still culture shocked from being back in the U.K." She paused for the titters and noises of sympathy from the floor to die. "He proposes, therefore, to speak not about his exploits, and I suspect anyway he is far too modest to do that, but to give us his personal impression of events in The Republic of the Nile. Ladies and Gentlemen, I have said quite enough..."

"Hear! Hear!" repeated purple-nose, surfacing for a moment from his post-prandial torpor.

"Martin Thomas." The Chair of the African Commonwealth Society smiled at Martin who was sitting in the front row, and ceded the rostrum to him. As she stepped down, her rubber flip-flops caught on the top edge of the dais. She tripped and fell heavily forward into Martin's arms, almost knocking him back into his seat. Martin helped her to her own place, averting his eyes from the continent of flesh bared in the upheaval. While she, flustered, re-adjusted her jumper, Martin clambered up to the lectern, losing half his notes in the process. As he fumbled to put the remaining sheets together, he remarked of his collision,

"I suppose that was another example of being in the right place at the right time." Such was his popularity that the polite applause of welcome swelled into a noisy appreciation of his wit. Even the Minister for Central Africa permitted himself a smile and his two senior colleagues, one of whom had been on his promotion board, shared a nod.

"How am I going to keep this up?" wondered Martin. For a second he recognised the old panic rising and the warning throb started up in his right temple. He sorted his notes and the room crashed into expectant silence.

He began ritualistically, "Madam Chair, Your Excellencies, distinguished guests, colleagues, ladies and gentlemen, it is a privilege and a pleasure to have been invited to share my thoughts with you here today." He paused, stood his notes on end and tapped them down on the lectern as a card player does to even up the pack.

"Your introduction, Madam Chair," (What a ridiculous title, he thought, though the French 'Madame Chair', meaning Mrs Flesh, would have been appropriate.) "was far too generous. While I was only too happy to demonstrate that I still am or have a safe pair of hands..." he paused for a titter to run through the audience and told himself not to flog that horse dead, "I fear that I am going to disappoint you all. The events that led up to the evacuation were not a bit as reported. Compared with the daily business of survival, they were a picnic." (Blast it, he thought, that gives quite the wrong impression, making out that they had survived an even tougher ordeal.)

He stopped, laid his notes flat and tried to read the first page. But the text swam in front of his eyes. He would have to ad lib.

"It wasn't like that at all." Now he remembered how he was going to start. His head cleared and he straightened up, "There are many definitions of an expert. One of them is: an expert is someone who has flown over the territory, preferably once in daylight." He paused but his audience did not get the joke and he continued hastily. "I was not in the Republic very long, but I was there long enough to realise that I understood less about the country with every day that passed. I was there too long to call myself an expert." And Martin could not help adding, with a sidelong look at the row of Foreign Office staff. "I am sure that if anyone wants a political analysis they will find plenty of expertise in this room. Expertise, dare I say, unsullied by the subjectivity of direct experience."

"Hear! Hear!" came a familiar cry.

"I do not know what effect, if any, my work had on Gondo or on the Republic in general. Words may not hurt, but at the moment the people prefer sticks and stones. I do know some of the effect that Gondo has had on me. And if you will forgive this Cook's tour of the darker cells of my ego, it is this I should like to share with you.

"Many of you here will understand what I mean when I say that time telescopes the older you get. The years get shorter, fold in on the life you have already lived, and your future is encompassed by your past.

"One moment your ideas had seemed new, and because they were new, better than the ideas of parents, teachers, bosses.... You were riding a wave of innovation, surfing along in front of the flotilla.

"Next moment the wave has slipped from under you, gone rushing on ahead carrying with it younger, nimbler colleagues, friends and competitors. To your shock and amazement, your ideas are regarded as old-fashioned, irrelevant. You have been left behind.

"To continue the surfing metaphor, you have been knocked off your board; there has been no spectacular crash. You have through inattention, lack of application or through sheer bad luck let the wave escape you. You have failed to keep abreast of all the forces and currents of that onward surge.

But this image is incomplete. It does not account for a shift in values. You still have ideals, you are still capable of making a judgement. You did not deliberately let that wave slide away, you are not yet aware that your view has changed.

"All of a sudden you are considered a reactionary, an obstacle, old-fashioned, obsolete, redundant. All those words. Between one wave and the next. Between one age and the next. And yet it is what you have retained that makes you so. You have a questioning spirit. Dangerous! With it you used to question the old values and methods. Now you apply it to the new. Is that the difference between a reactionary and a revolutionary? One questions the old, the other the new? Not in your case, you think. You make no such distinction between the old and what appears the merely fashionable.

"You might claim to have achieved a deeper insight, the wisdom of experience. No one believes you. You are in the way. You must be dumped.

"I was only dimly of all this when Britwords offered me the post in Gondo. No one else wanted to go, they told me. I could not understand that. I saw it as a great adventure, an escape from the rat race and my last chance to do something 'real' with my life. I suppose I half suspected this was Britwords' way of dumping me. And in saying so now I am not implying criticism of my colleagues who sent me there." Martin could not resist adding, " Even though one of them is present with us today. They, as we have to say instead of he or she, they were as much a victim of the system as I was."

He noticed his tired-looking director muttering to a colleague sitting beside him. He dimly remembered this as the man who had asked him to put a price to his poetry.

"I see you fidgeting. You may have come here to listen to tales of derring-do, anecdotes, action. Well, despite everything you have been told, there was very little action of that kind. For me, it all went on in my head. As you can see, I have returned physically safe and sound, but," he paused before admitting quietly, "I am not sure it is the same Martin Thomas who has come back." There was an earnestness in his voice now that for a moment longer held his listeners' attention.

"I was invited out the other night. A private dinner party. The room was bathed in music. Someone began to extol the virtues of the sound system. Such perfect reproduction seemed irrelevant to me, but then I suppose I never have been able to see the advantage of the CD over the LP, the LP over the 78, if its end use is to provide background noise to dinner party chatter. I prefer unreprocessed silence! I do not want to ride this hobby horse to death, but let me give just one more example of the way we allow technology to lead us along a false path. We all use word processors. Very useful they are. But because they are so quick and simple, so labour-saving, our speeches, our theses and reports, our novels are 20% longer than they used to be. I wonder if that extra 20% carries any more valid a message? Shouldn't we have invented something slower than a typewriter, less wieldy than a pen? A distillation not a dilution is required. We should perhaps all become stonemasons or poets. In fact I once admitted to someone here present that I used to write poetry.

"It was not my intention to stand here and whinge. Neither is it my intention to deliver a profession of faith, for in truth I do not know what that faith would be. I have been lucky, I suppose. I have achieved a moment's notoriety. But I did want to hint that there is very little substance in the flattering stories that have grown up around those events.

"Let me, then, take you for one or two steps in the evolution of my thinking. Nothing new, nothing startling, I assure you. As I said just now, it is a Cook's tour of one man's small ego. Since I have had five days' fame thrust upon me, do not blame me for taking advantage of it. Let's be positive.

"Back to the beach, then! If you perceive life has passed you by, how do you fight back, catch up? Time goes in only one direction so far as we know. Our occupation of it is linear. We proceed from birth to death. We may be strong enough to live without the approbation of society, but at the very least we have to live with ourselves. And most of us have to earn a living. That is the crunch."

Martin shuffled nervously with his notes, could not find what he wanted, and with a quick glance up at his two senior colleagues, continued, "Now, what I am going to say next may upset some of my colleagues. Please bear with me. I promise you positive things are to come. But first we have to understand the negative.

"You all know about compassion fatigue. It occurs when there are so many disasters that the public grows weary and donations to the charities dwindle. We can take only so much suffering at a time. Well, I contend that the same goes for innovation. Fatigued by the ever new, we begin to see change as fad and fashion rather than as offering us any improvement.

"In an organisational culture like Britwords where employees are daily enjoined to welcome change, few would admit to themselves and certainly not to their colleagues, who might be informers, that rather than continuously contemplate the corporate navel, they would prefer to be left to get on with the job in their own way using their own language. A language in which words like 's/he', 'spouse', 'visually impaired' and, I must say it, 'Chair', are best avoided. A language in which a spade is called a spade, where black is black and white is white and no shame attaches to either.

"Britwords, my organisation, professes to encourage risk taking. The area of that risk is circumscribed. It does not mean risking a compliment to a 'human resource' of the opposite gender, for example. That would constitute sexual harassment which is a deadly sin. It does not mean risking being seen smoking a cigarette, or worse being spotted in a pub not drinking alcohol. No, taking a risk means risking the taxpayers' money and achieving a high return. By definition risk-takers are winners."

He saw that his director was scribbling something on a scrap of paper. His companion was reading it and nodding. Martin cleared his throat and gave them both the kind of look a teacher gives to pupils not paying attention in class.

"Innovation fatigue at the workplace leads to apathy and apathy to lethargy, a kind of 'what's-the-use-ism' that spills over into the worker's private life. The spiritual malaise gives rise to psychosomatic illnesses - tiredness, loss of appetite, headaches. We have invented a name for this phenomenon. We call it stress."

He saw that the note was being passed forward towards Madam Chair in the front row. She had a forced smile of perplexed intelligence on her face and those behind her failed to attract her attention. The note progressed as far as a middle-aged woman a few rows behind her. This pillar of society did not realise she was part of a chain of communication. Furtive signs from the authors of the message only confused and embarrassed her. The note burned her fingers. She tapped the shoulder of the old gentleman in front of her. He turned, took the note in disbelief and with a broad wink slipped it into his pocket. His neck reddened slightly.

Martin saw this all happening but did not take it in. He gripped the lectern with both hands and launched into a kind of confession. It was unpremeditated, as if the trip around his ego was also something of a voyage of discovery for him.

"I thought I was escaping all this when I went to Gondo. I wanted new experiences, I craved a change, a break. Well, I certainly got that. But I discovered something I had not bargained for. A different kind of innovation fatigue. After the initial euphoria, the anti-climax and the levelling out which we all go through in new places, a lot of things happened rather close together. I found myself sated with novelty, most of it of the anxiety raising kind. And I realised that I had not had the imagination to prepare myself for life in Gondo. I had left it too late. My anxiety was replaced by fear, verging on panic. It was only by actually coming to Gondo that I could have had this revelation. This was not the life for me. Not any more. Having dreamed all my life of getting away from the routine that was my life, I discovered in Gondo that really I was not made for adventure. I thought of my former life, my office job in London and concerts on the South Bank. I never imagined I would be homesick for that safe and sound and dull routine.

"I am sure many of you here have been through these feelings. And got over them. They pass. But I discovered another thing in Gondo. Something I had not noticed here at home. I had become middle-aged. The things that had appealed to a younger man, the attraction of foreign places, the need to sip at, if not to get drunk on, new experiences was now less urgent. In that case, though, I had never been young. I had had the dreams of a young man; the shadow of those dreams still imprinted themselves on the aspirations of the older man. But it was too late now. I had not translated those dreams into reality in my youth. And if what I was experiencing in Gondo was reality, I said to myself, then I preferred the dreams, the wishful thinking, the inaction.

"If I got out of this, I promised myself, I would no longer feel trapped by the nine to five routine where the biggest adventure is whether the trains were running, the bus drivers working to rule.

"Have I convinced you yet what a boring fellow I am? A very low flier! I've nearly finished. Let's just go back a moment to Gondo. I had had this insight. If it was a flash of self-knowledge it should have led to peace of mind. But it didn't. It resulted in bitter disappointment in myself. Imagine. Everything I had dreamed of all my life, everything I had enjoyed vicariously at work from the accounts of my colleagues posted overseas, everything I had envied them, suddenly turned to ashes when I experienced it myself. And I can tell you that more than enough occurred in the space of a few months to convince me I did not have the taste for it! Why not? Because I was a coward.

"That is the whole irony of this lecture. That is why I am telling you real truth. Did I say I would take you on a trip round my ego? That ego took quite a bruising in Gondo. It was dried and shrunken. Perhaps it should be put in an obscure corner of the Museum of Mankind along with its museum piece of an owner and labelled 'boring old fart.'"

He waited for Purple Nose or someone to shout, 'Hear! Hear!' but there was complete silence. He noticed the director mutter to his neighbour and rise from his seat.

"Please stay," Martin appealed. "Please sit down. I said I would come to a positive conclusion and I am about to arrive at it. I am sorry I have led you by such a devious route." The man reluctantly settled back in his seat. Martin continued in some desperation, "We had to pass via Gondo, not simply because it is the excuse for this lecture, but also because without that detour I could not have given this talk. You understand? We shed a lot of luggage on the way. I lost some of my illusions. Not all.

"There is still one thing I cling to. I share the central belief of Britwords. Words still matter. Words matter more than ever. I do not think that is old-fashioned. I do not think we have been left behind at all. I think we are a lap ahead. Those within the organisation obsessed with the visual, with logos and with branding, with appearances and with the corporate image are merely circling in a backwater. Oh, we all profess to welcome change, we have to! Change is the new orthodoxy. But why then are we still exporting the word, not the image? There is a new Logo. But why has the name itself not been changed? Surely Britwords should have long ago have become Britpics! Wouldn't that be more modern? Yes, but I think we still all share a belief in the word. My worry is, which word, which words. And why this compulsion to export them? Do we not want them ourselves? Aren't they good enough for us?"

Whether or not Martin was leading to a solution or a punchline, he was interrupted by applause from his senior colleagues, desperate now to end this embarrassing performance. Chair at last took her cue and mounted the stage barefoot like a woolly nymph. Martin graciously gave way, standing a little behind her while she proposed her vote of thanks. She had prepared her 'few words' in advance and carried a prompt card in the palm of her hand.

"I am sure I speak for all of us when I say it has been a big thrill to share your adventures with you. On behalf of the Commonwealth African Society I should like to thank Martin Thomas for his revealing account of the turmoil in the Republic of the Nile. And our special thanks, of course to Britwords for their splendid hospitality and for lending us one of their star performers. I am sure, Martin, you have a bright future."

"Thank you," muttered Martin. He felt slightly relieved that she had apparently not been listening to a word he had said. He hoped fervently she was typical of the rest of them. But Chair, adjusting her sloppy sweater, had not finished.

"I am sure Mr. Thomas will be pleased to answer any of your questions."

Martin was as dismayed as his colleagues at this suggestion. There being no takers Mrs Flesh said after a short pause during which people were getting ready to leave, "There is one question I am longing to put. I should like to ask Martin when he was most afraid. Was there any one moment?"

She turned to Martin to pop this last question but he hardly noticed her. His mouth had crashed open, his eyes bulged, he was quite oblivious of the occasion. Mrs Flesh turned, following the direction of his gaze and she saw the reason for his state. A bronzed, and compared to her, young woman stood smiling in the doorway.

"Martin!"

"Alice!" In that one cry was contained guilt, love, doubt and the awakening of joy. In a film Martin would have leapt from the podium, rushed to enfold Alice in his arms. Instead he invited her to,

"Come in. Sit down."

"Am I too late again?" she asked, rooted in the doorway.

"Too late for what?"

"Your lecture."

"Oh, you've missed that. Just as well. Come in."

Because she had been holding the door ajar like a screen, Alice had not seen the audience, nor they her. When she realised the position she blushed and made a frantic mime to Martin that she would be waiting in the cafeteria.

"Don't go..." But the door swung shut, leaving Martin staring at it in disbelief. Some of the audience thought he had finally cracked. Madam Chair coughed discreetly and Martin remembered where he was.

"I said earlier our occupation of time is linear. I am not so sure I was right. I have just leapt out of time, and," he muttered to himself, "like a trout at the steps, fallen back into the mainstream." He told the audience, "You have just seen, or rather you have just not seen, the person who should have been giving this lecture. A real heroine. She came out to Gondo to visit me. Unfortunately our paths never crossed. I am sorry, but I have to leave the room. Madam Chair, please forgive me... Oh, you asked me when I was most afraid. If you do not count the waiting, the uncertainty, the answer must be now."

ALICE'S STORY. PART TEN

If I had been able to keep a diary during my captivity and escape, I should probably have recorded the hardships, the frustrations and the anxiety of it all. But setting it down after the event here in England, the bites and the bumps and the boils, the problems of hygiene, the monotonous food and the endless walking, walking, walking - this no longer matters except as the backcloth of discomfort against which people came and went... I wonder if I'll see any of them again.

I try to remember what happened at the end. The order of events. Delia and I did not get long to rest after the helicopter flight. We had both assumed we should be spending the night in the hut. We had been chatting like schoolgirls over a midnight feast. Delia had just told me she had met Martin when we were invited to another place to eat. All I could ask Delia was,

"Is he all right?"

"Who?"

"Martin."

"Yes, he should be out of the country by now."

"Has he gone home?" I was shocked. Despite Delia's reassuring presence I felt deserted, betrayed, forgotten. "Delia..."

We were shown into a poorly lit hut. Delia squeezed my hand. "It's okay. Tell you later."

The food was by no means a feast and by midnight we were marching through the bush again. No light and no sound was tolerated by our guide. I could not help thinking about Martin. I had come all this way to see him. He had not been there to meet me. And now it seemed he had left the country without me. There was no chance of putting to Delia all the questions that were buzzing round in my head like disturbed wasps.

We reached another settlement an hour or two after daybreak where we were told we could rest until darkness fell again. Both of us collapsed fully clothed into sleep. We awoke sweating and dry mouthed about mid-day. Delia got hold of some water. Both of us were proficient in bathing in a teacup. Most of the water we used to brew tea, in fact. We were watched by some infants who played in the dirt amongst chickens and small black pigs with long snouts.

As we sipped our tea and stretched out our bare, newly washed and much marked legs, Delia chuckled in her throaty way. She parted her thick lips to pronounce in ham Shakespearean tones, "Some are born great, some achieve greatness and some have greatness thrust upon them."

"Which are we?" I asked, wondering if my gawky companion were beginning to crack up.

"Us? None of them." She laughed, revealing her crooked teeth. "Unsung, that's us. I was thinking about your friend, Martin."

"Martin. Why? What's he done?"

"He's a sensitive chap, really, isn't he?"

"What's he done?"

"Lots of things. And they've all been thrust upon him." She moistened her lips with the tip of her tongue and told me of his "mercy errand" to Wok; she told me how, like Gordon on the Steps, he had outfaced a drunken rentamob. Her tone was ironical and I asked,

"But you do like him?"

"Oh yes, he's a genuine sort."

I was encouraged. She told me of their morning walk in the bush soon after I went missing.

"I wanted him to see the good side," she said. "I don't know if I succeeded."

"But why did he leave?"

Delia told me about the threat to Gondo. How Martin had been chosen to coordinate the evacuation. How he had not wanted to leave until I had been found.

"Nevertheless, he did leave," I protested on a note of rebuke.

"Martin only left because I promised him I would help you," Delia said, giving me a searching look, but at the same time embarrassed at her admission. It took a while for this news to sink into my selfish skull.

"So you persuaded him to leave?"

"Yes. There was nothing he could have done to save you."

"And you have put yourself to all this trouble for me?"

"For both of you, I suppose. Let's not be sentimental about it, Alice. I am enjoying it."

Shortly in to the second night's march we reached a river. Our guide told us to wait in a cave of vegetation on the sandy shore. "No lights," he warned.

Delia explained to me that we had been following one of the routes used to smuggle supplies in. And in this case me out. The tributary flowed into a wider river. Over the other side was Ethiopia "where we have many friends" she said, before dropping a bombshell of her own.

"I am afraid that this is where I must say goodbye."

"What!" I felt a new kind of terror. With the realization I could not take much more of this on my own, a rush of warmth for Delia, for her companionship and kindness, surged through me. I hugged her and said, "Thank you." That is all I said, but I think, I hope she appreciated the depth of those thanks.

Our guide returned in a flat-bottomed boat. I was introduced to a dark, silent man who stood like a heron in the stern. In the darkness he seemed to be perching on a long pole.

"This man will take you to safety," said the guide.

"Hop aboard then," said Delia. "I'm sorry there's only room for one."

"So am I! Where am I going now?"

"The boatman will take you to a camp. A Red Cross official will make contact. Good luck."

"Same to you." I embraced her again, shook the guide's hand and stepped into the wooden boat, settling somewhere in the middle. The floor was awash with water.

The boatman pushed off. He let the current do most of the work. It was a moonless night, deliberately so timed, I suppose. I thought how Martin would have enjoyed this dark ride. I imagined how he would have described it to me. There was very little to see, particularly when we joined the main stream. The river banks with their dark vegetation were just a smudge against the night. Reflected stars glittered brilliantly in the stiller patches of water, eddies occasionally slapped against the boat and a dank, warm smell of wet vegetation, wood and silt enveloped me. The calls and cries of night creatures from the shore, bats and frogs and insects floated across in bursts. Occasional plops and gurgles erupted closer to hand. I have always thought of a tropical night as a kind of aquarium in which we swim or float like fish. Being on the water enhanced this impression and I was immersed in a kind of dream world. Suddenly in front of us of us I heard a loud burp or tummy rumble. The statuesque boatman immediately came to life, exchanged his pole for a paddle and swung us round in a big arc, continuing downstream on the other bank.

"What was that?" I asked.

"Hippos."

"Hippos!"

"Yes."

I did not ask about crocodiles. I just hoped they slept at night.

I started thinking about what Delia had said about Martin, about the troubles in Gondo. I thought about Mary. I hoped she would find her husband. I wondered what had happened to Moses who was responsible for my predicament. Had he been pardoned or punished? I was woken from my reveries and perhaps a gentle doze by a lurch, a scraping and our boat running on to dry land. The boatman helped me ashore.

"Here you are free," he said.

Perhaps I was no longer a prisoner but I was about as free as a zoo animal released into the wild. When I reached the camp, quite a trek I must say from the river, no one seemed to be expecting me. I was asked the all too familiar questions. The young man who finally interrogated me must have been some kind of commander. Although he wore no uniform he carried a good deal of authority. He had been informed that I came from "across the water" and was suspicious. When I mentioned Delia's name, however, he relaxed and made arrangements for me to eat and rest and get a change of clothing.

When I next saw him he had made enquiries and told me cheerfully that a man from the Red Cross would be along in a day or two.

"What!" I exclaimed, ungratefully. I do not know what I had expected, but certainly not another delay, another wait. I had not thought it out. I can honestly say that the last week, the waiting, the bureaucracy, the doubt and the so-called debriefing was the hardest to take. I had exhausted all my reserves of patience and resilience. Finally I was flown to Kenya where I had a further session with British High Commission people. It became clear that they were interested in places and positions held by the rebels, intelligence they called it. I realised with an inward smile that Delia had never told me the name of villages or settlements nor even the name of the river! I told the officials

270

that I had been well treated and played up my confusion. I was not going to give anything away. Delia would leak anything to the authorities that she thought they ought to know.

They were kind enough to me in Nairobi. They were anxious to avoid publicity and I certainly was not seeking it. I was thankful for the rest and medical attention and the assurance that I had only picked up the usual parasites. I was given some medicines but what probably helped more than anything was a shepherd's pie and green vegetables prepared by a sympathetic diplomatic wife. She even supplied Worcestershire Sauce!

"It's not often we can be really useful," she half apologized. I was whisked away before I could get to know her properly. I felt she was more trapped in her sheltered villa with two fierce looking guards at the front gate than I had been throughout my own captivity. I had never had to be protected against intruders, as far as I knew.

The next evening I was put on the overnight British Airways flight to Heathrow. All very low key. I could scarcely believe it. I drank my free G. and T., watched an in-flight movie and felt pampered as never before.

CHAPTER FIFTEEN

Martin had run up the steps from the basement to the ground floor before he checked himself. The cafeteria, where was it? He dimly remembered registering the clatter of cutlery on crockery, the smell of fried fat, on his way to the auditorium. He looked about him in the artificially lit expanse. The entrance lobby housed an enquiry desk. Martin asked the porter where the cafeteria was.

"Well, it ain't out 'ere," came the reply.

He went back into the building, found some signs by the lifts and finally located a coffee bar at the end of the building. He lunged into the small, snug space. All the tables were taken. There was no sign of Alice.

He went up to a group of students.

"Excuse me... Have you seen..." They took no notice of him. It was as if he were the one missing. Anyway, what could he ask?

In the doorway of the lecture hall Alice had mimed lifting a cup to her lips and drinking from it. He had assumed she would be waiting somewhere in the block. But perhaps she had meant a cafe outside. He hurried out into the road, a concrete, treeless cul-de-sac. Darkness was already rising from the ground and the drizzle thickening to rain. He walked out into Russell Square. No joy there. He took the first street to his right. It led past a side entrance to the British Museum. The massive building stretched away as far as he could see in the murk. No cafes there, either. Where could Alice have gone?

The pounding in his head started again. That sick feeling that he thought he had left behind him in his flight from Gondo rapped on the door of his consciousness like an evil friend, like a familiar adversary.

"I'm going mad," he told himself. "Did I really see her? Or did I imagine it?"

One of the first things he had done on his own return had been to inquire about Alice. He had been told not to worry, that her release was merely a question of time and logistics. Her sudden appearance at his lecture, then, seemed unlikely.

He had her address somewhere. Tried to remember where she lived. In Putney. That was it. He had never been there. He had no phone number. She lived with a married sister. Martin did not know her surname. Through the noise in his head he tried to recall the address. He had written to her often enough from Gondo. He would have to go home. Untie the bundle of letters. Her address was sure to be on one of them.

As he calmed down his headache increased. The prospect of trekking across London seemed as much an ordeal as returning to Gondo. He was disappointed that he had not left these headaches behind him in Africa. During a routine medical examination at the School of Hygiene and Tropical Medicine on his return he had made light of his complaint.

"I might have had malaria," he had told them. "And headaches and things. I'm fine now."

They had taken samples of his blood and urine and had asked for a stool specimen when he could produce it. They said he might have to return for further tests. Preoccupied with the preparation of his lecture he had forgotten all about it. Until now.

He decided he had no option for the moment but to go home. He needed to lie down. If he felt better after a rest he could go and seek Alice out in Putney later. If not this evening, he would surely be all right in the morning.

His headache remained with him, however, throughout the next day. He was woken on the third by his telephone. The headache had lifted and he felt happy as he picked up the receiver. The call was from Britwords in London. A girl who had obviously just been on a course in telephone communication asked,

"Mr. Martin?"

"Yes."

"This is Britwords. My name is Chloe and I am ringing on behalf of Mr Jefferson. We are very sorry to disturb you. I know you are still on leave. But Mr. Jefferson wondered if you would be able to find time to call in here and see him."

"When?"

"Will 10.30 this morning be convenient?"

"Today!"

"If you wouldn't mind, Mr. Martin," said Chloe sympathetically, and Martin knew it was an order.

"Very well. I think I have a window," he tried to joke.

"Good. Half ten it is then."

"Ten thirty. I'll be there."

On the way out he picked up his mail. A small brown card requested him to report for an urgent appointment at the hospital. If he could not make it, he was to ring them at once. He looked at the date. The appointment was for today. At twelve thirty. He could probably just make it after Britwords. He did indeed have a window!

It was Martin's first visit to the office of the Controller of Human Resource Material since his fateful promotion interview there what seemed to him a lifetime ago. The appalling thing was that nothing had changed. Nothing that is, except that the green-eyed girl was no longer at her desk.

"I used to know your predecessor," Martin told the new incumbent.

"Yes. You don't know where she is working now, I suppose?"

Martin was confused. "Who, Alice?"

"That's right. Alice Tupman. They tell me she went away on leave and never came back."

"That's funny. I thought I saw her yesterday," said Martin, wondering what this conspiracy was all about. The new girl stared at him, suspecting he was taking the piss. There was no time to find out. Martin was called in by the Controller, the same man who had chaired the panel that had sent him to Gondo and subsequently had witnessed his performance for the African Commonwealth Society.

It was a polite bollocking. The Controller said that while he was fully aware that people's behaviour was sometimes modified by shock, such people were not required by Britwords. Moreover, Martin's disgraceful conduct at the African Commonwealth Society lecture had brought the name of Britwords into ill-repute. He regretted that it would no longer be possible to find a position for Martin. Finally he expressed the hope that Martin would enjoy the remainder of his leave and advised him to settle the rest of his affairs with Pay and Pension Division at his convenience.

Martin was neither surprised nor upset. He had known subconsciously that he had reached the end of the road. This interview had brought that knowledge to the surface. However he was angry at the way it had been done.

"Thank you for being so honest and so direct," he replied, "but you should have asked me if I had anything to say. You must know of course, that you have no right to summarily dismiss me, (even for using a split infinitive), without first giving me the opportunity to defend myself. And I am entitled to have a colleague in with me if you wish to charge me with a disciplinary offence." The Controller started to bluster but Martin waved his words aside. "Actually, I don't mind. In fact, I am rather relieved. I only have one request. Is it too late for me to resign? It would look so much better on my CV."

"My dear fellow," said the Controller. "I am not dismissing you. Britwords regrets, simply, that it is forced to declare you redundant. You will do quite well out of it. If you resign, on the other hand, you'll get nothing."

"Oh, Mr. Thomas," the receptionist said as Martin retrieved his coat, "I thought you were pulling my leg just now."

"What do you mean?"

"There's someone here I think you know..."

And there stood Alice, an empty cup in one hand, in the alcove where in the beginning they had made tea and coffee together. Another ghost?

"Alice?" he called.

"Martin," she smiled.

"Are you real?"

"Touch me."

Martin took her hands, searching her eyes for reproach. She seemed pleased to see him. He longed to hug her, to embrace her, to devour her. "I couldn't find you... You weren't in the coffee bar... I stood in the street... I was beginning to think I had imagined it all."

"I sat in the canteen for over an hour. I thought you were caught up with the dignitaries."

"Canteen! What canteen?"

"In the basement. Round the corner from the lecture theatre."

"Oh no!"

"I thought you didn't want to see me. I thought you were angry I had messed it up again. Just like I did in Gondo."

"You messed it up!"

They stood looking at each other, holding hands, embarrassed. A lot more answers, a lot more questions scudded through Martin's mind, too fleeting to find expression. He stood there, awkwardly, distantly in front of her, fighting tears. Too late. Too late now to kiss, to embrace. Too late for it to be spontaneous. He dropped her hands and stammered,

"What are you doing here now?"

"I came to fetch some of my belongings." She raised her mug from the draining board. "Have you time for a coffee?"

"Alice, I'd love to talk. Really I would. But I have to go to another appointment."

"Sounds important," she said. Again there was no reproach. She knew now that things worked themselves out in their own way.

"I'll tell you about it. It's all part of the same thing."

"What same thing?"

"The thing that I want to tell you about. That I want you to understand."

"I see," she said, but she didn't. Brusquely Martin took her by the shoulder, pecked her on the cheek and whispered,

"I'll be in touch, Alice. Soon, I hope." He could not look her in the face. He was ashamed she would see his tears. He turned and fled. He reached the hospital on time. He showed them his appointment card and was led into a small reception room. There were several people ahead of him. As he sat waiting for the result of his tests and the reason for the urgent recall the thought occurred to him that it would be safe now to read her letters. But it would be more fitting perhaps, to wait until they really were together again. Yes, that would be the way to do it. Ask her round to untie the bundle. A little ceremony to mark their rite of passage. There was only one small obstacle. Martin remembered that he still did not have Alice's telephone number.

I had been told during my debriefing that Martin was safe and well in England. They confirmed Delia's somewhat ambivalent account of his exploits and told me he would probably be resting before returning to work. I, too, felt like a "rest" before making contact with him. So the first thing I did on my return was to visit Mum and Dad.

"You back then?" said Mum.

"A man came from London asking us about you," Dad said.

"Alice might have written to us a bit more often," Mum grumbled to Crowbar, the dog. They had no idea I had "gone missing."

"It's a funny thing," Mum told me, "but one day we thought we saw you in the porch. We'd just been for a walk. We both did."

"A trick of the light," explained Dad, rationally. "We had been talking about you."

"I said, 'I hope she's all right,'" said Mum.

I went for a walk with them and Crowbar, a tame, one hour ramble around wet fields. It was a good, secure feeling, but I realised the impossibility of communicating what I had been through.

It was the same with my sister and her family. When I returned to "my room" she said they could have done with me last week. The kids wanted to know if I had brought them any presents. I tried to tell them about the Republic of the Nile. They found it about as riveting as some one else's holiday video. But my sister did remember having seen something in the evening paper about a lecture at the Royal Academy or somewhere by Martin Someone and did I know him.

"Martin Thomas?"

"Could have been."

"That's not Martin Someone," I cried. "Where's the paper?"

She could not find the announcement but felt sure the lecture was at the Royal Academy or the Royal Geographical Society, anyway the Royal something! I followed up these leads and tracked down a woman who knew about the talk. She thought it was sometime that afternoon. I hurried over to the School of Oriental and African Studies and arrived just in time to catch the end of Martin's address.

It was very embarrassing. I opened the door to the lecture theatre. There was Martin with some barelegged scarecrow standing behind him. He was in full flow. Well, until he saw me. Then he just stared as though I were a ghost. I wasn't even sure he recognized me. I suppose I gradually took in the fact that the lecture had begun. I seem to have a gift for arriving at the wrong moment. I told Martin I would wait for him in the cafeteria. Well, I made a sign to that effect. The cafeteria was only next-door. You could hardly escape the smell.

I sat and waited. And waited. I could not at first believe he was deliberately avoiding me. I drank two cups of coffee, slowly. I went back to the lecture hall. It was empty. I guessed Martin had been whisked off by the hosts, or something. I had one more coffee and waited. Martin failed to appear. I drew the obvious conclusion. He had not wanted to see me.

I was still kicking myself for missing him again when I went into Britwords to collect a few of the belongings from my former life. There was a girl I took to be a temp occupying my old desk.

I had hoped also to go and make my peace with Alan, but he had someone in with him when I arrived. Imagine my surprise when that someone turned out to be Martin Thomas.

Twice I had written him a letter and I had torn the letter up. I had been on the point of phoning him, but didn't go through with it. I was convinced by now he was deliberately trying to avoid me. Why was I punishing myself? I think I still hoped he would get in touch with me. I wasn't at all certain, either, what I still felt about him, if anything.

I found out, however, when I almost literally bumped into him. It happened there in the office of all places. There he was, the same slightly stooping man, lost like an absent-minded professor. I was so pleased to see him, and pleased I was pleased! I wanted to fling my arms around him, but in the office, you know how it is. Especially at Britwords. And that girl looking on with a contemptuous expression.

Martin did not seem a bit pleased to see me. Hardly even had time for a cup of coffee. Invented some lame excuse about an appointment. He was just - embarrassed. I had become a huge embarrassment to him.

He wasn't normal, though. He pounced on me. Shook me. For a moment I thought he was going to throttle me. I even experienced a kind of thrill. Well, it was a long time since I had had any physical contact, violent or tender, with a man.

He didn't kill me. He gave me a... what? A kiss, a bite, a nuzzle? I don't know. Before I could react he was gone, leaving me disturbed. And angry. I had rather a large bone to pick with him. He had led me on and twice let me down. Firstly by not being there to greet me in Gondo. Secondly by deserting me. But I was more angry with myself. Why was I, a mature woman, perhaps even more mature since my "adventures", still chasing him around like an undergraduate pursuing a college lecturer? It would have to stop. I told myself to get a grip.

That was nearly a month ago. The first days of anticipation were agony and the ensuing weeks worse. I didn't try to contact him. I wanted to, but I thought it about bloody time he made a move. If he cared he would be sure to contact me. I kept thinking about that peck on the cheek. What had it meant? To him?

Then I heard he was in hospital. They had put him in an isolation ward. He was under observation. That explained everything. His detached behaviour, his reluctance to kiss me properly and perhaps pass something on (so I wildly excused him!), his general behaviour. It explained his preoccupation and his absence. I felt guilty again and angry because I felt guilty. I phoned the hospital and asked to speak to him. There was no phone in his ward. They took my number and said they would ask him to call back.

"He's well, then?" I asked.

The administrator did not know but told me there "was no undue cause for concern at this time."

Martin, you're out of the isolation unit now. I suppose they told you why you had been called in: the initial tests had shown up a new virus. New to them. Since your blood count was very low, they judged you might not withstand a second infection. Hence the panic. In the event they found nothing wrong with you, anyway. Nothing they could explain. I wonder if it's me! An Alice allergy! We'll soon see, because I'm coming to visit you soon. Just as soon as you have read this. My story.

I started writing it for myself. To sort myself out. The trouble is, just as I think I am getting up to date, something else happens. The story moves on.

I was going to come and see you yesterday, complete the story. But two things happened.

The bad news first: I told you about the sympathetic wife in Nairobi who made me a shepherd's pie. She wrote me a letter about ten days after I left. She said she shouldn't be telling me this, that she was not supposed to know these things, but that our brief acquaintance had left a deep impression.

When I read the first few lines of her letter I thought I was going to hear a personal confession from a sensitive woman trapped in the world of formal receptions and dinner parties. But she was far too well bred to complain about her own predicament.

She told me that although her news was bound to cause me pain, she judged (her words) that I would want to know that Delia had been killed. A helicopter carrying Colonel M'Bang, the rebel leader, had been shot down. His companion, a white woman, had died with him. My head span as I read on.

"I understand there is no doubt that the white woman was your friend Delia. For political reasons the incident is being played down. This is why I should not be writing to you. But I thought you would prefer to hear it from a reliable source now rather than through the rumour mill in a week or two."

She went on to say that she and her husband would be on home leave in London early in the New Year. If I cared to come round for a chat, she would enjoy meeting me again. She signed her letter, "Yours truly, Daphne."

It was brave and kind of her to write this note and I resolved to thank her personally next year. I wept a few tears of gratitude to this intelligent, thoughtful woman before giving way to my grief for Delia. Delia, in her own words, the unsung hero. The bitter thought briefly crossed my mind that at least she was spared coming home, adapting to the humdrum. I told myself that this was an infantile thought. That I was lucky to be alive. But once again, Martin, I hope you will agree, I had good reason to postpone our reunion. (I do not think our encounter at Britwords can be called a reunion!)

That was the bad news. Now for the good news. Yesterday I received two more unexpected letters. One of them was from Britwords, actually. From Alan, Mr. Jefferson, no less.

It appears Britwords have finally realised that I did not deliberately go AWOL. Not only have I come back but I have resigned, they have discovered. They, Alan that is, but no doubt someone else drafted the letter, express their regret at my "unfortunate experience". They offer me counselling. Counselling! Now! Alan hopes I will reconsider my resignation. And here's the laugh! They are offering me an overseas posting. They do not say where, mind you. It is part of their strategy to "speed the advancement of women into senior management". Apparently I have demonstrated that I possess the "requisite attributes." But there's a give-away. Someone at Britwords has got wind of the fact that I am to be interviewed on BBC Woman's Hour. Alan wonders whether I would welcome some "coaching" from Britwords P.R. Department. Fat chance!

It's a seductive offer, though, isn't it? Manipulator Oceania might be nice! But I don't know really, if I could do a job I no longer believe in. Does that shock you? You've given so much to Britwords. For me, Delia's death has put things in a different perspective. Britwords, it seems to me, is a bit of an irrelevance. No doubt you, who have after all lectured on their behalf, will be able to convince me otherwise. Do you think I should give it a go?

The second letter is far more important. It is addressed to both of us. When it arrived I looked at the Canadian stamp on the envelope and wondered who I knew in Canada, or anywhere for that matter, who would associate you with me.

The letter had in fact been forwarded from the Republic of the Nile and sent on to me by Britwords. It is from Therese, the girl I found living in your house when I arrived in Gondo. The girl I, in my small way, helped to leave the country. It is a very long letter. Therese apologizes for not writing sooner.

"Life for us and everything was not simple for us at all and we didn't see what to write to you. It was a situation difficult to understand or explain."

I know just how they felt. There are pages about how they were quizzed for hours, tested and examined medically; about the waiting, about the uncertainty; about their transit in Vienna and Amsterdam and about their arrival in Montreal. I like this bit:

"We were given warm clothes and taken to YMCA hostel downtown. We stayed there nine days and they found us an apartment where we are living now. It is good. It has kitchen, bathroom, bedroom and sitting room which is big enough to take Jacques' bed and still leave enough space. It is on the third storey and we enjoy town view. We are learning the buses and finding our way."

Therese goes on to tell us of how she has a place in the school, Jacques at the university. She tells us of her impressions of the city, the mixture of races. The whole letter is infused with a sense of relief and elation. At the end Therese writes:

"I often think of you, of Martin especially because I know him longer. Particularly I think of the little bungalow and garden where he allowed me shelter. But it reminds me too much of the African sun. We are glad to be here, of course. Here we have tomorrow.

We both ask you to understand and forgive us why we did not write. It is encouraging to write to friends that you are well. Jacques says we are friends now. We hope you will come and see us. With love, Therese (and Jacques)."

So you see, Martin, for Jacques and Therese this story has a happy ending. A happy beginning.

THE END